Shooting Angels

Christopher Hope was born in Johannesburg and is the author of nine novels and three collections of short stories. His novels include *Kruger's Alp*, which won the Whitbread Prize for Fiction, *Serenity House*, which was shortlisted for the 1992 Booker Prize, and *My Mother's Lovers*, published by Atlantic Books in 2006 to great acclaim. He is also a poet and playwright and author of the celebrated memoir *White Boy Running* (1988).

Shooting Angels

Christopher Hope

ATLANTIC BOOKS
LONDON

First published in hardback and export and airside trade paperback in
Great Britain in 2011 by Atlantic Books, an imprint of Atlantic Books Ltd.

1 2 3 4 5 6 7 8 9

A CIP catalogue record for this book is available from the British Library.

Hardback ISBN: 978 1 8488 7338 4

Export and Airside Trade Paperback ISBN: 978 1 8488 7369 8

Printed in Great Britain by the MPG Books Group

Atlantic Books
An imprint of Atlantic Books Ltd
Ormond House
26–27 Boswell Street
London
WC1N 3JZ
www.atlantic-books.co.uk

For Eleanor

Yesterday, upon the stair,
I met a man who wasn't there
He wasn't there again today.
Oh, how I wish he'd go away.

William Hughes Mearnes

Part One
A Man of Some Extinction

CHAPTER I

My name was Winston, but I answer to Charlie, for reasons that will become clear. I have a noticeable limp, and one other small identifying mark, almost invisible now: a hexagonal scar across the back of my right hand. I know when it happened, but I don't know why. Not knowing why had been a source of enormous puzzlement to me all my life. I'm known around this town as 'the supplementary' – or, worse still, 'the remedial'. The title refers to my job. I supplement – or remedy – the defective English of my students at McLeod High, a name that flatters the two-storey structure of beige face-brick and corrugated iron roof, in the middle of town, where farm kids are corralled for a few years of book-learning before heading back to the land and the flocks, or clearing off to the cities.

On this particular Friday afternoon the school was closing for the Easter holidays. I'd finished marking a series of bad essays on picnics, shooting expeditions and car chases, locked the stationery cupboard, switched off the lights in my small office beside the boiler room, and I was setting off for home. I stopped, as I often do, at the school gates to look again at the man on the gatepost. The gates are fashioned of old, heavy wrought iron and must be chained and locked each night to prevent their theft. Good move, that. After all, the gates of

Zwingli Junior, next town down the road, plus the entire school hall, were carried off one day and never seen again.

On the right-hand gatepost, blocked out in jet-black, stark against the whitewash, is stencilled the figure of a gunman. The sleeves of his sweatshirt are sliced away to show his biceps and he bristles like the goddess Kali, with many arms: machine gun across his shoulders, pistol in each hand, several others strapped to his belt, alongside grenades, kris and bayonet.

This gunman is a hero to the kids I teach, and a noted killer, but only, they tell me, in the movies. When I look disbelieving they grow intent, almost frantic, needing to make me see they are not joking. He is also an American senator in what they call, with a slightly embarrassed grin, 'real life'.

'He is really *real*, Mister,' they tell me. 'In the movies.'

They are baffled that I do not know the stencilled figure on the gatepost, that I have not seen the movies and cannot understand the different lives of the gunman on the gate and the senator he is in real life.

'We seen him, Mister. Truly! He's like a politician, but he's also like an avenger. In America.'

Avenger? Amazing how their word-hoard swells momentarily in the presence of an assassin. They have no interest in the other 'real life' of the man who plays the avenger; it's not his political role, it's his weapons they like – bless their cruel little hearts. They have scant idea where America is and they do not care: it exists in the movies and that is enough. They have seen the killer on the screen and he is a video game they play endlessly. He becomes most alive when they play him – no, when they *are* him.

I blew into McLeod one day in much the way a ball of tumbleweed is pushed by the wind, snags on the barbed-wire fences that serrate these plains, and kicks for weeks. It is a town without features – except for the old slave bell, a clangourous slab of iron, slung from a stone arch in the main street. 'McLeod,' say the locals, 'is the back of the back of beyond.' A desert town set on a vast plain of tumbleweed, rock and scrub. Icy in winter and blazing in summer; where nothing breaks the monotony of the huge sky except the distant ridges of the Snow Mountains many miles away. Scottish pastors emigrated to these immense stony plains, married local women and gave their lives, their names and those of their religious leaders to heat-struck hamlets: Knoxton, MacTaggart, Calvinton, Lutherburg, Zwingli, Stormont, Wesleyvale. The main street is wide enough to turn a wagon; its broad dusty length contains the farm equipment store, the café, the Central Hotel, with the defiant date on its peeling gable – *Est. 1888* – as if daring anyone to credit it with lasting that long. The concrete sluices that run alongside the streets once led water to gardens and vegetable patches, but no one grows anything in McLeod now: they bring in almost everything from the capital, many miles away.

An old cottage at the end of First Avenue, where the town straggles into the wilderness of the desert, was free, and I rented it. One day Miss Tromp, the Head of English at McLeod High, wandered down to the end of First Avenue. Did I speak English? Would I come and speak it to her kids? She wanted to impress her senior students by showing them a real live Englishman speaking real live English.

'I'm not qualified to teach English. I studied science at university. To be honest, I don't really care about English.'

'That's good, Mr Croker,' she said, 'neither do they.'

I took the job and the kids were appalled, then bored, but she was pleased and soon I was taking classes a couple of times a week in remedial English. My position is vestigial. I am not a member of staff and my salary is paid out of a fund reserved for extramural 'arts' activities (netball, fencing and needle-work), activities so remote from the everyday interests of the kids around here that anyone mad enough to take up any on offer would be mocked to death. So the special fund goes to pay me alone.

Of course, there is no remedy for the defiant rejection of the language by my students. When English became increasingly the official teaching medium throughout the land – because that was what the faraway government in the capital wished – the kids began to fight against it even more fiercely, rejecting what was so evidently useful for them, deliberately harming their chances in life, knowingly cramping their world. I knew their anger – if they couldn't improve themselves, then they could work really hard at self-mutilation, and I liked their fighting spirit. They are out of tune with the times, but yes, of course, we all are.

Everyone agrees in principle that if we knew each other better we might loathe each other less, but no one wants to be the first to give up the acid dislikes in which we stew, because they know from history that those who have done so are not around any more. Mutual revulsion may not be nice, but it is freely available and open to all, it is our only real democratic value – we detest everyone equally – though there are penalties for saying so, and we talk like this only around our kitchen tables with the few people we trust.

Our one consistency has been the even heat of our mutual dislikes. Violence is our common characteristic. Our predilections are for rape and revolution and hard contact sports: mud-wrestling, kick-boxing, head-butting, though from time to time we organize festivals of reggae and repentance. No one mistakes these promises for anything but war-talk. We know how and who we are. The ambition of each remains the extinction of the other: the rules are crooked, the umpire blind and every aspect of life is a duel that you either win or go under.

The cliques, clubs and coteries that have mismanaged our land – all of them demanding freedom and fairness – have done their level best to stamp out this demon of hatred, because it isn't easy or useful constantly having to mend bones, mop up blood and cover the funeral expenses of your citizens. Every regime from the year dot has pledged more fairness, freedom and equality. They, and we, fit our lips around the great abstract nouns, and this tradition continues right up to the present.

Watching my class thumbing the buttons of their phones is to see them giving mouth to their muscle: punching out blunt hieroglyphs that spell out war and fun. Their memories, their interests, stretch back no further than a week or two. They live, for the most part, in a continuous and violent present. But clearly sometimes they are forced to think back and it hurts. History is something that hits you, rather like cramp. We all suffer these spasms; remembering how it was and who you were. They cannot endure for long anything that cannot be viewed on a screen. Inert, immobile chewing reflectively a lock of hair, they linger in a kind of frozen adolescence, inward, remote; occasionally they will laugh or jump or shake something, or scream with laughter, then return to the huge lassitude that is their nature, and stare transfixed at their phones with the dreamy pleasure you will see on the faces of the macaque monkeys when they groom each other. Their T-shirts read: *Speak the Mother Tongue or Drop Dead*!

It was soon clear that my job was a waste of time – Miss Tromp agreed, but as she pointed out kindly, 'it's a useful waste of time'. I might try to help the kids to write a business letter, to read without moving their lips, to stay afloat in the language. And that is all: my role is the equivalent of a rubber tube for paddlers. I lend them scraps of grammar, a nibble of *Macbeth*, perhaps a sip of Keats. And how they hate it! No amount of talk about a universal business language impresses them. They want to grow up, dress up and, if at all possible, shoot up someone or something very soon. They are hardly out of the classroom before they jettison any pretence of being able to manage a decent English sentence, and revert to the slangy, slippery patois people speak in McLeod.

The kids think that because they're speaking the patois I can't understand them. I spoke it as a matter of course because I grew up in the capital, where it was essential, if not obligatory, since, at that time, it was the language of the ruling clique. It has a sound that slides and grates, like a stream over gravel, and vivid scatological riches. It mixes indigenous words with borrowings from overlords, imperialists and pastors, as well as scraps of Indonesian, donated by the flourishing slave population of the early years of settlement, and a taste of Gaelic, Swiss-German; and even the odd word of Spanish, attributed to the shipwrecked crew of a galleon who interbred with local people and vanished, though they continue to haunt our nightmares – 'Suave as a Spaniard' is still a vile insult.

Though I've been in McLeod for a while now, people still slow down as they drive past and stare at me. I hear the voices: 'There he goes: Mr Croker, the supplementary English teacher, the walker, the photographer, the odd bloke who keeps to himself . . .'

Behind me now I hear someone say: 'Hey, it's Hopalong Cassidy!'

Hopalong Cassidy goes back way too far for them – to the era of silent cowboy films. Would they make fun of a lame man? Of course. What's the point of having a local cripple in town if you can't make fun of him?

I am tall and rather thin and I tend to swing my stiff left

leg ahead of the right and this, together with my height and skinny build, makes my limp seem more pronounced than it really is and gives me a list to starboard. It is something that does not go unnoticed in an arena like this. I broke my left leg falling from a second-floor window of St Jude's Home for Boys when I was fifteen. Then again, 'falling' is not quite right. One evening, after prep, as we were all getting ready for bed, Trevor Lockett picked me up, carried me into Mr Buttleby's room, held me over the sill, and let go. He did so because Mr Buttleby's window opened wide, unlike the other slatted louvre windows of our dormitory, which did not allow him to push a classmate over the ledge.

It's not only the way I walk, it's the fact that I walk at all. Walking in McLeod is a rare thing. Walking is for wimps or wackos. Walking exposes you to the eyes of everyone and to the dangers of the world. Walking strips you naked. And that is what I like about it – the way it incenses just about everyone, because they don't do it. The farmers drive, the police drive, even the dirt-poor travelling people move by donkey cart along the broad length of First Avenue. If absolutely obliged to go on foot, citizens move at a fast trot between hotel bar and bank or church, like soldiers crossing no-man's-land. Keeping their heads down they make a dash for it, and then hurry back to the safety of the waiting car or the truck. As if there were snipers hidden in the belfry of the tall ugly church, as if a desert town where nothing ever happens is really a carefully contrived doomsday machine ready to rub out the world.

All the way along First Avenue I hear the voices – there is Levant, now Birkett and now Jessup. 'Mister!' they call, always 'Mister', like the hunchback in the park in Dylan Thomas's poem. We come from such different places that even when we aim to meet, we miss each other.

Their voices must have masked the whispering,

7

midnight-blue BMW, which suddenly drew level with me; the window opened, and I heard a pent-up whisper, pitched between a gurgle and a low snuffle.

'H-h-hop in, Charlie.'

The driver shifted his bulk behind the wheel, leaning across to open the passenger door.

I heard myself say: 'Joe di Angelo, as I live and breathe.'

'Glad to know you're still doing both, Charlie. I thought maybe you'd gone to the big hostel in the sky. Am I going your way?'

I climbed in, wondering why I should feel suddenly guilty, as if I were playing truant.

'How did you find me?'

'Some guy told me a while back he'd seen, at some little gallery, a show called *Nowhere People*. These guys who live on donkey carts and go from farm to farm, and the photos were taken by a guy called – Croker. And he lived in a tiny place no one had heard of. And I thought. "That's got to be him, hidden away. Chasing shadows." I made a note and forgot about it. At the time I wasn't thinking of looking for you.'

'What changed your mind?'

'Life.'

The polished, liquid walnut of the dashboard sparkled with tiny orange lights, and the meaty fragrance of good leather was strong.

'What do you want, Joe?'

'I need you in the capital. I don't have a lot of time.'

'The capital and I don't get on.'

'Remember how it was with us, Charlie?'

I said nothing. The engine hummed along softly with the whispering air con. I couldn't see his face, but I guessed his lip would be curled in the old grin, full of the scorn he felt for himself, and for the world; the blood would drain from his

8

face until his freckles stood out like polka dots on his dead pale skin.

'What did you come here for?'

'The same reason you did, Charlie. I want to fix something that went wrong a long time back.'

'Such as?'

'I can lift the weight, Charlie. I swear it with all my heart.'

I'm not an easy laugher, but I almost laughed. 'You don't have a heart, Joe. We both know that.'

'Maybe you owe something, Charlie. Have you thought about that?'

'We had this talk a long time back. Remember? I don't owe you.'

'Maybe you owe her.'

'She's dead, Joe.'

'That's not the half of it. You don't know why it happened that night.'

'I saw it. I know exactly what happened.'

He slowed and stopped. 'It weighs on you, not knowing. Else you wouldn't be in this dump in the desert, chasing shadows. Come to me in the capital and I'll tell you. It's a trade.' He opened the glove compartment and took out something and handed it to me. 'This will get you there. When you hit town, phone me. Only, remember, I was never here, in this place, OK?'

I wanted him gone from McLeod and it was something I wanted very much to agree to – and, anyway, what had I seen in the dashboard lights? A fuzz of stubble, a glimpse of jowl. It would be easy to forget it all.

'I never saw you here, Joe.'

'That's my boy. See you, Charlie.'

He took off fast, back wheels slithering on the sand. Overhead the black sky climbed and climbed, powdered with stars; so many and so clear they made my eyes prickle. I was holding what I saw now was a large envelope, soft and unwelcome. I remember thinking, 'Pass-the-fucking-parcel. Thanks a lot, Joe.' Father Daintry had once told us about messengers from nowhere. 'They turn up wanting to say something. Only they can't find the words.'

Watching his tail lights wreathed in dust, it did occur to me that Joe was driving very fast and the dirt roads around McLeod could be deadly. All it took was for a buck to jump into your headlights, you hit the brake and you were gone. That would have been something, and a good bit of me didn't care. But then, nor would he – when it came to mortality, his own or anyone else's, Joe Angel had always been wildly indifferent.

Chapter 2

Again, the voices.

'It's Long Tall Sally, out for a gallop!'

Long Tall Sally? One of the great rock 'n' roll songs of long ago. How the kids come up with my nicknames beats me. They know nothing of rock 'n' roll, nothing of anything, you might say, and they flaunt their angry ignorance. The kids are wrong about just about everything; being wrong is important to them. They are proud of knowing as little as possible – ignorance raised to this level is a form of rebellion. And I know a thing or two about deliberate and monumental blindness, having made such a success of just that all my life.

Miss Tromp, she does her best – bless her heart – to make up for the fact that my students and I will always be aeons apart. Just as mine is a kind of non-existence, so she and I have what I think of as a non-love affair. Miss Tromp also called me 'Mister' when she came to my cottage one night and we went to bed together. Then we moved on to – but never went further than – our full first names: we were Beatrice and Charles, and there was a relief in this distance, this formality, in a town where most things began with clamorous intimacy and ended in noisy assault. Going to bed with her was like visiting a foreign land, a small and perfectly white little island of unruffled sand surrounded by clear water where her sighs

II

were the sound of the breeze. We met and made love and talked of nothing, said not a word, just faint cries and sighs, yet our silences were wonderfully wicked, even subversive. By such strategic discretions we made sure no one would know what was happening – ourselves especially. Nothing was ever mentioned afterwards. We met like spies to exchange secrets and afterwards we resumed our daytime identities.

Miss Tromp despairs at her students' resistance to a world language. She likes to remind my sullen charges that I have a degree, and once worked for a newspaper in the faraway capital.

'You should be glad,' Beatrice Tromp tells my class, 'to have to teach you a man of some extinction.'

I think that is beautifully put. I have no interest in the future and not much in the present. What moves me most is what isn't here any longer; that which is not. If oblivion is a great wheel that will roll over us all, I try to throw a very small spanner into its iron works.

McLeod is terrific if you're in the extinction business. It sits on a plain that was once a vast, shallow inland sea – later an immense swamp – that saw giant epochs come and go. The desert plays a long game. It is dotted with tiger-striped, leathery bushes, and here and there a single iron wind-pump churns and grinds. The tops of the Snow Mountains are worn down to their granite shoulders, and high clouds have their edges whittled into spikes by the wind. I go walking in the shadows that lie between the great vanishings which had happened over billions of years, when, say, the Triassic age gave way to the Permian. I have found, with a feeling of almost manic excitement, traces of my extinguished predecessors, relics of reptiles and proto-dinosaurs that walked a wet and steamy world in Triassic times, and the petrified claw-prints of an Upper Permian cynodont scored deep in the rocks of what had once been the mud bank of an ancient river. Much, much later came faint remains of the hunter bands who once owned the countryside, and were shot out by punitive hunting parties of the first farmers. I find tiny oval beads cut from ostrich shells, pierced for threading on a necklace; sharp arrow heads and flint scrapers. In the rocky overhangs that overlook the plains are flaking paintings of sprinting hunters, and magical rain creatures sprouting heads and horns.

In time, everything goes and there is nothing you can do about that; and for that reason I decided I would do something. I cannot make time stop, but I can visit the scene of the crime and make notes. I love arriving before the last traces have blown away or been covered, and making a note, as it were, with my Leica. These are not compositions; they are evidence of disappearances which excite no one but myself, rather as a police photographer might record the scene of a crime, as evidence of violence done by time, malefactor or circumstance.

I go to the desolate little graveyards of the early pioneers who farmed and failed in this great dry world of sheep, thorn and tumbleweed. On a rusty gate, in white paint on blackened tin, the notice reads: *God's Beloved Sleep Here*, and five or seven headstones lean among the thorny shrubs, showing names and dates. These were homesteads of the families who long ago quit in despair, sold out to a neighbour and vanished. I photograph their abandoned houses, room by room, untouched since the last member of the family escaped or died – the brass bedstead stripped down to its metal bones and above it the framed embroidered sampler offering prayers to the Lord of All. The dust thick on the yellow-wood chairs, the stout leather thongs of the seats still tightly stretched; a paraffin lamp, loaded with fuel on the dining-room table, waiting to be lit; the floorboards of the front stoop lifting and warping as if time itself were turning in its sleep; the fireplace with its mantle of slate, above which hangs a photograph in a mahogany frame of the wedding pair: flustered Claradyn in her bridal veil, and bearded Hermann in his stiff collar, both staring into the world with wild eyes, as if they were about to be blasted off into unknown worlds – and so they were, into the far reaches of time from which these hot, thirsty vistas proclaim: there is no going back, and no one who cares.

I have my defiance: 'Yes, I care!' I care precisely because it doesn't matter to anyone else. This is my private war against forgetting, my refusal to let oblivion have it all. Caring is useless, I know. These people, these creatures, are all gone. But I make my notes because someone has to speak for the dead. I do it because it is something I was raised with – I've been trained to do battle with the bony enemy. Death may give no quarter, but it behoves you, said the Brothers who raised me, to make sure you give him hell in return.

Once inside my cottage, I locked and bolted the door. The wind was blowing and it came loaded with fine grains of sand that rubbed the skin raw. They called it 'the Scour' and it had a grievous effect on some. A farmer chases a drinking partner from the bar of the Central Hotel, hoisting a frozen leg of lamb. It lifts, it falls; there is air where someone was and business for Govender, the undertaker, in his white Toyota van, and another murder docket filed in the Calvinton cop shop, an hour's drive away.

I sat down at my kitchen table, resisted an impulse to pull on a pair of gloves and tore open the buff envelope that had once been addressed to *Dr Joe Angel D.Litt, Ph.D, ACM*. Joe had never in his life been near a university and these academic bouquets were rewards for services rendered. This hedge of pretty letters had the useful effect of smoothing over any hint of Italian excess – it was a far cry from, say, Giuseppe Roberto di Angelo – they lent his name a reassuring weight, gently pointing up its celestial connotations, backing it up with a string of hiccupping honorific degrees. It sounded the right sort of moniker for a philanthropist and patriot, yet stood, too, for honesty, sobriety, a real Honest Joe. But that final 'ACM' had me stumped.

The addressee's name had been crossed out with parallel strokes of a magenta pen and, above it, in the spiky hand I remembered from the covers of school exercise books, Joe had written *Mr W. Croker*. It looked meagre beside the grand titles of the original addressee. The 'W' was a nice touch. Someone wanted to show he really did know a lot about me.

Inside the envelope I found an air ticket and a brick of cash in five-hundred notes, wrapped in a linen bank bag. The notes were new, shining, smelling of ink and slightly slippery. Counting the stuff seemed pointless. The weight alone told me the wad amounted to thousands – more than I knew what to do with. The five-hundred note is a pink lozenge bisected by a transparent strip that neatly divides the first word of our country's new motto, 'Together', from its companion, 'Forever'. A fatuous injunction, since mutual detestation has always been our engine of propulsion.

On the band of paper that held the wad of cash, Joe had scrawled: *Open return ticket. Business class. Plus something to tide you over. Need you in town! My numbers are below. I'll be waiting.*

'Well, I won't be coming,' I said aloud, and immediately felt rather silly.

I did not want to have anything to do with the man pricked out in these preposterous titles. For Joe to believe he was calling in an old debt – and for me to allow him to think this – was to negate the many years I'd spent trying very hard either to forget what I owed him, or to decide plainly that I owed him nothing, and that if the truth be told, the obligation ran the other way – that he had survived at the cost of my happiness and of all that I had loved; that he had got off scot-free to lead the life he did.

What that life really was I had only the vaguest idea, picked up from what I'd seen or heard on TV or in the press. At one time it had been said that Joe was a turncoat, a prodigious, shameless hypocrite, a shameless apologist for the Furies he had once despised. Then suddenly, it seemed he had been nothing of the kind; in fact he was a hero, a visionary, a selfless benefactor, and this entirely new history of Joe Angel was the version enthusiastically accepted when the balance of power changed in our savage land. You needed to go to something like quantum theory to offer even a remotely convincing explanation of versions of this man. Joe Angel was the human version of Schrödinger's cat, a creature more mysterious than even its Cheshire cousin. He was two things in waiting: he was saint and sinner, fool and hero – but only when you decided to look at him did his real nature show itself.

I had my own reading of Joe Angel from a long time back, when I reckoned I had known better than anyone. The boy I knew was called Giuseppe Roberto di Angelo, and he preceded the man in the Merc by a good four decades. He had been a skinny, foxy little guy whose complexion was so pale it always reminded me of aspirin, and this allowed his freckles to show vividly. He was nervous, quirky, watchful, agitated, scurrilous, sneering, funny, as well as deeply and constantly uneasy – about what I could not say – but it made him very attractive, this feeling that his life was forever balanced on the finest edge.

Then, later, there was his successor, Joe Angel, the man who had called to me from behind the wheel of his car, all gleaming grill and jutting bonnet. A chunky slab of a man with a square, fleshy face; thick black hair fell in waves over his ears and his lips were fixed in a pout, as if he were constantly surprised that the camera was so interested in him. He was noisy, weighty, famously rich, repeatedly married to – and regularly separating from – ever-younger wives, who were prodigiously – and publicly – rewarded for being dumped. He was constantly in the papers, several of which he owned, and which celebrated his profligate talents and passions, his racing sloops, vintage cars and art collections. He was, apparently, a virtuoso on the flute, a consummate mimic, a powerful supporter of the disadvantaged, who ranged richly through the many areas of deprivation, donating time and money and expert care to everyone from disabled seamstresses to AIDS orphans. The Angel Academy for the Promotion of Academic Excellence took in the poorest children with talent and raised them to be princes of the future; the Angel Endowment Fund, the Angel Art Awards, his ballet troupe, his opera company and his string trio. In remote rural areas he had been supporting seamstresses, who crafted monumental tapestries tracing the history of our country from the ominous arrival of the first settlers to the tumultuous coming of democracy. He worked to revive the old bardic tradition of oral poetry by sponsoring a praise-singer in neglected country communities. He rode, he hunted, he loved the arts and made millions: he was a schemer, a dreamer, a Medici in the new Renaissance, much of which he subsidized and which he embraced with the devouring passion that marked his every move.

There were, too, his spectacular share deals, his mansions, his marriages, his gold and diamond mines, his vast construction projects, the gigantic shopping malls, the casinos of marble and crystal. I knew – the entire country knew – of his immense residence on the Northern Ridge of the capital, with black basalt eagles rampant on the gateposts, buried sensors beyond tall beautiful walls, armed sentries day and night; a mansion once owned by Pompapisto, reputedly a leader of the Cosa Nostra – who skipped bail and vanished, and before him by a cousin of a cousin of the Queen of Greece.

The mansion had been radically remodelled in severely minimalist style, a subtle suite of greys and whites, by Bermuda Barclay, the Knightsbridge designer, at the behest of his last wife (his fifth, or was it sixth?), a pretty girl about half his age and whose name I could not remember . . . Carita or Cordelia? I had seen pictures of their wedding – 'our own royals': the hills of caviar, her bejewelled running shoes, his collection of autographed baseball bats. His papers, magazines and TV channels sprayed the couple with adjectives that revealed the abject level of public discourse within the country. Joe Angel was 'a rough diamond', 'a golden boy', 'super-stock-meister' and, to remind us that – his immense fortune notwithstanding – his roots were modest and real: he was, at heart, plain Joe Angel, 'the concrete king'.

Of course, that was it. I had got it at last and it made me smile. ACM: Association of Concrete Manufacturers. This was more like the boy I'd grown up with, who had entranced and appalled me; and whose fortune and prestige were founded on dodgy cement his dad had suckered the old regime into buying during the building frenzy that had marked their years of power; a form of daffy, pharaonic overreach that led its spokesmen and apologists to constantly boast that under their rule there had come to pass the biggest dams and widest roads and longest bridges in the country, on the continent, in the world. And so on, and on.

I knew something about concrete. I had a store of arcane and unconnected bits of knowledge in my head, which I tried, always unsuccessfully, to forget – tommy guns, for example, tulips, Chicago and Calvinism – lodged there courtesy of the writer of the note I held in my hand. I knew that concrete resembles a kind of currant bun. The crushed stone or rock forms the currants, and a finer aggregate – this would be sand – provides the base. Mix in water and a binding agent – Portland cement, say – give the mixture a good stir, and it will harden in whatever mould it is poured into, and stay that way for decades. Joe once told me that in each year around a cubic yard of concrete is produced for each person on the planet.

I told myself I would not be taking up the offer. I would forget the visit Joe had paid me, and would go on with my life as before. The Easter holidays had begun, I was free and I had started a project that fascinated me. For some weeks I had been photographing a family of travelling folk. They were the 'shadows' I chased, and Joe's name for them was not far wrong: shadows fade when you shine a light on them, and wanderers vanish when you look at them. They are unseen in the towns they pass through, and they have no name for themselves. 'We are just us,' they would say, 'and we are nowhere.'

Yet the funny thing is that the farmers who came to stay for ever have abandoned the old homesteads around McLeod, but the nomads are still here, they exist. If you see them in the flesh they seem to be invisible; only in my pictures can you see how real they are. The early farmers who came to McLeod believed they had arrived somewhere; they would make something of it and themselves, and would stay on their lands for ever. But McLeod is nowhere and it is the nomads, not the farmers, who understand this. Like elementary atomic particles, they pass invisibly through the world, but sometimes I have been lucky enough to record their passing traces, evidence of their existence. Why do I do it? Because it gives me pleasure, because I am angry, and I can do nothing with my rage – except record, remember.

The family I followed now were Old Saul and his wife Sinna

and their teenage daughter Chantal. I've travelled in their cart, along the dusty roads where the wind stings like the whip Old Saul flicks across the backs of his two shaggy donkeys. We are always stopping to patch and pump the balding tyres. Water is taken from the round cement reservoirs below the straining steel wind pumps; tea is brewed in the kettle that hangs like a dead guineafowl from the back of the cart. I have slept in their rudimentary camps and listened at night, as I lay in my sleeping bag, to the donkeys cropping at the few small grasses that struggle to grow in this great desert. I have watched the men sharpening their shears before sitting the surprised sheep on its tail (the same position to shear or to slaughter) and peeling away its fleece in one slow, unstoppable slice. I have treated the burns of the children who come too close to the brushwood fires spitting in rusty tin cans in winter. The kids wear rayon and nylon skirts or jerseys, and as they crowd the brazier in the bitter cold their clothes sometimes flare up, and then the smell of scorched flesh accompanies the scent of coffee.

The next morning, early, I was packing my gear when the name of Joe's last wife suddenly came back to me. I remembered seeing pictures taken shortly after her divorce, where she stared into the camera with the agonized look of a deer caught in the headlights of a hunter's four-by-four. Her name was Cameron.

Another bit of useless knowledge to add to concrete and Calvin and Capone.

In a mood of wild anger, and rather silly daring, I left the fat brick of cash in the window facing the street. 'You never know your luck,' I told myself, feeling a gambler's surge as I pushed the notes up against the pane for any passer-by to see and left the window ajar, making it very easy for someone to reach inside and help himself. And I drove out into an icy morning, beneath a dawn sky as white as the frost on the windscreen.

I was heading for the big Mackenzie farm, east of McLeod, at the far end of a dusty road near the Snow Mountains. Redwatersridge is a spread of several thousand hectares, mostly scrub, but it has a big muddy dam, and water is riches in this achingly dry place.

I found Old Saul and Sinna behind the sheep pens, sorting through their bits and pieces. She was scraggy and laughed a lot, showing not many teeth, and she had very bright eyes. Their daughter Chantal was an dreamy, silent child of around fourteen. The remains of a sheep carcass were suspended on a string of barbed wire over the remains of a fire, its severed head lay to one side, on its own, the eyes glazed. This was part-payment for their work, and they had slaughtered the sheep the night before and feasted. Sinna was tying the kettle and cooking pots to the back of the cart with baling wire and Old Saul was folding his whips. He wore a dark woollen jacket over a filthy sweatshirt that said *Princeton*, and whistled up his dogs, skinny runners he called Wind Hound and Dirty Dog. Sometimes they hunted rock rabbits, sometimes they went after the jackals that had been killing sheep. Saul was proud of his dogs.

I said, 'It's cold this morning.'

'Very cold,' Old Saul agreed.

There never was much talk, and today they were hardly aware of me. That was what I liked, to work among them unnoticed, almost a ghost. I had heard Chantal was staying behind, and they agreed, because she wanted it, but they did not like it. Work when you must, move when you can, drink till you drop. Money, though useful, was neither here nor there. Having no past and no discernible future, movement was all. 'My mood is ready', they would announce one day, and a few hours later only the wheel tracks of their carts, a dabble of donkeys' hooves in the dust of the desert, remained; and they vanished over the huge horizon, gone into the empty sky.

I began photographing the rich clutter. The wanderers find work, food and water where they can. They are shearers, tinkers, hunters, boozers, bums, travellers, trackers, fence-menders, wall-builders – occasional trades – and a nomad camp is a jumble of blankets, spare tyres, scraps of strips of corrugated iron for building walls against the wind, tin kettles, blackened cooking pots, plastic buckets, baling wire, threadbare blankets, pipes, woollen hats, whips, enamel cups, needles, string, bridles, brandy, animal traps and lots of knives. Saul shaving, holding up a shard of mirror to the light; Saul trimming his fingernails with a long knife – probably the one he'd used to butcher the sheep the night before; Saul stacking corrugated iron sheets; Sinna folding blankets; Saul harnessing the donkeys to the wooden cart, with much whistling and cursing; the girl, Chantal, was playing with an old bicycle wheel long stripped of its tyre, using a crude wire whip to make it run. I turned the camera on her. I wanted to catch her self-absorption as the wheel rolled, fell, rolled again.

I knew the farmer had come up behind me; I felt his heat before I heard him cough. 'They're a mess,' he was saying, 'these things. They're just a mess.'

I kept shooting, knowing each snap of the shutter on the Leica pushed the man deeper into his buzzing incomprehension of a God who allowed such 'things' to exist. When I'd got what I wanted from his shearers, I turned to face Mackenzie. He had a fierce hawk face, high cheekbones, a skin burnt dark as oiled teak. Even more taciturn than Old Saul, he had trouble speaking three words in a row before the effort became too much and he cursed and began kicking stones and punching the air in noisy confrontations with some devil in himself. He was the ultimate pragmatist; he believed only in what he could kick.

He hated me because I gave myself over to taking pictures of people so low they brought human beings into disrepute. It incensed him that I spent so much time looking hard at their faces, and their work. What was the point? He meant the people themselves – he could see no sense in their existence. The men of McLeod often had this fissile quality: they would move from inertia or nullity into furious action, unleashing huge energy, and striking out with a fist, a boot or a knife. Mackenzie's form of madness was so widespread no one really gave it a second glance.

Mackenzie's wife came out of the kitchen now and called to the girl who didn't seem to hear her, so deep inside herself was she. Geena Mackenzie was a pretty woman of about forty, and she wore her thin blonde hair drawn into the nape of her neck in a tight bob. Her lips were plump and generous, and contrasted oddly with the narrow rectitude of much of what she said. She was deeply pious, an evangelical snob and a pedant. She had told me why she had decided to keep Chantal on to learn the work of the kitchen.

'I want to see if I can help her. To be better than she is. That's not a bad thing, is it, Mr Croker ? We're told to love our neighbour.'

'You're taking her from her family. Doesn't that worry you?'

'I believe it is best for her.'

'What if you're wrong? The road is the only life the girl has known.'

'If I'm wrong, then I will have to face my God.'

'That may be too late for the girl.'

She gave me a small, pitying smile. 'You don't understand my faith, Mr Croker.'

As it happened, I understood more than I cared to know

about what she believed. 'Eternal life is foreordained for some and eternal damnation for others,' John Calvin had written. Straight and direct. But we never know who is or is not elected. In theory, Chantal might be saved already, though that seemed unlikely when you looked at her, as Geena Mackenzie was doing, and saw a grubby child riding a wheel. It was equally possible that Geena herself might *not* be saved. But Calvin allowed that we might glean a hint of our fate by observing the way good people lived. Not that good works would save anyone, only faith did that, and yet a well-led life might signal salvation. Geena Mackenzie knew that a lot of work would be needed to transform a wild child of the road into a decent girl. Yet God wanted it, and so did Geena Mackenzie, and trapped in this pincer movement the child had very little choice but to do as others thought best.

Old Saul put his hat on at a rakish angle and lifted his thick moustache into a wide, vivacious grin. Now he took the reins, raised his whip and, with the pots clanking thinly, and with Dirty Dog and Wind Hound loping in the rear, the cart slowly moved away. Chantal kept riding her wheel, and every so often reaching down and smoothing the skirt between her thighs. The farmer Mackenzie turned and spat in the dust.

Geena Mackenzie called again: 'Come, child. We'll wash you and feed you and do something with your hair.'

The cart rolled out of the gates and along the sandy road that climbed gently towards the vast horizon. Old Saul and Sinna did not look back. The dogs ran beside the cart, the whip spat, and I got a last shot of them as they slowly crested the small rise and vanished.

When I got home that evening, and every evening that week, the cash was still in the window. Safe and sound. I'd not really expected anything else. Murder happened in McLeod, along with rape, battery, incest, on a pretty regular basis – but somehow or other very little was ever pinched.

Each evening I worked in the darkroom and the pictures of Chantal astride the old and rusted bicycle wheel were all I had hoped: the dreamy, locked-in air of the child, total absorption in her inner mood. Untouchable, you would have thought. Unreachable. A state I had reached until Joe's intrusion. To go back meant remembering it again, after a lifetime of forgetting. But I felt the pull: a strong, unavoidable attraction which had nothing to do with affection.

I had read Erwin Schrödinger, as anyone interested in particle physics will do, and he explained how two particles which happen to knock up against each other may, for obscure reasons, find themselves forever linked if they are just a hair's breadth maybe, or light years, apart. There is no real independence between either of them, so tightly tangled are they. If one spins anti-clockwise, the other will react by spinning in the opposite direction. Somehow information passes between them. Each mirrors and matches the other. Somehow it seems that particle A knows what particle B is up to and it makes no sense to think of them except as two in one. It is what Einstein called 'spukhafte Fernwirkung' – ghostly goings-on at a distance. 'I find the idea quite intolerable,' he wrote, and said that if it turned out to be true then he'd rather be a shoemaker or a croupier than a physicist.

Joe and I had once been so close you could not tell one from the other; but then we flew apart and I imagined that was the end of the story – but the entanglement turned out to be as strong as ever. I read Joe's note again. What did he need me for? More to the point, how did he know I would do as he asked? Even as I thought about it, even as I was refusing, yet again, to have anything to do with the man who trailed me down Central Street in that absurd limo, I was reaching for the phone.

CHAPTER 3

The jet roared down the runway. The land below opened and began unscrolling like a screen to show stone, scrub and sheep, and then they vanished as we climbed and there was only the utter emptiness of the plains. Looking down from thirty thousand feet you had some idea of the curvature of this country; it is like a banana, some say, referring to its narrow, winding form. I'd have said it was more of a serpent, with a long tail to the south where it touches the sea; its huge midriff is an immense arid plain and then, to the north, where it comes to a head in stumpy hills and big skies of the rough country, the capital rears up out of nowhere.

Nothing in the deserts and dams below gave any clue as to the immense turbulence of the land and its people. The countryside glowered, it slunk, it darkened, but of the blood and agony there was no hint. We have in the past been ruled by royalists and republicans, by tribalists, colonialists and capitalists and, for a brief few months, by Rosicrucians. We once had a royal family, but it lasted precisely two generations before it was wiped out in a blaze of gunfire by persons unknown – no first family since the destruction of the kingly rulers of Nepal has been despatched so completely and so efficiently. Indeed, once again the rumour was that it had been so succinctly done that it cannot have been carried out by 'our' people and must have been, in the choice phrase here, 'an internationalist plot': the implication being, yet again, that only foreigners could have done something so cruel, and so effective.

Ours is a land marinated in aggression, hatred and anger. We follow a pattern of destruction which began in the time of the indigenes, who were wiped out by the incomers, who were in turn massacred by the settlers. Then came the colonialists, who decimated the setters, and who were then stamped upon by the imperialists, and so on. Subjugation, followed by oppression, followed by a succession of tyrannical ventures passing themselves off as governments, culminating in a religious tyranny, when the imperialists were eliminated by a small band of despotic zealots.

My special interest is a moment when the zealots took over. They were protestant puritans from some sub-strand of that creed – originating in some forlorn sliver of Low Country polder, a place of bog, boredom and incest – who somehow crossed the seas and implanted themselves among us. They practised a dour Calvinism. They did not laugh or dance or gamble or drink and they interbred often, this being preferable to contaminating the tribe by sleeping with foreigners. In the wider scheme of things they were never more than a marauding posse, as it turned out, destined, like all our rulers, for ignominious extinction and eternal mockery. But for a while they were, they believed, the chosen of God, and they decided that the Catholics among them, an even smaller and more risible fraction, were the true enemy and must be eliminated. And they were cruel and silly enough to take themselves seriously, as only the Chosen Ones may do. But then, as their victims, we took them seriously, too.

This mini-war of religion did not last long and it is barely remembered now – except by me. These zealots have been replaced by a fresh band of reformers who call themselves (I have trouble even writing the name) the NFD: the New Free

Democrats. Never trust a movement that identifies itself by its initials: my life and failure is proof enough of that. They have tried various ways of encouraging – or enforcing – fairness or 'enhanced equity'.

Everyone rather liked their idea of tag-team wrestling for the under-fives, made compulsory in kindergartens and for both sexes; with the quota system at its heart which saw candidates chosen by lot and by ratio, so that when the toddlers stepped into the ring to do battle they reflected a fair cross-section of the community.

Then, too, their decision to take all polo clubs into state ownership. If a few rich people insisted on silly, expensive games in private enclosures, then the state would oblige the wealthy to join in chukkas with the poor. Soon municipalities owned strings of ponies, and on the enormous green fields where the matches were played, limousines parked next to modest cycles and rickshaws, and refuse-pickers drank state-sponsored champagne with the nobs.

But, as it always happens, both sides retreated into unhappiness and headaches the morning after. Now the polo fields are deserted, the water sprinklers play on empty pitches, and the only happy souls are the merchants who have contracts to feed the ponies languishing in the stables. And everyone is relieved to have found a way of getting back to reassuring animosities. Ours is a curious place, and if you went out and about with a lamp looking for a peaceable person, you would be mugged for your lamp before you got very far.

The fiery ideologues of the NFD have grown into unctuous careerists; they have proved to be neither novel nor libertarian. The summit of their achievement has been to overturn a despotism where the skinny poor many were forced to serve the fat rich few; and transform it into a system where the poor merely subsidize them.

The plane dipped and we began our descent, and I could not help noting that the weather was on its best behaviour: the skies ominously clear, the sunshine worryingly benign. The capital is known for fierce, tremendous electrical storms; thunderbolts jolt the head, and lashings of rain carry away whole settlements in boiling floods of mud the colour of ox-blood. But sometimes these storms end in nothing more than noisy bluff, empty sky-clamour, a bit of heavenly body-building. When the last lot ruled, weather reports were forbidden and loose, meteorological chit-chat was dangerous. You had only to say, 'We're in for blustery winds and a deep depression' or 'the forecast is for flash and fizzle all next week', and everyone knew what you meant, and if you were overheard using this Aesopian lingo in public you might end up in jail.

What was alarming was how absolutely the last lot had vanished. So large, so important, so unpleasant an impression had been left on our collective psyche that it was hard to believe they had ceased to exist as anything except a dull ache. That they should have come to so little was more than disappointing. It was infuriating. All that huff and puff, all that moral certainty, had faded. The small Puritan–papist war we once fought in a distant corner of the capital, and which had given us ideas above our station, now seemed a passing spat between posturing clowns, the one as fatuous as the other. Yet the war had happened, and I would not forget it.

We began our approach. The plane dipped, the downward pull was alarming. I was falling towards something and there was no way out or back. I had gone over what had happened so often, and yet I had missed something crucial.

As I came through the exit doors into the concourse, a line of drivers meeting passengers flapped their name cards hopefully, like demonstrators staging some obscure protest against the companies or individuals whose names were scrawled on their placards. I was not expecting my name to be there – of course not – but I looked anyway. And then I looked for Joe.

The old airport in the capital had been designed to what I always thought of as Stalinist specifications; Moscow under the Soviets or some such model. The cardinal rule was to allow very little light – the old regime was allergic to natural light. It was said by some wag long ago that our last rulers embraced the political philosophy of fungi: keep your subjects in the dark; raise them pure, pale and dull and when they grow up, cut off their heads.

Our recently arrived masters, wishing to exorcize the old dull ghosts, had built – much as Christian churches supplanted Roman temples – a revolutionary modern airport with ads for fast cars and Scotch whisky, pulsing on the screens on the biscuit-blonde walls. Yet the furry-hat feel of the old place still hung on – and there was still not enough light.

On the big electronic board overhead arrival times flashed and vanished. The crowds of passengers seethed and ebbed as each new flight to touch down sent another batch streaming through the exit gates. When the crush thinned I was left stranded in the sudden silence, before the next wave of travellers burst through the automatic doors. What was I doing back in town? I'd been angry ever since Joe erupted into my distant life in faraway McLeod, but I recognized another emotion, riding below the anger, deeper and more alarming, more painful. Disappointment.

I found a bench beneath a line of presidential portraits, some long forgotten, others I remembered with a shiver: the butcher; the pipe-smoker who declared that only colonists got cancer; the brutal jailer; the furious fanatic, who declared there was no such thing as rape in our country because there was no word for it in his mother tongue.

The fat brick of cash was in my coat pocket and for two pins I'd have bought a ticket back to McLeod. That part of me which said it had been a mistake to listen to Joe when he asked – almost beseeched me – to come to town, now spoke sternly, telling me I was an idiot. Yet I looked for Joe, I expected him to be there. I'd taken it for granted that I'd see his swatch of pitch-black hair.

I knew it was a bad idea, but I pulled out my phone and called the cell number Joe had given me. The line of presidents looked down at me in dismay.

The voice that answered spoke in light, urgent tones: 'Joe Angel. Leave me a message and I'll bell you back. *Hunnert* per cent . . . cheers.'

His insouciance was exasperating. The self-important, breathy haste, the home-town slang: 'Hunnert per cent', 'bell you back' . . .

I said, 'Fuck you, Joe!' and tried his home number. This time I got an answer, a man who sounded almost as wound up as I was. His voice was deep, shaky; a man angry for being scared.

'What d'you want?'

'I'm a friend of Dr Angel. I've just landed at the airport and he was supposed to meet me.'

'And so?'

'Well, he isn't here.'

'And he isn't here, neither.' The 'h' came out as a strangled 'y', the 'r's rolled like drums – 'Ee'zznt yurr neithrr . . .'

'Do I have the right number?'

He was evidently astonished by my question. 'Look chief, if you didn't have the right number you wouldn't be calling his house. Would you? And I wouldn't be answering. Right?'

'This is his house?'

'Right.'

'But he isn't there.'

'Keerek!'

I could hear him breathing, feel his jitters. Whoever he was he knew more than he was saying. I tried to find the right tone – easy, calm.

'And do you perhaps know where – Dr Angel – is right now?'

'I don't know – exactly. But more or less.'

It was not really a conversation, it was a kind of verbal dance, a series of circumlocutions by means of which each of us bought time, trying to work out what the other was up to before deciding whether he could be trusted. Meaning would emerge, if at all, only in indirect ways that did not compromise either party.

'More or less?'

That was a mistake, he backed off: 'Who did you say you were again?'

I tried, and failed, to keep cool. 'Who did you say *you* were?'

There was a silence, a calculated pause, and then he let me have it between the eyes: 'I'm the police, is who I am.'

I was so surprised I said nothing and he liked that.

'I am the police at the house of Doctor Angel. Who is not here right now. But I am here. But not all the way in.'

He sounded calmer, as if being able to reveal who he was had reassured him. I began to get the rhythm. Slow and easy, like talking to a young, edgy kid.

'You are in Dr Angel's house, but not all the way in?'

'S'right. I am, like, in the entrance to the residence – a pretty big entrance, and I am not going any further in without good back-up. Would you go in without good back-up?'

I said I would not go in without good back-up.

That was the right answer. He sounded relieved. 'Well, me neither.'

32

I let out a bit more line: 'Can you tell me – if Dr Angel is not there where you are, where might he be? More or less?'

'Yes, I can tell you –' the voice spoke warmly, almost gratefully, as if I had found the key; as if I had asked the question he had been waiting for and to which it was possible to give the right answer. 'He is not here because he's dead.'

It took me a while to come back: 'Dead?'

He sounded glad to have cleared this up, almost jaunty now. 'Yes. And so, you see, he's not here.'

It was a blow to the head and it knocked me silly, but I knew if I lost the beat the other man would simply hang up. He was really opening up now, he was telling me how things were.

'And why is that?' I kept my voice light and casual, as if I'd been told that Joe had popped out for butter at the corner shop.

'Why is what?'

'Why is he . . . dead?'

'He got shot is why he's dead.'

The logic and the symmetry pleased my respondent. He was feeling positively helpful now; he had me marked down as someone new to town, who knew nothing about local ways. He was trying to guide me gently through the nature of things as they were in the capital, and in case I had not fully understood what he said, he told me again, in reverse order: 'Why he's dead is because he got shot.'

'And where is he now?'

He had to think about that. 'Maybe still there.'

'And – where is there?'

'Where he got shot. In his car. Where he was hijacked. Close by the golf course at, like, that off-ramp. Seventeenth hole. Unless they've moved him already. And me, I am at his house to see if there's, like, next of kin. I am in the entrance and there's no way I am going further without back-up. This

33

place is bloody huge. Would you go further without good back-up?'

I said again that no, I would not.

'Nor me, man. You go in without back-up and who knows what the fuck hits you?'

I slowly put the phone back in my pocket. He had it right: you go in without back-up and who knows what the fuck hits you?

Until then, I'd told myself, I had kept my options open. I could change my mind at any moment, turn back, junk the whole thing. Even now I could simply forget the voice on the phone and fly back the way I'd come. But I knew now how much I needed Joe to tell me just why I had come. By his not being there, his being dead – whatever that meant, had closed off my escape route. Joe had winkled me out of my hiding place, launched me into space, then vanished, and I was stuck. It made no sense to think of going back. I *was* back.

On the TV monitor set up for tourists I checked a list of hotels and, using the map of the city, I fixed on a place called Summerland, around the corner from the golf course, which, if the cop had it right, would be fairly close to the spot where Joe had been attacked. I called a cab and had the guy drive me along what I guessed was the route Joe would have taken. The news was already across town, because drivers in the stream of traffic on the three-lane motorway slowed and stared as they passed the off-ramp exit that led down to the golf course. But there was nothing to see.

The atmosphere of the capital had not changed: a mix of boredom, expectation and menace. An iron regularity. If I hadn't known they had long departed, I would have said the old lot remained firmly in charge. But then, what do you do after the fireworks of revolution sizzle and fade? You re-employ the flunkeys who do the books, the roads, the drains. Those on the streets had the look of unhappy men selected to administer an empire; civil servants, indistinguishable from their predecessors, still carrying the obligatory pigskin briefcases, scurried between offices; each regime had them: sulky pen-pushers consigned to paperwork, while their bosses made laws and money.

Summerland turned out to be not much more than a bar with rooms, a tacky dive popular with commercial travellers and girls on the game. The reception desk was red leather with a 'No Firearms' warning on the wall, beside a mirror showing a kilted piper advertising Black Watch Scotch. The dark little guy at the small reception desk wanted to know how long I'd be staying.

'No idea.'

'Give me enough for a week and we'll settle the rest later. The name's Gregoire. I run this dump.'

I peeled off several bills from the stash Joe had given me.

'Any machinery?'

'What?

Without turning he reached down and swung open the door of the back safe which stood behind him and I saw racks of pistols, each neatly tagged. 'Did you want to check weapons – to keep in the safe?'

'No weapons.'

'OK. It is just that some guys, they don't like to check their hardware and I won't have guns in the rooms. Not that it stops trouble. The other night I had a girl kill a bloke. He starts to beat her, and she pulls a knife and stabs him. Twenty-three times. We've still not got that damned room clean. I asked her, "Why twenty-three times? Wasn't he dead enough?" She told me she remembered the room number, and gave him the same. I said, "Twenty-three times? Guy was dead by five or six, surely?" She say, "Maybe. But even dead I didn't trust him." Odd world, isn't it?'

'It is.'

'I am sorry for my English. I'm from Mauritius. You?' He tossed the cash I'd handed him into the gun safe.

'I'm from McLeod.'

'I never heard of there.'

'No one has.'

'Come into the bar when you unpack and have a drink. I given you best room, very comfortable, very clean.'

My room was vast and dark and everything in it was brown or purple. From my window I could see a tall, cantilevered tower, which I learned later from the guys in the bar was Angel Reach, the tallest building in town, where decks of luxury apartments were stacked above a slew of restaurants, car showrooms and boutiques. Summerland was on a major boulevard and I found it sensible to cut out the view and keep the curtains drawn against the traffic thundering below. Two rickety cupboards stood against the wall opposite the bed, framing a huge antique TV that did not work. I hung a few things on the wire hangers and packed the rest of my stuff in the splintered drawers.

I sat on the bed with its ugly purple cover, and forced myself to open the linen bankers' bag and count the cash Joe had given me. It came to close on twenty thousand, far too much to simply 'tide me over', as Joe had written. It was more cash than I'd ever held in my hands. More like a stake in a new life, except I didn't want one. I needed suddenly and very desperately to have my old life back. I had little doubt that the cop on the phone had spoken the truth and that Joe was dead, but that raised more questions still. Why, and how, and who? And what the hell was I supposed to do?

So much cash in its raw state lying scattered across the wretched bedspread made me feel slightly sick. I knocked out the flimsy bottom panel of one rickety cupboard, dropped the banker's bag on to the baseboard of the other cupboard and laid the panel over it to make a false drawer. After taking a shower in lukewarm, rusty water I went downstairs to the bar.

And there he was, on the screen above the bar, as if he were alive. Again and again they showed his picture and there was something distantly familiar about him. But his later capaciousness, his bear-like bulk – which I think was probably deliberately acquired, much as a sumo wrestler puts on enormous weight – had swallowed up the thin boy I'd known, with his complexion that alternated between dead white and a rather unhealthy yellow. Now a helmet of rich dark hair framed his face, and his heavy jowls hung like stage curtains, closing off the lean look of the younger man.

Well into that night and each evening for all that week I sat at the horseshoe bar of the Summerland Hotel, among the commercial travellers, pensioners and pimps that drank there, and watched – on the big screen bolted to the wall and flanked by giant vodka bottles – reporters recounting in obsessive detail the events surrounding the murder of Joe Angel.

CHAPTER 4

He had been shot eight times at close range. Whether he was still alive after the attack, no one could say, but, instinctively perhaps, he had jammed his foot on the accelerator and the car had continued on to the road bridge, where it nosed into the stanchion near the exit ramp leading to the motorway, and stalled. The BMW would have looked like just another car about to join the silver snail-tracery of nightly traffic on the triple carriageway below. Until, that is, the guy following on behind got out to investigate why the car did not move, and found a dead man at the wheel. That Joe got as far as he had was taken as evidence of superhuman endurance, or plain doggedness.

The TV crews had arrived soon after Joe had been taken from the car, and the clips ran over and over. The left-hand indicator was pulsing, the driver's window down. The camera poked its nose into the empty space behind the wheel where the driver had been. I saw, again, the soft orange dashboard display lights and breathed the rich leather upholstery. It was the car he had been driving the night he trailed me down First Avenue.

He had died a few blocks away from the immense shopping mall that carried his name: Angel Plaza. Indeed, for some commentators, his death was harrowing as much for its geography as for the cruel details. That a multimillionaire could be murdered in what was virtually his own backyard seemed all the more chilling for being both ironic and senseless. It was accepted that money did not spare you from being murdered, quite the contrary, but it was chilling to be shown so brutally that immense bravura, a huge business empire and the ear of important figures in the administration offered no protection, either.

Earlier, Joe had been at rehearsals of his opera company for a production of *Fidelio* at the City Hall, with sets designed by a young painter he had found begging on the streets of the capital, and whose education at the Beaux Arts in Paris had been funded by Angel Endowments. There was Joe, singing along with the chorus of the opera in rehearsal; Joe conducting the orchestra; Joe at the gala opening later that evening; Joe hugging a couple of AIDS orphans he brought along to the first night and whose crèche he sponsored. Leaving the hall, his last words – according to some sources – had been, 'Oh well, tomorrow's another day.' Then he climbed into the BMW and slid into the night, apparently heading home to his big house in the Western Suburbs. Instead, he stopped off to see his ex-wife Cameron and then, according to her, still in the best of spirits, he left for home.

That the 'Angel Affair' should arouse such emotions was remarkable in a town which, after all, had grown inured to quotidian violence, to shootings, stabbings, hijackings, the bombing of ATM machines, cash-in-transit heists, multiple road fatalities and ever more frequent cases of rape, few of which ever made the papers any longer. The two emotions felt widely were shock and loss. The general conclusion, in those first days, was that Joe had been murdered in a botched hijack – a common event on the streets of the capital. So quotidian indeed that, for the most part, it took a murder of exceptional brutality to stir emotions in a public surfeited on a daily diet of violent deaths: whether a noted chef knifed at a stoplight for her cellphone; or a reggae artist ambushed as he drove his kids to school; a nuclear scientist garrotted and dumped in a river down which he floated for weeks before arriving one horrible morning at the very marina where his family kept their yacht. But here was the death of Joe Angel, headlining newspapers, topping the talk shows, leading the TV news, condemned from pulpits and political platforms.

The drinkers in the Summerland bar studied the details of the case with the same regard they gave to post-game analysis after an important rugby match. When the cameras slung beneath the choppers panned once more over the enormous lawns and fountains of Joe's monumental residence, Monomatapa, several of the guys clapped and the girls wept a lot.

I got to know the regulars rather well. Tony Tucker, who wore a small pork-pie hat indoors and wheezed when he laughed, was a traveller in ketchup. Mannie Kahn sold bricks, was fat and amiable with an endless patter in old saws: 'If you worry – you die; if you don't – sorry, you still die. So why worry?' He was seen as pretty much an authority because he had once sold bricks directly to Joe di Angelo.

Sometimes one of the girls would be in the bar, wearing a frilly robe and sipping camomile tea, ready for the night shift. Gregoire, the sleek Mauritian, chatted to the salesmen or chided the girls for not ensuring that their clients took their condoms with them when they left. Pretty soon I knew by sight most of the girls who worked nights at Summerland, but I never got the names right. Jayne, Krystell, Vibranca . . . the girls might have up to five different *noms de la nuit*, depending on how they felt or what they called themselves in the advertising fliers, the personal columns or the cards they pasted inside phone booths across the neighbourhood; or whether their pimps could spell.

The bar was increasingly at home now with all the technical details: as familiar with ballistics as with the ball games, being constantly interrupted with fresh details of the killing.

We got the calibre of the bullets used, the brand of petrol in his car, the size of his settlement on his last wife, Cameron (many, many millions). We even got the results of the official post-mortem, which was leaked almost immediately to the press. Joe's last meal was described in some detail. He had begun with mulligatawny soup (he had an old passion for boarding-school fare, perhaps related to his early days in St Jude's), followed by two dozen oysters and a T-bone steak, and he ended with chocolate profiteroles. The wines had been a Chardonnay, and a goodly quantity of pinotage, a variety he particularly liked, and it was seen as typical and admirable that he had chosen wines produced on his own estates – as a digestif to round off the meal he had chosen an Armagnac of unidentified vintage. Then, as always, the report ended, several people whistled and the match was back on the big screen; and when a player hugging the ball to his chest dived over the score line, the crowd waved flags and the drum majorettes shimmied and flashed their frothy knickers.

If the drinkers at the horseshoe bar, like many others across the country, were fascinated by what had happened to Joe, they were also very scared. It was the manner and timing of his death that haunted everyone. They took his death person-ally; they looked for some hidden message. If this could happen to someone who 'reached out', 'spanned the ages', 'healed the rifts' and 'moved beyond hatred', then who was safe?

Tony Tucker spoke for everyone when he said, 'This is so weird you wouldn't believe it if you saw it on TV.'

'Could have happened to anyone,' Mannie said.

'Damn right,' said Gregoire.

Each day now brought something new, and the constant diet of ball games on the screen was interrupted by news flashes and investigative reports. The regulars around the bar bore it all with patience. A government statement was read out, hinting that whoever had killed Joe had done so because he represented the spirit of tolerance and reconciliation in a deeply divided society; that he had been a legendary fighter against the prejudice and Puritanism of the old regime and had given his life to the struggle for a better life for all. The murder of Joe Angel was becoming the martyrdom.

There were, from the start, dissenting voices: some suggested that Joe Angel had been a reckless wheeler-dealer who cared for nothing but his empire. There were questions about the legality of his share deals and his mining operations. It seemed he had stopped the car and opened the window in a lonely spot – actions almost unthinkable for anyone who knew the dangers of the city after dark. The assassin – one or more, so the powder burns suggested – had got very close to him. Maybe there was more to this killing than we knew? But those who said so tended to be shouted down. His admirers – and clearly they were in the majority – rejected these accusations 'with contempt', if not always with conviction. They fell back on the insistence that Joe was a man whose generosity was endless, who could not pass a beggar without reaching for some cash, who sponsored soup kitchens and drug rehab clinics.

The fact that Joe had kept right on going despite those bullets in him fascinated everyone. I can't say I found it very surprising. It would never have occurred to Joe that he was supposed to die on someone else's terms; and anyway, death was his familiar. He'd always had what I thought of as a kind of philosophy *in extremis*: he began with the terminal and worked back from there. 'Anything not the end means I'm doing fine,' was how he had once put it to me.

Try as I might I couldn't get out of my mind the preposterous thought that I had been taken for a ride. I'd exchanged a carefully calculated obscurity, which, after nearly thirty years, suited me well, for a frantic, convulsive focus on someone who was proving to be even more inscrutable in death than he'd been in life, and that was saying something.

Summerland itself and the run-down streets and elderly apartment blocks around it were, I soon learnt, on Joe's list for redevelopment and would have made way for a towering new hotel, a casino and a brace of luxury car showrooms. This made the hotel a tenuous island in a sea of change, and the news of this unexpected reprieve left the drinkers around the horseshoe bar unsure what to feel. They were genuinely shocked by the killing, and yet it was hard not to be cheerful at the thought of this little bit of warm nightlife continuing for some time to come. For the moment, all development plans were in limbo. And so, it seemed, was I, like all those who sat there night after night, marooned in this small bar in this crumbling dive, surrounded by towering skyscrapers, which, for the moment at least, had stopped growing. Everything, for the moment, had stopped, while the country tried to adjust to the killing of Joe Angel.

I'd been there for three nights when Gregoire said quietly, 'Funeral is set for next week. Should be a hell of a thing or a thing of hell? Which do you say?'

To my surprise I heard myself say, 'Both. Where is it to be?'

'Three o'clock, Thursday, St Peter's, they says.'

'I think I'll go.'

Gregoire was impassive. 'Really? Maybe you need invite. Like family?'

'We were at school together.'

'Then I guess you kinda owe it to him, being an old friend. You knew him.'

That's what Joe had claimed. The words sounded oddly like an accusation. But I did not know him – or owe him. I knew the boy he'd been and I had been there when the boy I knew split from his old self and was launched on the trajectory that culminated in the man in the BMW. I was there at the moment which ended for ever the life of the white-faced boy, who survived by reducing himself to a grinning, servile clown, the Damascus moment when he saw not the light, but the dark – when Joe came up hard against the power that he knew would destroy him if he did not fight it off. And fight he did, for the rest of his life – or his lives, for I have reason to suspect (and I will come to this later) that even the later Di Angelo was engaged in this struggle right up to the end. He'd got richer, plumper, stranger, perhaps, but he was still at war. But the enemy was more formidable and more resourceful than even he – who knew more about it than anyone I ever met – had been prepared for.

My plan was simple: I'd see Joe buried and then I'd be off back to McLeod. There was nothing more for me in the capital and I wanted to get home. I was already late for the start of term and I knew that the derisory duties of a provisional English teacher were hardly likely to be missed. Even so, I made myself phone Beatrice Tromp.

She sounded unsurprised to hear from me, if a little reproachful. 'Where do I find you, Charles?'

'I'm in a place called Summerland. It's a hotel, in the capital.'

'You missed the start of school.'

'I have to go to a funeral.'

'Is it the funeral of the man who got shot?'

I tried to keep the surprise out of my voice. 'How did you know?'

'It's all they talk about here. They say he came for you, in a big car.'

Of course. All McLeod would be aware that Joe had hit town in his absurd limousine. And when I vanished, the rumours would have started. The tall English teacher no longer limped through town, no longer wandered the countryside photographing ghosts and graveyards. I'd been seen getting into his car, and then I'd vanished.

Miss Tromp said, 'I will be seeing you, I know, in the near offing, I very much hope.'

I was confused. 'Will you be coming to the funeral?'

'They say it will be on TV. I will be watching for you. One more thing, Charles: what must I tell the people?'

'Which people do you mean?'

'The cart people, those nowheres. They came to the school and asked me, "Where is the mister who takes the pictures?" I said I didn't know. But now I can tell them. Shall I tell them, Charles?'

She was making no sense. 'Tell them whatever you like.'

'Charles, I will.' She sounded relieved.

Summerland – with Gregoire behind the bar, a lock of shining black hair over his brow, his very white hands reaching across to jam the glass on to the spigot of the giant vodka bottle, without needing to look where it was – gave me the reassuring feeling that I was well hidden.

It was in this mood of satisfied blindness that on the following morning I found, neatly centred on the mat outside my door, an envelope, and in the envelope a photograph.

It showed three boys: Lockett, Joe and me sitting on the grass, dressed in school uniform, all of us grinning our heads off because, I remembered, the boy – a blond named Mayer – on the other side of the camera had called out: 'Smile, you bastards!'

I took the picture into my room, locked the door and looked at it again. We were at the air-force base and our government – I forget which it was – had just bought a lot of Mirage jets, capable of blasting potential enemies to smithereens, and all schools were to go and pay homage to these machines, and the Brothers of the Holy Cross, knowing that this was not a battle they wished to fight, warned us to look respectful at all times.

Of the three boys in their shorts and blazers, with their fifteen-year-old faces, only I was alive now. And someone knew that, and knew where I was, and wanted me to be aware of it. But what made it notable and worrying was the writing on the envelope: it was the same looping script on the envelope stuffed with new banknotes I had hidden at the bottom of my cupboard.

Later, I lay on the bed with the hideous purple cover. I could smell the dusty carpet and the furniture polish on the sagging easy chair and boxwood bedside tables, and I said to myself, firmly and hopelessly, 'Joe is dead.'

When I asked Gregoire about the envelope, he shrugged. 'Found it on my desk this morning.' And then: 'Tell me – this Joe Angel, when you knew him at school . . . was he crazy, like the guy who got shot?'

'Crazier, I'd say.'

'Maybe you'd better have a vodka for the road.'

The bar waved me goodbye, as if this was some sort of grand reception I was off to. Vibranca, who roomed next door to the girl who had stabbed someone, sipped her tea and told me I was a rare and special person to have known Joe Angel. Tony Tucker told me Joe Angel was the sort of guy who gave him hope for this rotten fucking land of ours. Mannie said, 'Frankly, I think he was a crook. But he kept going, and I really have to hand it to him for that. Didn't know he was dead.'

Part Two
Home from Home

'You get further with a gun and a smile than a smile alone.'
Al Capone

CHAPTER 5

I climbed out of my father's car on Bonaventure Drive and waited outside the big teak door, over which was painted in gilt letters *St Jude's Home for Boys*, and saw three golden tears leaking from each 's'. I was too scared to knock, but my father would not leave until I did, so there could be no progress on either side. We were stuck together, but aching to be apart and it had always been that way.

A second car pulled up and a boy walked up to the door and rapped loudly. He had spiky, coal-black hair, a pointed jaw in a chalky face covered with freckles, and he looked me over.

'I am Giuseppe Roberto di Angelo. Joseph to you. That is Joe, in English-speak. What're you called?'

'Croker.'

'Croker before, or after?'

'W. Croker.'

'William, Watson or Wilberforce?'

It took a moment, but Joe seemed the sort of boy you told things to: 'Winston, actually.'

His grin cracked open his pale face. 'Oh, that's bad. I'll call you Charlie, OK? How much do you know about Al Capone?'

'Nothing.'

'Stick with me, I know a lot.' He left off knocking and shook my hand. 'Glad to meet you, Charlie.'

Behind us the cars of our fathers idled at the kerb; the green humped bug my father drove and the sleek red job, the make of which I did not know, belonging to Joe's father.

'Where's your ma?'

'Don't have one.'

'Must do. Everyone does.'

'She – went away.'

'Where?'

And I told him, as if telling him was easy. When I'd finished he said, 'So when did you work out what had really happened?'

The truth was I still hadn't worked it out. I had been around ten when she went away, and I told myself she must have gone to visit someone. One day my father took me to see her and she was in hospital. She looked tired but happy, and she kissed me and said, 'Winston, I want you to be a really good boy and help your father. Promise me.'

As far as I could see my father did not need the help my mother asked me to give him; he drew his strength from the bank. He often talked of 'the bank' in tones I did not hear again until later, when, in the capital, politicians talked of 'the future', 'the nation', 'the people' and 'the youth'. Such large undertakings, such vacuous words, which, it seemed, bred even more words like 'solidarity' and 'loyalty', but which meant that someone you did not like wanted you to do what you did not want. I would have tried to tell my mother, but I did not have the words. She lay back and looked tired in her pink nightdress, so I promised her as she had asked.

Some days later when I came home from school, my father was there. He looked worried, and he said, 'Winston, I am afraid she's gone.'

'Gone?'

'This morning. I'm very sorry.'

I knew the words referred to my mother and I knew, more or less, what they meant, but I would not let my mind run away with me. My father had said 'gone'. He had not said 'dead'. So 'gone' it would be.

Whatever funeral arrangements my father made I knew nothing about, so there was never any formal leave-taking. My mother simply vanished and might, at least in theory, still be alive somewhere and thus contradict my father's certainties, which seemed to me to be in considerable need of contradiction, but I could not find the words or the means of doing so. I tried to assume the state of sadness I felt was expected of me, but I could never exclude the possibility that she might suddenly reappear, secretly, and we'd go off somewhere.

The bank moved my father from town to town over the next few years and I was able to keep just ahead of my name in a succession of schools which I left before anyone really knew who I was. I wrote 'W. Croker' on my books and, if anyone asked, I said it stood for Wellington or Washington.

One day, a very good day, my father said, 'Winston, I've found a place. A boarding school for boys just like you. Isn't that a bit of luck?'

'Oh, yes.'

'That's settled then.'

And so I came to be standing outside the door of St Jude's Home for Boys, in a suburb in the capital, talking to Joe, who called me Charlie.

Joe said, 'And your old man, what does he do, Charlie?'

'Works in a bank.'

'They're the real racketeers, so Al Capone said. My dad, he makes cement and concrete. I think he's probably a crook, too. Why don't you bang on the door a bit?' Joe took hold of my hand and knocked loudly. That's when he saw the scar on the back, with its diamond shape and its pale gleam.

'Lots of blood?'

'Yeah.'

He was impressed. 'I'll bet. You might have bled to death. Who did it?'

'Some guys, with a piece of glass.'

'It's a good scar. How did it happen?'

I told him how the bus had dropped me, one day after school, near the strip of suburban shops, as it always did. I walked past Rocket Tea Room, the pharmacy of Mr Schevitz, Bennie's Bottle Store, Universal Hardware Supplies and, lastly, Mr Benjamin, the rug doctor, turned sharp left and walked through a dishevelled plantation of gum and fir trees that grew behind the shops.

They were waiting among the trees, boys I didn't know, and one of them held a triangle of jagged glass on which the letters *psi* could be read, and he stabbed me on the back of my right hand, saying as he did so, 'That's what you get for walking that way!' and I called out, 'What way was I walking?' But they ran off, leaving me watching the blood spill over the edge of my hand and splash in the dust. I thought of turning back to the shops, but what would I say? I considered going home, but I knew my mother would be horrified. 'What on earth have you done to yourself, now?' she would ask and I would have no answer. I took hold of my wrist tightly and squeezed, not because I thought this would stop the bleeding, but because I hoped it would make the blood run all the more quickly and so stop dripping, imagining vaguely that each bit of me contained only so much blood and if I squeezed my hand hard, like wringing out a sponge, the spattering pool would stop spreading in the dust. After a while the dripping stopped and, carefully reaching down, I wiped my brown leather shoes with grass. No one noticed that I kept my hand palm-side-up for weeks until the skin healed and I grew a snow-white,

54

diamond-shaped scar. I would turn my wrist and consult the scar now and then. What if I had died? The thought was not unpleasant. Maybe it was like a light going out. I remembered the boy's smile and how he had enjoyed doing it and that always puzzled me. Why did he like it?

I asked Joe now and he said, 'Because we do. It's what we are. Al Capone would have fixed those guys who knifed you.'

'How?'

But before he could tell me, the big front door opened. We stepped into St Jude's and everything changed for ever.

Chapter 6

St Jude's Home for Boys smelt of raw cement, floor polish and plastic tiles. It was a double-storey barracks of yellow brick, with louvre windows running the length of its front face. The parish of the Blessed Redeemer, in a fit of perverse ebullience, had built a spanking new boarding establishment on the western edge of the capital. Completed just weeks before we arrived and built in record time, with the vague idea of providing shelter for boys of impeccable Catholic credentials, to staff it with the best international teachers that could be recruited, and for it to serve as a conduit for boys who felt called to become priests.

St Jude's became instead a receptacle for boys whose parents had separated, died, decamped, lived too far away from a Catholic base, or were incapable, for one reason or another, of looking after their teenage sons, or had simply gone missing. It was an orphanage in all but name because, technically speaking, most of the boys had at least one visible parent.

To the left was the dining hall or what we later learnt to call 'the refectory', and beyond it, separated by a curtain of heavy plastic, was the miniature chapel painted blue, with two steps leading to the altar on which was a simple tabernacle, with doors of chased silver depicting in relief the Holy Ghost as a dove, arising from the sacred chalice. Directly ahead of us was a flight of stairs softened along their concrete edges with rubber treads. Carrying our suitcases, we walked up those stairs to the dormitories that ran left and right the length of the second floor. Twenty-four boys to a dorm, two rows of steel bedsteads, each separated by a bulky steel locker and, as one came through the swing doors, the housemaster's room, behind a stout wooden door. Along the walls of the dormitory, slatted louvre windows sliced the sky into lozenges of light, which fell on the metal lockers and painted refracted rainbows on the dark brown floor tiles.

Thirty years later I can still move in my mind down the row of beds: mine was beside Joe's; his was beside that of Trevor Lockett. He was the other force that marked me, throughout my life, though in some ways less so than others whose marks were far less visible. Broad as a tank, hazel eyes and a sallow skin, with hewn, handsome features, a strong jaw and very strong – if there is a word for Lockett's looks it was 'chiselled'. He had a cleft in his chin; he had perfectly positioned cheek-bones; he had a very symmetrical forehead, and his soot-black hair grew with utter precision in glossy waves of well being; his eyes were sea-green and his teeth brilliant.

Lockett was probably eighteen, but looked to us around thirty, and arrived at the Home riding proudly on a black, growling Harley Davidson, and in the time he was there he changed our lives. He kept a set of clothes for walking out, which he did on Saturday afternoons. He wore a pink string tie held with a brass clasp embossed with a silver 'T', a cream sports jacket that reached down almost to his knees, and his hair was lusciously oiled and combed and sprayed along the temples with silvery mist. And he carried a flick knife. Who else would have had exactly the right gear for lifting weights, the right nightclothes, down to sumptuous silk smoking jacket and cherry-red Turkish slippers?

57

He kept soft leathers for riding his big Harley with a nurse, Julia Morgenstern, riding pillion, and looked utterly right, when the rest of us did not even own pushbikes. According to Lockett, the delicious Julia met him at the café near the railway station – 'True as God, Di Angelo' – wearing a full-length fur coat, but without a stitch on underneath.

As we stood in the entrance that day, Joe and I understood nothing at all. But there was no going back, and no one else knew any more than we did about the world we had just entered or the place which wore so awkwardly the name given it: that of the patron saint for hopeless cases.

Our territory, and its appendages, measured six square blocks: the Church of the Redeemer with its gardens, palms and parish hall; the Convent of the Sacred Heart with its hockey pitches and playing fields; Holy Cross College, the day school across the road from St Jude's, with its red corrugated iron roofs and whitewashed gables, rugby fields and tennis courts, and the Scout Hall, of biscuit-brown brick, in the shape of a ship. The Scouts were nautical types, though the city was five hundred miles from the coast, and some in the troop had never set eyes on the ocean. As Joe was soon to tell me, we had landed in the middle of a battlefield and the enemy had us surrounded.

A gigantic Calvinist College, with a campus stretching several miles, hemmed us in and grew all the time, bolstered by lavish state stipends, its business being to hand out degrees in everything from mathematics to agronomy to students who accepted the values of their fathers. It was not an academy of free enquiry – it was a mental boot camp where the ideals were obedience, discipline, loyalty; and detestation of the small feudal outpost of Catholic Rome, spawn of the Beast of Babylon, a treacherous fifth column camped in their front yard. Beyond stretched the capital city, owned by men of the same mind, who did not know what to do with us – but knew that we were dangerous and unreliable: servants of the damnable pontiff in distant Rome.

St Jude's, then, was an unwelcome arrival in a deeply disturbed town. It had no form or pattern; no one knew what to expect, and no one knew what to do; not the Rector, nor the new housemasters: willowy Trevor Buttleby from Australia and the saturnine Wim De Kok from Amsterdam, who, having taken the jobs in the belief that they were going to some 'normal' school, and had come to the Home expecting to find some form of meaning and value, found instead confusion among the boys themselves, who fought incessantly; and between the boys and the barefoot Calvinist students on the borders of our enclave; and civil war between the boys and their teachers, the Brothers of the Holy Cross in the college over the way, who ruled by the rod, the fist and the leather strap. Their pupils responded with kamikaze insolence, and the general tenor of the place was a kind of jovial brutality, alarming to foreigners but pretty much normal, and indeed enjoyable, to the combatants themselves.

Oblivion was always close, and we occupied the lowest level in the pecking order of the Catholic parish of the Blessed Redeemer, itself lost in the Calvinist kingdom of the tall ones, the shaved ones, the superior ones. Our numbers at St Jude's hovered around fifty; every roll call was an experiment and every morning there were more, or less, of us. Boys vanished. Some were expelled; two died in motorbike accidents; some went into hospital and did not come back; new boys showed up and replaced them and they, too, might vanish a few weeks later. No one said where they went, and we never asked. We always had the feeling that if all fifty of us were to have been wiped out, our absence would cause no stir.

Joe's family had 'fled' (his word) Sicily a few years before and he was vivid about life on the island: 'We lived in a cave and we were so poor we had nothing to eat except a stick of salami hanging from the roof, to keep it away from the rats.' We were impressed by this history, just as we were by his ability to stand up to whatever life threw at him. He hated St Jude's because it lacked 'even a smidgin of style'.

Mr Di Angelo, to begin with at least, came more often than most fathers, and looked, in close-up, like a more solid version of Joe, his face so well-fleshed that his eyes receded like buttons in some plump cushion, his black hair smoother than Joe's, longer and oiled over his scalp. He drove a blood-red Hudson Hornet with a miniature Great Dane reposing in the rear window, its head swaying to and fro when Mr Di Angelo took off down Bonaventure Drive after depositing his son at the Home at the end of a weekend's leave. He took off at some speed, a resonant swoosh of the sort only big American cars made, as opposed to the apologetic throat-clearing of small British cars like the pale green Vauxhall that my father drove. A car that knew nothing of Sicily and caves or dried sausage, and would not have wanted to know anything either, thank you very much.

My father had never met Joe, but he lost his temper when he asked if I had any friends and I said, 'Giuseppe Roberto di Angelo.'

'Damn little wop! I think you care more for a lot of dagoes and Eyeties and Yids than you do for your own family.'

I knew then that I had found a way to stop the visits altogether. I said, 'Joe di Angelo's from Sicily, and his family lived in a cave and all they had to eat was dried sausage. He's my friend. Can I bring him home with me?'

My father's visits thinned down to biannual interludes, at the beginning and the end of each term. And even these faded out after my first year at St Jude's, when an uncle who owned a sheep farm sent me a train ticket, and from then on I spent every holiday on the farm where I soon knew how to ride, to shoot and to slaughter a lamb. I learnt to sharpen the knife on a whetstone, to look the lamb in the eyes when it seemed to offer its neck; I learnt not to take my eyes off the neat edge of blood left on the knife as it slid around the pulsing neck of the lamb. I saw its eyes dull and then glaze over. When jackals got among the sheep, I saw what they did. They toyed and tore; they ripped a neck, an ear, emptied the guts. Savagery was their setting, taking the pleasure that pain had to give.

When, later, in our English class, Brother Duigan, a pleasant man with a wave of white hair, and a fine shot, read out the lines of Blake which make the tiger so terrific you'd think it a privilege to be eaten by such a great burning beast, and spoke the awestruck challenge: 'Did he who made the lamb make thee?' I knew there could be only one answer: 'Damned right he did.'

CHAPTER 7

Father Daintry, the new rector, arrived from England on the same day – and offered us tea and chocolate cake, though he never did so again. He seemed alarmingly improbable, with thin grey hair curving in oily comb-strokes over his faintly freckled scalp, and the flushed, strawberry pallor of his broad face with its several jowls. He wore black elastic-sided boots, which he threw outwards as he walked, leaning slightly backwards to counterbalance his belly. Everything about him was round and soft and faintly flushed and he showed, sometimes, a bead of sweat on his upper lip or his forehead. His hands, pushing limply from his cassock sleeves, edged with frayed leather, were clasped loosely across his middle.

'Pale hands I loved beside the Shalimar,' Joe would croon.

Boys soon vied to shake one of those pale hands, and went away marvelling at 'the dead fish'. Drawing your fingers into his moist palm, he subjected them to a brief, jelly-like, dying quiver that made this greeting famous for miles. His fat fingers, bearded with surprisingly wiry black hair between his knuckles, had the limp flaccidity of scallops. Between index and forefinger there lodged eternally a lighted cigarette with its tiny elephant's trunk of ash fluttering, a flake at a time, on to his curving midriff.

Father Daintry was not merely English – he was England incarnate. And as a result we patronized him, laughed at him and were utterly beguiled by his plummy London tones. His encouragement of Mozart, in a neighbourhood where boys were beaten up for carrying violin cases, was positively dangerous. And yet I saw very soon that he had qualities which, if grasped, would be devastatingly useful.

Joe got the message fast. Daintry spoke Italian very well. He loved Verdi. He taught us to say 'reffer-tory' instead of 're-fec-tory', for what we called the dining room; and he made us answer *'Adsum'* – 'I am here' – when he called the roll each morning in the yard, after Mass. He made us read *Lives of the Saints* in the 'reffer-tory'.

The close-cropped young men at the great university – storm troopers of the one true reformed faith, who lived in Zwingli Hall, the student's hall of residence just a few doors away in Bonaventure Drive – seemed the worst of all, perhaps because they were so close. They enjoyed haranguing boys from Holy Cross College with what they took to be mild quips; a favourite being 'little cunt-creepers'. The insult had an even deeper, rounder tone in the patois and evidently delighted the young men, who shouted it again and again, and fell about with manly laughter. Sometimes, when in open country where escape was possible, we would answer back (before running away): 'Fuck off, piss-willy Puritans!' I saw Father Daintry watching this carefully, and very soon he was seeing how we were and what we felt – fear, anger, but no sense of who or what we were fighting. He wanted very much to help us survive and he knew what it took.

The Brothers across the road in the College had other ideas: they were determined to save our souls. What we learned in class at Holy Cross College was to be frightened to death – by death. They taught not preparation for life but a crash course

63

on how it closed. Extinction was guaranteed, and if there was some short administrative delay, we should not get our hopes up. Death was on its way, sure as shooting. Mortality was measured out in sporting terms. The Brothers who readied us for that final fixture believed in dying to win. Life was rehearsal; death the real thing. Hard training was needed if we were to be licked into shape. Heaven was won in the sweaty gymnasium of the soul. Readiness was all. I confessed my sins, begged divine forgiveness, strove to make my nightly acts of contrition more and more perfect, for only then would I be safe. Daily spiritual exercises; nightly acts of contrition to counter a sneak attack while asleep; plenary indulgences to mop up accumulated time in purgatory; frequent confession and hourly prayers to patron saint and guardian angel.

Sometimes these measures helped. But too often, minutes after falling asleep, I would jerk bolt upright, heart battering my ribcage, choking and screaming soundlessly, as if my mouth were stuffed full of feathers, sickened by the utterly certain knowledge that this was my last night on earth and the moment I closed my eyes again I'd be gone. This pattern would last until exhaustion finally knocked me out.

And though no one actually said so, it was taken for granted that we were headed straight to hell. Not that anyone gave us a particularly good portrait of Hades, only that it was hot, interminable and infinitely removed from the joys of paradise. But then heaven didn't look like much either: praise and adoration and angels. Nothing that compared with the blessed life we led within the brick walls of St Jude's.

We waited, poised, on the rim of eternity, on the outer edge of the world to come. And that added seriousness to our lives. If it hadn't made us happy, I could say with some confidence that, after such an eschatological crash course, it took a lot to rattle us. Our views of death, though deeply felt and horribly well informed, tended towards sedition – we might be in awe of its inescapable power, but we reacted and rebelled by subverting its sombre dignity. If teaching children about sex too young robbed them of innocence, then what did the frequent and graphic introduction of the terrors of death do to teenagers? It robbed us of respect for the old ogre. It gave us a fierce desire to spit in his eye. It meant we never developed a sense of proportion. It led, in short, to perversions – which were our own and which we enjoyed expressing. The world to come looked like a totalitarian state, a rather more interesting version of the city in which we found ourselves, with its sublime hauteur, its pompous rituals of pride and propriety, its stifling self-esteem – and we were learning how to subvert it.

In order to do so we needed to know its pathology, to see it up close, to study, and classify its different genres. And the Parish of the Redeemer offered rich opportunities for doing so.

Generally speaking, death came in two varieties: big and small. Crude though this division might have seemed, it helped us a lot.

Take the first case: a Tuesday morning Latin class, for example, around ten, with the heat getting up, it being summer. Usual Tuesday, usual teacher: Brother Bassett, a huge, square man who wore a steel plate planted in his flat, pale forehead to cover a hole gouged out by shrapnel in the First World War (for some reason he was late that Tuesday). Usual text, Caesar's Gallic Wars, and, as usual, one of the class, Graham Mays, innocent provocateur who said nothing, did nothing, sat with arms folded and with the faintest of smiles on his very thin lips. This was enough, usually, to goad Brother Bassett beyond endurance. He would be reduced to foaming curses and tears of rage and began bumping his armoured head against the blackboard, like an aged, ailing buffalo.

But this Tuesday there had been the order to go into the quad that resembled a prison yard; its high walls formed the square, with balconies and columns stretching up to a patch of sky. Here we were formed into a line, three abreast, and marched down to the Church of the Resurrection, just a few blocks distant.

Rumours in the lengthy marching column of boys, passing beneath blossoming jacaranda trees, spoke of astonishing things. Old 'Bassett Hound', last seen in the very fury of good health, landing six of the best with his long leather strap, on some stooping white-faced victim, was said to be gone. Just like that, out of the blue.

At the church we filed into the pews of the Lady Chapel, blinking bemusedly, unsure which expression to assume. The mid-morning sun, shining through stained-glass visions of saints, virgins, evangelists and martyrs in the windows over-head, painted on our white cotton shirts disconcerting emblems: a lily emblazoned across Trevor Lockett's broad back; Joe's neck striped black and yellow, as gaudy as tiger's hide.

We contemplated the coffin on its bier below the altar steps, with its six tall yellow candles standing guard, and we had thought, 'That's Bassett Hound in there, a man so tough he once tossed Di Angelo across the classroom, and he bounced off the blackboard like a shuttlecock; a guy for whom Ernie Di Longhi's plump, blonde mother had a purple passion, despite Brother Bassett being celibate, and a homoeopath to boot.' But here, now, Bassett was in the box, we had the rector's word for that. He had spoken of the sad demise of Brother Horace Bassett. 'Demise? . . . Horace?' It was all we could do to keep from collapsing with merriment. Gone, well OK. But since when had he been Horace? It was absurd. What would ample, soft Mrs Di Longhi say? She who wore heavy gold bracelets of chunky Aztec charms, and drove a Pontiac. One minute he was having a mild flirtation and the next Horace – NO, he could not have been called Horace – and the next, Brother Bassett, old Bassett Hound, had upped and died.

What had he been thinking of? What did it mean?

The statue of Mary, Queen of Heaven, stood on the Lady altar in the side chapel where we filled the pews. She was dressed in blue robe and creamy veil and her crown was a wire halo representing the star-studded night sky. The Christ Child on his mother's knee had carelessly kicked off a sandal. Trevor Lockett was also staring at the Virgin with a look of deep awe. Lockett had told us that he didn't give a scrap for any of the Catholic faith, even if he was forced to go through the motions. He did not believe in Jesus or Mary, he believed in Elvis Presley and, probably, Julia . . . Yet the look he gave the Queen of Heaven was one of extraordinary solicitude. As if he wanted to dart forward and retrieve the Christ child's sandal, or hold up his hand and say, 'Please Miss, your little guy is about to lose his shoe . . .'

What on earth had come over Lockett and turned him (briefly, it was true, but sincerely) from street-fighter into boy Scout?

Death had come over Trevor Lockett. Intimations of mortality; the sure feeling, as he stared at the coffin before the altar, that death would one day take him, just as it had taken the late Brother Bassett. Just as it would take us all, sooner rather than later.

So it was that we began to know not just the horror but also the extraordinarily anarchic character of death; its appalling manners; its rough intrusion into unsuspecting lives; the way it took what it wanted without asking or paying or apologizing; the confusion it caused. It silenced the school bell, destroyed the timetable and turned famous rebels like Lockett into plaster saints, right before our eyes. Death, then, might have its advantages. But no one could be sure of its humour: it might take those more suited to being taken – or it might suddenly, horribly, take you.

No matter how often it happened we were always surprised. Seeing Brother Bassett buried did nothing to familiarize us with the reality. We never got used to it. Men who seemed so vital and indestructible in their heavy, rather greasy black cassocks, rough with the fumes of tobacco, Lifebuoy soap, brandy and the leathery tang of the arm-long straps they kept in their back pockets for beating errant boys suddenly and violently and helplessly vanished.

On the other hand, it paid dividends. The mortality rate among the teaching staff was probably quite normal, but because it made such an impression, we had the feeling that it happened regularly. And to go to the funeral was shocking – but it brought an unexpected bonus: no more lessons that day. Yes, there was black crêpe and muffled bells and solemn prayers for the soul of the departed, but there were compensations – after the requiem came the reward: no more lessons; death brought grief, sadness, fear – it also brought welcome half-holidays.

That the loss of a Holy Cross Brother could be a cause of secret celebration might have shocked our teachers, but in wartime you took comfort where you could. This was not a combat of our choosing; we had been drafted without consultation. We found ways of fighting back. We were battle-hardened veterans in the field of final things, and we took no prisoners. We lived close to death, but extended exposure led us to rebel. How close might you get to the edge of life without falling off? And if you did fall off, how original could you be? I'm not sure if this training strengthened Joe di Angelo's already wild and desperate spirit, but it gave him a taste for the macabre. Some kids collected trains; we took notes on the four last things: death, judgement, heaven and hell.

But only Joe took classes, studied it close-up in the movies, three or four times a week, whenever the local cinema ran another gangland series of shoot-ups and bootleg sagas. Death was an abstraction, too ephemeral to get hold of. Better, said Joe, to look hard at what dying meant, and to do that properly you had to consider bumping people off.

'Literally killing them?'

'Of course not. But seeing what it means, and how it's done and why it's done.'

'And how do you do that?'

'You watch movies.'

He was obsessed by the mayhem that had decimated the gangs of Chicago, and the versions that played out on the screen of the Monte Carlo Cinema in Jeweldeane, matinees 2.15 to 5 p.m., twice a week. Though it was strictly forbidden, Joe and I slipped out to watch *The Doorway to Hell*, *G Men*, *White Heat* or *Gun Crazy*. These ingenious celluloid depictions of manslaughter came to represent for him a shapely and utterly desirable world, one with style and smooth, sexy charm. We sat in the dark, watching men get beaten with baseball bats, shot repeatedly in slow motion, or cut into pieces with Tommy guns – this being a filmically attractive prop, because it enabled the shooter to become a one-man army and to murder many people within a very short space of time with panache, in the repetitive universe of kill-flicks.

When the end credits rolled he'd stroll out of the darkness, blinking like a cat and yawning in the sharp sunlight, to find me waiting, stupidly, in the lobby, under the Tarzan posters, alongside those of forthcoming attractions, showing Tommy guns, fedoras, floozies and sharp suits, his look somewhere between pity and real sympathy for a guy who could be so dumb, so blind not to see what a lark it all was, how natural and healthy.

'This is just a movie. Can't you tell the difference? Don't take it so seriously.'

It never got any better, though he would urge me on: 'Next week, it's all gang flicks, a festival. Let's go, it'll be knock-out stuff. You'll see. But it isn't real, OK?'

Looking back, I guess he was right – it was all just a load of fun: Lucky Luciano, Mad Dog Coll, Pretty Boy Floyd, Legs Diamond . . . the funny cops and even funnier killers – the hats, the girls, the tommy guns. But for me it was too real to be borne. I was simply too dumb to get the right perspective on what is a human and universal phenomenon – and in this reading the depiction of bloodletting and the real thing are poles apart and everyone is entitled to thrill to the faithful depiction of cruelty, and to confuse it with the deliberate extinction of another is just silly and not even particularly cruel.

I watched Machine Gun Kelly or Dutch Schultz lift his weapon and fire a bullet into the head of a trembling rival, and I distantly took Joe's point: that making murder a game was allowed in movies because filmland is a privileged place. Where else – outside a civil war or inside the mind of a pathological killer – may the deliberate snuffing out of life be exhibited in loving detail, and celebrated in images and music, to the delectation of those who buy a ticket, and for whom watching it happen is a natural right, whose only benchmark is whether or not it is done with style? For whom it is an art form, and as much fun as skipping a rope, and who rejoice in it – this was Joe's way – he loved its wild innocence! For happy doters on lyrical bloody fun, nothing matched grievous bodily harm being done, and cheering it to the rafters. As Joe said of *The Rise and Fall of Legs Diamond*, a film he saw fourteen times: 'It's not just blood and bullets, you dope. Look at the lapels, the suits, the hats, the spats. Lighten up a bit, Charlie.

Hear the music they make when they talk. Feel the texture and rhythm.'

Joe wanted to kill someone, but he wanted it to happen in the way it did in *Scarface* or *Little Caesar*.

'Thank God for Little Caesar. He teaches us how to stick up for ourselves. He's got such class! I'm from Sicily and I know what I'm seeing. There's a war going on. And we're sitting ducks. We'd all better get ready to fight, or go under.'

In the gospel according to Joe, formulated so pungently over those years, we were 'the Pope's people' (sometimes the 'Roman Resistance'), locked in a struggle to the death with 'Calvin's Crew'.

Once a week, Brother Duigan marched us down to the school shooting range behind the rugby pitch. There were a dozen booths for the marksmen and behind the targets stood the butts, mounds of fine beige sand peppered with lead.

It turned out because of the early training on my uncle's farm I was pretty good with a .303 and I got better. I enjoyed seeing the target after a session, with the bullseye cut away by clustering hits, not one beyond the second ring.

Joe's shots threw up puffs of smoky sand as his rounds pocked the butts behind the target, and he simply did not get it.

'Do not fire the weapon, but rather use it to reach out and touch what you're aiming at, like a painter applying a dab of paint to a canvas,' said Brother Duigan. But Joe shot the way he'd seen it done in the movies: too rushed, too stiff and mechanical.

'You're a wonder with a gun. I'm hopeless,' said Joe. 'Getting to the target, seeing what you aim for and hitting it, that's a talent, Charlie.'

'It's no big deal, shooting straight.'

'You never know when it could be useful.'

'Useful?'

'Yeah. When I need a hitman.'

I grew up with a murderer-in-waiting, and he was my best friend. I liked him: he had once lived in a cave and lived off salami, and I was tremendously impressed.

'It's only a matter of time before they polish us off. We're doomed, but I want to go down fighting. Little Rome against the world. I'm gonna take as many of them with me as I can.'

And he meant it. I never knew anyone who looked so frankly at destruction, and smiled. But it had to be – I reach for the words – shapely mayhem. Elimination was to be aesthetic, something that looked the way it did in the movies, where bullets were beautiful and murder had form and rhythm, where it had – I'll use his word, vague as it is – 'class'. The origins of that higher desirability might be summed up in a single word: America. Only in America did people pull off such photogenic homicides, only in America could it be good to see, great business and such fun. But between the way he wanted it to look, and the way it really was, there loomed a great gap. He soaked it up in the movies, lived every moment of it, and he read moral lessons into murder. But when it came to real shooting, it turned out he was hopeless, and I should have thought about that very hard.

CHAPTER 8

God the father, who was so often invoked in the home, in school, in church, was a shadowy, shifty figure, rather like all the fathers – Di Angelo's dad, in particular, who sometimes lavished on him cash, tape recorders and string ties (red and gold and black with brass clips, reading *Di Angelo's Concrete Services PTY Ltd*), and sometimes never showed up for weeks on end and left his son looking ill, his brown eyes smouldering in his dead white face, saying things like, 'I think maybe my old man's dead, or something.'

And I'd say, 'No, he isn't, Joe. He'll turn up.'

'Don't make much diffs, Charlie. I don't care. I got someone better.'

Unlike other boys, who pinned pictures of film stars or rock singers or saints to their locker doors, Joe had stuck there a picture of a man with dark hair, a podgy profile and a half-smile, and on the man's right shoulder was the notice *Miami Police Department* and a stencilled number: *3500*.

'Who is the bloke?' I asked.

Joe looked at me with an expression of such solemnity that I had to laugh.

'That's no bloke. That's the true Al Capone. It's the police mugshot.'

In a gesture I had only ever seen someone make before a

73

crucifix or a statue of the Holy Virgin Mary, he knelt before the picture on his locker door and crossed himself. It would be wrong to say Joe worshipped Capone; it was rather, as he said to me, ' It is what you do with saints. You use an image to raise your awareness of the real thing.'

One day, as Joe knelt before the poster of Al Capone, the Rector walked in. For a fat man with a waddle, he was a very quiet mover; you hardly ever heard him until he was right on top of you, cigarette smoke drifting like a veil over his face, eyes half-shut and watering behind the blear of his glasses.

'Praying for something special, Di Angelo?'

'To be anywhere but here, Father.'

Joe flung out his arm to encompass Little Rome: six square blocks of real estate, contiguous with one another, cradled an entire and self-sufficient Catholic universe. The Convent of the Sacred Heart and its hockey fields, Holy Cross College for Boys, with its red corrugated iron roofs and whitewashed gables. Beyond Little Rome lay the capital with its broad streets, its jacarandas, the towering blocks of student flats that loomed above our Catholic enclave like watchtowers, its statues of famous rebel fighters, its throng of churches, spires like rocket ships, its army and police force, its squadrons of civil servants with short hair and briefcases and their mute, self-important obedience to their church, their regime and their gruff God.

'Where would you like to be?'

'New York, when Capone was growing up.'

'Can you tell me more?'

Joe got out his maths exercise book and in blue crayon he drew a map. 'This is Brooklyn's Navy Yard, in New York, where Capone hung out as a kid. Around that time, 1918 or so, it was a stinking slum, with gin, girls and gangs,' Joe explained happily. 'You had the Irish gangs, the Neapolitans, like Capone – and you had Sicilians, like me. You also got Jewish and Irish gangs. East of Flushing Avenue belonged to the Sicilians. In the north-west you got the Irish; Jews held the north-east. Capone joined a gang called the Five Pointers in Manhattan, on the Lower East Side.'

'Wasn't he from Chicago?' Father Daintry asked.

'That's what people think. But he was a New Yorker and the cops were after him, so he headed for Chicago.'

'Why were the police after him?'

'They said he'd knocked off a few guys.'

'True?'

'Here and there. In the line of business. It was good practice.'

'Murder was good practice?'

'He had to keep things on the level.'

'I've heard something about St Valentine's Day.'

Joe smiled. 'It was never proved he did that. Anyway, those guys were muscling in. And he wanted straight dealing from his partners.'

Father Daintry considered: 'What do you mean by straight dealing?'

'You know about dinner at the Hawthorne Inn ?'

'Tell me, Di Angelo.'

With the Rector leaning on Joe's locker, occasionally glancing at the mugshot of the man numbered *3500*, whose profile showed a neat sideburn, a shapely ear and a pug nose, Joe told us about the Hawthorne Inn.

'A bunch of bootleggers planned to double-cross Capone. So what he did was to invite them out for a great dinner. He fed them and filled them with wine. And then, just as they thought it was all very nice, in came his guys and wired them to their chairs; then Al walked around the table with a baseball bat, breaking every bone the bat could break. Afterwards each of them was shot through the head.' Joe's eyes were bright. 'Isn't that something? And they were Sicilians. My own people. But they had it coming. They messed with Big Al.'

'He was a killer, Di Angelo, a hoodlum.'

'He was a good-hearted guy who gave out food parcels at Christmas. Widows and orphans thanked him. The so-called respectable folk, they drank his bootleg booze, used his brothels, but they called him a crook. I say he was what he was. He ran a business, and he was better at it than everyone else in a crooked world.'

'Admirable loyalty to your saint, Di Angelo, but you are missing something.' The Rector nodded and lit a cigarette. 'Here was a man who carved out in Chicago a complete parallel universe, lived brightly and bloodily alongside the legal universe of law and politics, and alongside his straight customers, who bought his bootleg hooch. He exposed the lies and double-dealing of the so-called respectable world.'

Joe was pleased. 'You've got it, Father.'

'Yet he went to jail, I seem to remember. Your picture – your shrine – shows him on his way to Alcatraz, is that right?'

Joe nodded. 'The Feds set him up. Non-payment of taxes. He got ten years. Capone never snitched, never complained when he went inside. He said, "I played my cards – I lost . . ."'

'Yes, yes. But you're not hearing me, Di Angelo. Others did far worse, and got rewarded. Where did Capone go wrong? Tell me why – in your reading – did the hoodlum with the good heart pay for the sins of others? If a man with that degree of power goes under, what did he misjudge? How might he have done better?'

Joe shrugged. 'The way it is.'

'Why is it the way the way it is? You're missing something important. He lost and you should ask yourself why. Perhaps it has to do with the disposition of forces. Maybe he lost control.'

'Of himself? He went too far?'

The Rector looked hard at Joe. 'Maybe he didn't go far enough.'

'How do you mean, Father?'

'The question really is this: how far is far enough? If you play a hard game, you had better play for keeps.'

When the Rector had gone, Joe said to me, 'He's crackers, isn't he, Charlie?'

The Capone compulsion, and Father Daintry's challenge, provided Joe with the need to study in detail anyone who might offer the merest clue to the nature of the world as it was. But – and this was absolutely vital – no matter how he lowered himself, Joe's eyes were on the stars; he loved class, expertise, he worshipped shapely deportment within the world and efficacy in all things, but he was still trying to answer the question why Capone had gone wrong.

'You're doing God, or you're going around kicking people in the goolies. Only question is – are you good at it?'

Capone had high-octane glamour. He played a large game. He was a pro. He lifted the show. In a city like ours, so ugly, so inept, so dedicated to the suffocating certainty of its own righteousness, Capone looked a classy guy. And so, by association, did Trevor Lockett. I guess he took what he could get and Lockett was the closest thing to being good at what he did, though what he did was not very nice.

The Rector showed what a hard game he played with a simple announcement the next morning after roll-call.

'Gentlemen, I seem to have landed in something of a jungle where the law is to kill or be killed. I prefer the former. I have decided to appoint Trevor Lockett head boy of St Jude's. Lockett gets my blessing because he has natural authority and that gives him privileges.'

We listened, astounded. Lockett had authority all right,

but it relied on the fist, the boot and the headbutt; he ruled in the manner of the lion or the warlord – he tended to maim those who disagreed with him.

The Rector was not finished: 'I regard him as a fine Christian gentleman. Take a leaf from his book. I wish more of you boys would be more like him!'

It seemed outrageous then; but I think now it was sublime. Daintry had our measure. He had just invited us all to dinner at the Hawthorne Inn. We soon came to realize that this strange man with his pale, watery eyes saw deep into us. He knew Joe oscillated always between guns and God. He knew that I was, even then, locked away inside myself, unable to move. And soon he was offering us ways out of ourselves. It was a terrible generosity from which we never recovered.

One of Lockett's first acts as head boy was to push me from Mr Buttleby's second-floor window, because, as he told me as he forced me on to the sill, only the housemaster's window opened wide enough to allow me to pass through. I landed in a flower bed outside the refectory, and when the story got around the school, the symbolism of my fall (into a bed of roses) amused the otherwise tough and intellectually incurious Irishmen who taught us. The roses I fell among carried labels identifying them as 'Bel Ange', and as I lay there – thinking, 'Well, I'm sure the pain will not be so bad in a while' – I noticed that the petals of the Bel Ange were soft pink with darker undersides. Such details were comforting, if not very persuasive. The boys of my dorm looked down from the windows in a semi-interested fashion, and I remember Di Angelo sticking his head out and saying, 'All right, Charlie?' I said, 'I don't think so,' and he said, 'Oh, you'll be OK,' and his head vanished.

I tried but failed to get up and the pain did not go away,

and then the ambulance arrived. When I got out of hospital a fortnight later, Joe said simply, 'That's a keen limp you got there, Charlie. I'm impressed.'

He was even more impressed when Lockett decided that St Jude's needed a fagging system like they had in England.

'But we'll have a better tradition. You will be my valet, Di Angelo.'

In the evenings, wearing his olive-green silk dressing gown, maroon cummerbund, a yellow silk handkerchief foaming in his breast pocket, Lockett would remove the ivory holder and its unlit cigarette from his mouth and boom commands: 'Di Angelo, you may lay out my night things.'

'Yes, Trevor, yessir, certainly, O Lord and Master.'

'Di Angelo, draw my bath!'

'Yes, Trevor, sir, right away, your Royal Highness.'

'You make a good worm, Di Angelo.'

'Thank you, sir.'

Lockett tormented Joe, and Joe bowed before him, his white face a doe-eyed ovoid, his mouth a helpless droop, the brisk upward thrust to his spiky black hair his only defiant note. But you caught, sometimes, a glimpse of his other side – the pointed chin, the sharp teeth: the outline of a weasel or a stoat or a fox, yes, all those names applied to Joe, but they were not quite right. Looking at him, I was sometimes reminded of a burnt match, charred, thin, brittle with a whiff of sulphur.

'A hatchet with hair,' Lockett once called him. 'A Lucifer.'

And he got hold of something. Joe was pride incarnate and yet it came across as humiliating self-abasement. He would prevail, no matter what it took.

He was both victim and director of his own long cruel comedy; he was in rehearsals for something far bigger than we ever knew. And he was reckless beyond our comprehension. He did not just court disaster, he rushed to meet it.

Joe had the gall to question whether Trevor Lockett's girl-friend Julia Morgenstern, a blonde nurse at the General Hospital, five years older than him, really arrived naked under her fur coat at their trysts at the station café.

Lockett took him along to the café in question, where they ordered toasted sandwiches, and when Julia arrived, Lockett said to her, in the same imperious tone with which he instructed Di Angelo to shine his shoes or do his homework or polish his motorbike: 'Julia, open your coat for Joe, and show him that you are beautifully naked.'

She did, and she was, and we all knew Lockett would stomp on him later, but Joe seemed prepared for that. He believed Lockett had the makings of a beautiful killer, and he was ready to stake his life on it. And if it was worryingly apparent to anyone who took a good look that Lockett was only a cut-price Capone, he was the closest Joe was going to get to the hoodlum of his dreams, the Capone who sailed over the moral barricades and exposed the hypocrisy of those who erected them.

It was a great deal for Lockett to live up to and Joe egged him on. He praised his style, his swagger and his Chinese flick knife, its plastic handle adorned with scarlet dragons emblazoned on the sides and a secret silver button, which, when pressed, whisked out the blade like a striking snake and held it to Joe's throat.

'Peekaboo, Di Angelo.'

'Yessir. Peekaboo it is!'

Like the Rector, Joe was beginning to play a hard game.

CHAPTER 9

On an evening like many others, the usual bedtime routine unfolded in its sleepy way, when the head boy in his silken gown, followed by his valet and soap-bearer carrying mug and toothbrush, began his procession towards what he called his 'ablutions', and very few of us bothered to watch. We had seen it before: sometimes, for no reason, Lockett would screw Joe's arm behind his back or stomp on him and Joe would go white and take it all with a helpless shrug of his coat-hanger shoulders. But when master and valet reached the dormitory doors, beyond which lay the bathrooms, Lockett halted.

'Please stand against the wall, Di Angelo. And turn your back to me.'

'Straight away, sir.'

Joe turned his back and we all watched as Lockett took from the pocket of his gown a handful of darts with brass points and tartan flights. With an easy flick of the wrist, he sent a dart looping through the air, then the next. We heard the soft meaty thud as each hit home between Joe's shoulder blades.

'Every one a bloody bullseye!' Lockett exulted. He hadn't meant the pun. Whatever pleasure pulsed through Lockett's synapses when he inflicted serious pain had the effect of blocking any flow of intelligence.

Joe straightened slowly, as if to make sure he did not shake loose any of the darts, standing out from his back like quills. He had turned even paler and because his face was always chalky white, his freckles stood out in stark relief, and his short black bristling hair seemed spikier than ever. We saw three intersecting circles of deepest red seeping through Joe's white school shirt.

'Bad is it, Di Angelo?' asked Lockett.

'Not too bad, Trev. Thank you, sir . . . Will you take your bath now?'

'First, a little blessing for being so brave. Please kneel, Di Angelo.'

Pouring the water from his tooth mug over Joe's curls, Lockett made the sign of the Cross: 'I hereby christen thee – Holy Joe Angel. What a cherubic name! But if you're an angel, you've fallen one hell of a way.'

Joe gave his little laugh or his cry; we couldn't really tell the difference because he wore his trademark pale corpse-pale grin. 'Do you see,' it demanded, 'what I can stand?' But it worried us to see what he could stand. We wanted to say to him, 'OK, now please stop it.' But then we decided he was laughing, and we all laughed too, and it was our laughter that brought the Rector into the dorm. Father Daintry paused in front of Joe and looked at the red bullseyes on his white shirt and the feathered shafts drooping and about to fall.

'Who did this?'

No one spoke. We were embarrassed. Our laughter still seemed to echo, and although we did not look at Lockett, we waited for him to say something, and when he didn't, we waited for the Rector to give us a way out of our embarrassment.

'Get up, Di Angelo. You give a very bad impersonation of St Sebastian, riddled with arrows. This an act of gross stupidity, and I ask once more: who has done this?'

Again the silence came, and stayed. The Rector looked at us with deep contempt.

'I will not shame you further by asking a third time. If I thought it would help to pray for your souls, I'd do so. But it would be a waste of breath. You, Lockett, will remove those darts from Di Angelo's back – carefully. We don't want any more blood. And you, Di Angelo, you will report to the sickbay and have those wounds cleaned and dressed. And you, Croker, will see me in my study in the morning.'

When he'd gone, Lockett said to me: 'Say one word to Daintry tomorrow morning, and you're dead.'

I did not care and I was not at all frightened. Challenged by the Rector, Lockett had kept quiet. What had he been scared of? Capone would not have ducked the question; he never snitched, never complained when he was jailed – 'I played my cards – I lost . . .' Even when Capone was down, he had a pithy way of seeing things. 'Overpaid dumb bastards,' he said of his lawyers when his appeal against his jail term was thrown out and he knew he was going to jail for a long time, 'they couldn't spring a pickpocket.'

When I knocked on his door the next morning, Daintry waved me to a chair.

'How close are you and Di Angelo?'

'We're friends.'

'More than that, I'd say. Two sides of the same coin. My guess is that Di Angelo wants war. He's ready to bet his life's blood. He wishes to go down shooting.'

'He thinks life is a film.'

'And you think he's wrong?'

'I don't like movies. I look at them and I see the lies.'

'His way is to throw himself at the world. You step back and look. That's good because, mostly, the world does not bear looking at. And it could not care less. Yet someone has to do it. Did I say you and Di Angelo were two sides of the same coin? That's wrong. You are opposite ends of a pantomime horse, and your other half is hell-bent on ruin. If you can't stop him, at least you can make a record of how you got there.'

He handed me a camera, an old-fashioned reflex. 'It's one I use from time to time and now it is yours. Use it to see.'

'I don't know how to take pictures.'

'Just point and shoot. Look on, Croker, and say nothing. That's what you did last night, in the dorm, when Di Angelo played the martyr. Make a record of what you see. Now and then you'll find something that wasn't there when you pressed the button. The Victorians thought the paranormal worked this way – ghosts, ectoplasm – caught on camera. Those were fakes or tricks of the light. Truth is stranger than trickery. Take observations of light. Look for evidence of light as individual particles and you find them. Look for light as a wave and a wave is what you find. As if the evidence adjusts itself to confirm the expectations of the observer. What you find depends on how you look at it. On your motives. The world, someone rightly said, is not just queerer than we know, it is queerer than we can *ever* know.'

I'd bring him my first snaps: dogs, boys, waterfalls, fields and sunsets, and he'd stare at them, shake them, hold them upside down: the ash on his cigarette would grow longer between his yellow fingers and fall in flakes on to his belly, his weak blue eyes, watering behind his misty glasses.

'No good, Croker. Not an angel in sight.'

I thought he was joking and I nearly laughed.

'I don't understand.'

'I'm not speaking of feathery wings and halos, Croker. These can be terrible things.'

One day he brought me a picture I'd taken of the municipal

dam, with the sun setting over the water and glinting on the topmost branches of the single willow tree, the only feature in a stretch of muddy water in a bland landscape.

'Consider this. Until yesterday your picture showed no more than a stretch of water. I've just seen the papers. Now it is the watery grave of three people, stabbed to death by a man who weighted their bodies and tossed them into the dam. Then he camped for the night under the willow. Look again at your photograph, it speaks. It's a crime scene. Angels, you see.'

So I began to look in another way. The pale diamond scar on the back of my hand; the line of suburban shops; Mr Benjamin, the rug doctor, and Schevitz, the chemist; the clump of gloomy firs where the boys had waited with the sliver of glass. You made pictures of your life by means of something you put into them. Joe wished to mow down the world; but I wanted to see it in court. My pictures were not about what I saw – they were about what I felt. They could be prophecy, clues, evidence.

I was present twice when Joe went though hell and came out the other side even more exultant in his ability to endure, then to triumph. First, he was St Sebastian under a flurry of darts. The next time it would be more terrible. If heroic virtue is a mark of signal holiness, of significant sanctity, of someone who will willingly relinquish his life for his faith, then Joe always had the makings of a saint.

CHAPTER 10

We had taken to watching, on Wednesdays – from a strategic gap in the spiny hedge guarding the hard-baked pitch – the girls of the Convent of the Sacred Heart playing hockey. Girls in gym skirts went scudding across the pitch, hockey sticks flashing, hacking at the ball. Along the chalky touch-lines raced the nuns who served as referees, habits floating to show greying plimsolls, whistling up fouls and yelping encouragement: 'Oh good girl, Bethany!' and 'Pass the ball, Constanza, for heaven's sake!'

It was Joe who had the idea. 'Why don't we wait for those two after the match?'

'And then what?'

'We'll walk them home.'

Bethany and Constanza, back now in school uniform, flushed from the game, strange in their panama hats and plain black school shoes, pushed their bikes through the convent gates and Joe went straight to them.

'We're from the Home. Where are you girls going?'

Bethany looked him over, amused. 'Where do you think? We're going home.'

'Can we walk with you?'

Bethany looked at Constanza, who shrugged: 'It's a free country.'

'No, it isn't,' Joe gave his bitter smile. 'It's a hellhole.'

'Is he always this bolshie,' Constanza asked, 'your skinny friend?'

'Always.'

So it was that a long walk on Wednesdays, illicit and wonderful, became for the summer our afternoon occupation, the girls perched on their bikes, pedalling very slowly, and Joe and me walking beside them. With the sun on our backs, we made our dazed way up to the high green suburbs that lay in the lap of the hills, called South Ridge, where the houses of the better-off and the diplomats looked down on the town. Sometimes the pace slowed until we stopped entirely and the girls would balance on their bikes unmoving, making tiny adjustments of the handlebars to keep upright.

Strange how hot you got, how your heart pumped, how everything seemed brighter, how you went deaf to everything except what the girl beside you said from time to time, and what you said to her. Not that I ever said anything interesting, but then it wasn't words that mattered; it was the wild singing inside me.

Bethany, smooth, blonde and compact, seemed to me to have been sewn into her blue-and-white school gymslip, so perfectly did it fit her, so carefully tied was her matching belt. Her face was broad, her chin small and firm, and there was something about her green-grey eyes that suggested a kindly wisdom tinged with reserve, as if she knew far more than she allowed us to see, but was too tactful to show it.

Constanza had the delicious habit of letting her curly auburn hair tumble in springy coils over her heart-shaped face with its pointed chin. She would seize one of these curls and pull on it, as if it might ring a bell, and sometimes she'd gnaw at the end of it with bright teeth. I admired everything about her, her neatness, her efficiency, the way her skirt dropped exactly to the backs of her knees. Ah – they made my mouth dry – the backs of her knees! From these slight hollows her calves began, curved balustrades descending into short white socks and black shoes buttoned snugly over little feet.

Constanza's place was a modest bungalow with a front stoop of polished concrete, as red as ox-blood, corrugated iron roof and a long driveway ending in a garage with green wooden doors. The garden was a collection of rumpled lemon trees, dahlias and heather, so typical of the capital, which mixes microclimates as it mixes its mutual detestations. Her mother was a bookkeeper at the bakery, her father was a civil servant and a Knight of da Gama.

Bethany Greene lived some blocks higher up the hill, in a vast house with acres of lawns, which seemed always to be dotted about with gardeners, tree surgeons, cleaners who swept the tennis court, mowed, raked leaves or scrubbed the swimming pool. We began it that summer, and others followed, drawn by the pool, the music, the staff, the ease of it, until we had a small crowd gathering on Wednesdays at Bethany's house.

We swam in the pool, which was enclosed by a trellis-work of Japanese canes on which grew thick bunches of roses the colour of strawberries in cream. Boys always changed first in the playroom, so we were waiting and watched, bewitched, as Bethany and Constanza and their girl friends emerged from the changing room in severe but elegant black costumes, wearing tight white rubber caps that gave them the look of strange but friendly space aliens who had dropped in to spend a playful few hours with a bunch of privileged earthlings. The clear blue water was shot with darts of silver and so heavy with chlorine it reddened the eyes. The sun lay like honey on our shoulders as we stretched to catch the warmth. Beyond the trellis surrounding the pool we heard the gardeners wheeling their lawnmowers across the perfect green, the blades whirling like wings, and the cut grass breathed out the gentle scent of perfect content.

I have a little snap, a simple photo in black and white, on thin paper, very creased now, which shows some of those who used the pool of Bethany Greene throughout that delirious summer. There is Dottie Wheel and her little brother Zeke, who was sickly and said he would be running away soon to join the Foreign Legion, but later became instead an investment banker, which deeply disappointed his family, who were a thrusting lot. Mimi Roux is flexing her biceps, which I prod tentatively and grin at the camera – Mimi could beat any boy at arm-wrestling. There, too, I see Arnie, Marnie and Dale – triplets from a family of fifteen, all in school uniform, a family so poor that they took it in turns to wear the one small grey woollen swimming costume they owned and could not agree who should wear it for the photo. There also came to Bethany's pool on those hot afternoons the Boshoff boys, who both got ringworm, three years in a row, and had their heads shaved; in the picture their bald heads are painted pink and they look like walking targets. Imelda Connolly is there, goalie of the Sacred Heart Convent hockey team, whose parents later founded Pink Pussy Safaris – offering charter flights to foreign brothels in Amsterdam, Bangkok and Hamburg. Hermie Broast, his red hair like a lamp and his freckles a pointillist pattern on his dead white skin, screws up his eyes against the sun.

Looking at the old picture now, I feel under my hand the smoothly shaven lawn upon which Constanza has been sitting, trailing her hand in the glassy blue water of the pool. The grass has patterned the backs of her thighs in lines of ribbed indentations which I can see, though she does not know that as she proceeds me into the playroom, her towel over her shoulders and her hips moving as if she were dancing, though

I know she is simply walking. For me that summer, in my heated state, everything she did looked like dancing.

We swam or sat on the lip of the pool, we said nothing, and it was summer for a long time on those afternoons which, looking back, were the most perfect of my life. Wrapping ourselves in huge towels as white as clouds, we sat in the playroom, played music, and ate chocolate eclairs off bone china. There was no relation between the real world and the world of the pool and the garden. We never assumed there should be. What counted was how completely we escaped. Though we always knew we were there like men who have broken out of jail.

One Wednesday, Constanza took my hand, waved goodbye to Joe and Bethany and led me into her house. Her mother was at work and her father had his weekly meeting of the Knights of da Gama. We sat in the small front room on a sofa, very close together, staring straight ahead, holding hands.

I had never imagined how much country a hand contained as I traced and retraced clefts and valleys and paths, from her fingertips and her palms, and saw the amazing juncture of the wrists, their bony edges flanked by sunken squares of soft flesh. It was the most intense experience of my life and hours, or years, later, when I stood up and sleep-walked my way back to the Home, I was a blind man feeling his way.

After that, every day that we could we would sit on the hard little sofa, the wiry horsehairs poking through the fraying brown leather, and kiss. Shallow, shaky, very new, not very good, kisses. And then stop and sit in a daze, then come out of our reverie, and there would be more nose-to-nose, pouter-pigeon kisses. I was so in love with Constanza I was quite happy to sit on the prickly horsehair sofa for ever, sunk in dazed tranquillity, feeling her hand in mine. I'd trace the sacred joints of her fingers, test the soft flesh between thumb and forefinger, taste the slightly salty savour of her, breathe the soap-flakes used to wash her school dress. My arm around her shoulders would go to sleep, and I did not move it because to move it was to lose the moment. And movement was not what we were after. We did not know what we were there to do, except to merge, to melt into each other and to stay like that.

Constanza was organized, efficient and brave; strengths which made her so formidable later on – and so dangerous, then and later. She soon decided that sitting on the horsehair sofa exchanging bird-like kisses was not getting us anywhere, and so she took me into her narrow little bed in her tiny neat bedroom, and she showed me how to roll on the French letter she had bought. On her bedroom wall hung a highly coloured painting of St Teresa holding a bouquet of lilies, the saint's face was paler than the flowers, and she followed our love-making with a tender and faintly reproachful, yet never condemnatory, glance.

Making love with Constanza made me very conscious that I was nowhere and no one without her firm hand. It was that hand that laid me on her bed and carefully undressed me, and then she undressed herself and made me lie very still while she kissed and lightly bit my ankles, kneecaps, nipples. The sense of sin was hugely present always, but like the soft look of St Teresa it left us unscathed and even all the more excited, untouched by guilt. Strange that, when I remembered it later. I had known, and so had she, as we were continually taught, that what we were doing was forbidden, that it set at risk our souls and our hope of eternal life.

And we did not give it a thought.

I lay watching her rock-hard little breasts with their tiny upright nipples, dark and sharp as pencil points, moving to and fro. Then, having extracted from me, as we lay in her narrow bed in her small room under the ceiling under the eye of the saint, the final surge, the last gasp, the extreme end of my stammering passion, she allowed herself that little sigh of content.

Orgasm was too messy a word, too overblown, to fit her triumph. She felt well because she had done well – and what her happy, slightly breathy sigh signified was not so much orgasmic but organizational delight.

'I'm glad we did that, Charlie,' she said as she made the bed and turned her room back into what it was before, like rewinding a film until there was no trace of what we'd done.

I might then, perhaps, have begun to see something of the commanding drive in her . . . but I hadn't. Of course not. I had simply and helplessly adored her. I loved her for her capacity to surprise, and also, of course, for the little sigh of pleasure for a job well done. To some small extent I contributed, but mostly it was all hers in the making and the guidance and the expertise.

When I asked Constanza how she got to be so good at this and to know so much, she simply laughed that small light laugh of hers.

'I just have a feeling. I read. I think about it. And then I go ahead and try it.'

'You got this from reading?'

As the summer floated by I became more and more sure that it must end badly: we had no right to be there, we had no connections with the pretty girl in her huge house, circled by silent servants in crisp whites. We would be found out and sent home, the dream would end.

Joe and Bethany were side by side on the grass at the poolside where the blue water licked its lips and sparkled. Bethany was wearing a red polka-dotted bikini and Joe wore his really tatty old aubergine costume, torn in places, where the pale flesh of his buttocks showed. Bethany noticed the circle of small scars, fading to white now, that stippled Joe's back and which, she suddenly saw, were too careful to be made anything but deliberately.

'What are these?'

'That's where Trevor Lockett got me.'

Bethany very gently counted to six. 'Got you? What do you mean?'

'He threw a bunch of darts into me.'

She sat up. 'Why did he do that to you?'

Joe said nothing. He shrugged and buried his head in his elbow.

'Lockett's head boy at the Home,' I told her. 'He can do what he likes.'

'That's no reason,' said Bethany.

'Charlie's right.' Joe did not look up. 'He has power, and when you have that sort of power you can do what you want. It wasn't a signal event.'

Bethany swivelled and brought her knees up. 'He could have killed you. One of those darts might have touched your heart.'

'Does he have a heart?' The words were out before I could stop them. I meant it as a joke.

Bethany turned on me furiously. 'He has a huge heart!'

I had meant it as a joke, but I'd meant it all the same. I knew then that she had fallen for Joe, his darts wounds, his skinny, bony body. I was sorry I'd blurted it out, but I knew I was right. If Joe had a heart, he didn't keep it where anyone could find it. That was the peace, that was the truce, that was time we spent on leave from the hostilities, and then, as always, we went home to the war.

CHAPTER 11

Once each year, to celebrate the feast day of the Body of Christ, we marched from the edge of the city to the Central Square in the middle of town. We processed through the city streets, behind a scarlet silk canopy, shading the priest carrying a great gold monstrance, whose crystal rays mimicked shards of sunlight, and which displayed the sacred host, the flesh of Christ, the true body of God himself, a pale disc gleaming austerely behind its protective glass window.

Joe and I were near the head of the procession. I was boat-boy, holding the silver jug of incense, from which I spooned fresh aromatic granules on to the glowing charcoal of the thurible, a brass beaker slung from brass chains, which Joe carried, swinging it to and fro in long arcs, throwing puffs of creamy blue incense into the air.

Was there anything very different about that particular procession that led up to The Event? No, it seemed simply another defiant, difficult Corpus Christi march, like all the others. 'Running the gauntlet for God,' it was called by all who did it each year. 'A marathon of the soul.'

The column was composed of every order, association and society that the Church could call to its standard and lasted a couple of hours. Kneeling in the streets in the hot sun to pray, the rubbery tang of softening tarmac in our nostrils, we knew to keep our heads well down and to hold our missals up to shield us against flying bottle tops, stones and coins. We marched, we knelt, we prayed and the pavements buzzed with titters, taunts and jeers. Each of us brought a handkerchief to wipe away the spit hawked by some of the watchers, but with every insult flung we prayed and sang all the louder: 'Faith of our Fathers, living still, in spite of dungeon, fire and sword . . .'

It was a gaudy show, a calculated blaze of papal pride in the very heart and temple of puritan, Protestant rigour. Hymns, bells, statues of the Blessed Virgin, nuns of every stripe, from sombre veiled Lorettans to nurses of the Little Company of Mary in white and blue; altar servers in white and scarlet; devotees of the Third Order of St Francis; first holy communicants in creamy silk; bishops in mitres of silver and green, swinging their golden crosiers like drum majors; Knights of da Gama in silk sashes and embroidered banners; acolytes of the Third Order of St Francis. There were reliquaries, crucifixes, plaster saints carried shoulder-high, holy water, hymns, rosaries and frequent genuflections. It was a show that must have seemed – to the scandalized eyes of the Calvinists crowded on the pavement – more outrageously flamboyant than any pagan extravaganza.

On reaching the town centre, we turned left and advanced towards the main square, and everything was perfectly normal. The usual hoodlums on the pavement this year included a group of students carrying a banner that would be translated into something like *Bump off the Dangerous Romans!*. The shouted insults were perhaps a shade more pungent. 'Roman whores!' yelled one of the large young men, his belly riding over his waistband in a sail of shirt front. But the derision of the onlookers, the spit and cigarette butts, the tar hot under our knees when we knelt to pray, all of this was as we expected.

Some of the newer marchers flinched at the abuse, but for us it was the sort of thing we heard from passing students every time we stood by the hedge and watched the convent girls play hockey.

'The harder they hoot,' I heard some priest say, 'the louder we pray.'

Joe was enjoying himself, and he swung the thurible heartily, giving off blue puffs of fragrant incense left and right. The students on the pavement held their noses, coughed ostentatiously or gagged noisily as the incense reached them. Joe turned his sharp profile ever so slightly in the direction of our tormentors, looked down his beaked Sicilian nose, lifted one hand and gave them the finger.

I said, 'Brilliant Joe, well done!' I also knew, somewhere in my sensible head, that it was not perhaps very sensible.

We marched, knelt, prayed and sang until we reached the finishing point, the Central Square. It had always been an eerie place, crowded with statues, facing a swanking city hall, adorned with a clock and bell tower, straight out of some Swabian village, and a Cathedral of grey stone and studded door of heavy oak, a miniature version of St Peter's Cathedral in Geneva; the square hedged about by banks and building societies, which seemed to hover protectively over the statues of heroes, as if they knew that this was where the money was.

The statues that dominated the Central Square were effigies of the leaders of our land since its first settlement: moustachioed men in spiky brass helmets, naval caps, berets, top hats stared into the middle distance and threw long shadows across the rather scruffy lawns. There were warriors with spears, bows, muzzle-loaders, carbines and machine guns. Altogether, this pantheon was a fantasy – many of the individuals commemorated had never existed, but it was judged politic to commemorate them all in bronze or stone because one or other faction needed to be placated and flattered by this concrete proof that their ancestors, tribe, invasion force, cartel or limited liability company had supplied the originators of our capital city, while in fact everyone knows we had no founding fathers, only founding fakes. As we got closer to Central Square, the buildings became squatter, more bunker-like. A sullen, sun-struck inertia still hung over the centre of town, a frown of disapproval that seemed cemented into place.

A mixture of public park and a parade ground, with walk-ways that traced a Maltese cross and a scattering of stolid figures on their granite plinths, amid stretches of grass where office workers and pigeons, tramps and lovers lounged at lunchtime.

Carved from granite, the seventh statue on Central Square, facing north towards the Blue Mountains and the rough country beyond, leaned on his muzzle-loader, naked but for a penis gourd. According to the inscription, he was the chief of a tribe called the Squamish by some, by others the Pukahoons, who were said to have lived in the area long before there was ever a city, before the settlers, the colonialists, the reformers, the royalists, the Puritans or the New Democrats. Each wave of incoming commanders of our destiny had its totem on the Plaza. We all knew our history was nothing but a series of wars, and we splashed about in oceans of rhetoric, which, we hoped, might dilute the true constants of our land: reciprocal hatred and exuberant violence. But the present governors of our country remembered their predecessors with statues and public holidays, not because they approved of them but because they had once been, however disastrously, the power in the land. And unless you prettified the brigandage of past regimes and justified their crimes, how could you defend your own?

The procession broke up in a swirling mix of discarded banners, sashes, vestments, veils, holy medals and missals, and all the marchers sat down on the grass, welcoming the long shadows cast by the statues, and ate the lunch of sandwiches and orange juice prepared by the ladies of the Catholic Women's League, and breathed happily, knowing that that was Corpus Christi done for another year.

Joe and I had our backs to the street, sharing a bottle of orange juice, when I heard quick steps behind me, and then I was being carried away. I could hear the chains of Joe's thurible rattling and I knew he was alongside me, though I saw nothing but the grass unpeeling fast under a pair of running feet. To the Corpus Christi marchers picnicking on the lawn, who would have seen what happened, it must have looked like a student stunt. Young men from competing colleges and universities, divided by race and language and creed, made hit-and-run raids on hostile campuses, and took hostages. They'd tar and feather their victims, dye their faces, shave their heads, or strip them naked, then let them loose in shopping centres or at sporting events. It was seen as natural high jinks, collegial horseplay among young men with a sense of fun – though everyone knew it was a form of warfare between tribes who hated one another's beliefs, clothes and culture – an acceptable form of headhunting because you did not actually kill your enemies – though it was widely understood that that was what everyone would have preferred.

Looking sideways I saw that a very big fellow had slung Joe over his shoulder like a side of beef, and Joe was trying – and failing – to hit him with his thurible, which rasped on its chain like a choking man.

I heard someone say, 'Now you bastards will see your arses!' The speaker spat out the words one at a time, panting a bit.

Another voice said, 'You wanna play games in frocks, hey? You wanna see what happens to guys in frocks?'

I knew then who had taken us. These were the guys on the pavement to whom Di Angelo had given the finger.

They had carried us clear of the square and, upside-down though I was, I knew we were passing Polly's Hotel, because there was the hotel's trademark, a parrot on a perch, and the legend *Dum Vivo Eloquor* – 'I live to speak' . . .

The words gave me a moment of ridiculous hope, because they were in Latin, the language of the Church, and we had been seized on a holy feast day of our Church, and I was hoping for a miracle, for someone to walk out of the hotel lobby and see what was happening. But this was Sunday, the hotel bar was shut, the capital was sunk in torpor, and no one noticed as we were carried into the narrow alley alongside the hotel and there we were dumped down hard. Then they all started knocking us around a bit. They saved most of their punches for Joe, who gave them the finger, yet the blows lacked conviction. It was almost as if they didn't quite know what to do next and needed to think about it, and that was a weighty and ponderous business.

A blond-haired guy with big yellow teeth, who had carried me, seemed to be the leader, and he kept promising we'd see our arse. He dwelt particularly on the syllable – leaning into it, drawing it out – 'aaahrse'. His use of the singular worried me, silly though I knew it was to think of it right then.

Taking up half the wall at the end of the alley was a huge enamelled advertisement for Schweppes Tonic Water. A slim, dark-haired woman wearing a diamond collar, a dress with a low neckline, and white gloves which reached to her elbows, held up a glass tumbler and stared into the distance with dreamy eyes. It seemed cruel, this woman looking on, while the young men punched us some more. There was no human help at the dead end of the narrow alley between walls like cliffs.

'Tell us to fuck off, hey? Well, we'll see what fucking off really is, you little cunt!'

99

Two of the attackers pushed Joe face first against the wall and took hold of his head and forced it down, bending him double. Another guy wrapped a big arm around his waist and anchored him, while the cheesy-toothed guy was doing something to his trousers.

I took it all in, the way you do when you can't look away and you can't believe what you're seeing. The woman in the gloves had her right arm raised and with one longer finger she pointed delicately groundward, over the bent body of Joe di Angelo, who, all this time, said nothing. His silence was terrible.

And then I saw what the toothy blond was doing and I still could not believe it, because he was fiddling with the buttons on his khaki shorts; he was slowly undoing the buttons of his fly while the other guys chanted 'Now, now, now!' like it was a rugby match. I tried to stop looking, but someone who held me tightly now got hold of my hair. When someone has a handful of your hair and is pulling it very hard, you feel the skin of your forehead stretching so high and tight it feels like it's coming away from your skull, and you have trouble closing your eyes.

Because I did not want to go on watching him, I looked instead at the woman in the Schweppes ad, with her white gloves, her pointing finger, and her snooty look. Above the bottle of tonic, it said:

In a class by itself
In a glass by itself
Or with a kindred spirit

I could hear the big guy breathing loudly, and then he yelled high and loud and everyone cheered again. I knew what it meant, but I still wasn't looking at him, I kept my eyes on the woman with the glass and the pointing finger. I wasn't really trying to get the pun, but when I did get it I felt quite pleased. I thought, 'Kindred spirit? That's gin, yes, or vodka? Pretty good.'

And then it was over. The three guys who held Joe let him go, and all four ran down the alley, their footsteps dying on the still Sunday air.

Joe stayed as he was without moving, then slowly he straightened and his cassock fell and when he stood fully upright again, the pointing finger seemed to touch the top of his head.

We walked back to Central Square without speaking and joined the others waiting for the buses that would take us home. We sat in silence as the familiar landmarks swam past the windows: Arcadia Hill, Paradise Crescent and Quiet Street. Something had happened and nothing had happened; this was – and was not – a perfectly usual Corpus Christi Sunday and we were going home; and the bus dropped us at the foot of Sunnyland Hill, outside the Monte Carlo Cinema, and it was screening that week *The Finger Points*, starring Clark Gable and Fay Wray. For the first time ever Joe hurried on past without so much as a glance at the poster. We walked, as usual, to the church, or rather more precisely to the vestry, because we needed to return the cassocks and surplices to the hangers, and still without speaking we started up the road that took us to the Home.

We were almost home when four guys came walking towards us, laughing and shouting, and it was only when we were abreast and they saw who we were that they stopped laughing.

Joe dropped his head. 'Say nothing, Charlie. Keep walking.'

That was all, but I have never forgotten the fix of his eyes, as if he were counting them, as if he were setting down every detail of their faces. Then they were past and they were our neighbours from Zwingli Hall. They knew who we were, but they could not let it be seen, so they went on by as if we were not there.

'What do you reckon, Joe?'

'For now, nothing.'

Back at St Jude's Joe went to his locker and, very carefully, he tore off the mugshot of Al Capone.

'Never say a word about this, Charlie. You will forget all about it.'

'How can I?'

There was something in his eyes that I could not read – wilder than I'd seen on the night Trevor Lockett tossed the darts into his back. He was smouldering. I could feel the heat he gave off, but it made me feel cold. Joe was on fire and he was freezing. I thought maybe this was what hellfire must be like.

I kept quiet because I did not know how to find words for what I'd seen, and if Joe was going to ignore the whole thing, then it left me even further out of it, remembering and seeing, yes, but unable to show it to others. Instead I watched Joe more carefully than ever. I couldn't think what he was going to do. What did you do after something like this?

Chapter 12

In an exquisite punishment, each evening at supper time in the refectory Father Daintry made Trevor Lockett read from *Lives of the Saints*, vivid accounts of mutilations and martyrdoms, which he intoned in a stumbling mutter as we pushed sago pudding around our plates. We heard how St Julian the Hospitaller had murdered his mother and father, before going on to holiness; how St Egwin shackled his feet together, shuffled all the way to Rome, where he found in a fish he bought in the market the key to his fetters – and freedom in his new life as a saint; and how the fierce pagan giant Christopher set off to serve the devil, but when he found that Lucifer feared Christ, he switched sides.

'Do you like our devotional reading, Di Angelo?' the Rector wanted to know.

Joe said, 'What I like about these guys is that they won't let anything stop them.'

'Everything yields to superior force; we hate to think so, and we find ways of denying it. Even in saints, what we find is the force of a Capone placed in the service of God. Sometimes I think it's a kind of narcissism. The saint's excessive love of God isn't far from an exaggerated love of self.'

When the Rector told us that a lot of saintly lives were myths, Joe was really shocked.

'Who made them up?'

'We did. Over time. But don't despair, Di Angelo, just because few of these saints existed is no argument against the exemplary quality of their legends. They defeated evil. They triumphed. Often it takes something violent to shift the proto-saints from their old ways towards the light. Something that comes close to destroying them. Do you follow me?'

'You bet I do,' said Joe. 'I had something like that happen to me. Maybe it'll make me a saint.'

'Tell me, Di Angelo.'

'I'd rather not, Father. It was personal.'

Daintry nodded, 'Then tell me something about these solid boys with the shaven hair, and these well-scrubbed young women who come and go to classes at the university – why are they so upset when they see me? They blush and mutter away in their lingo. What gives them this superior air?'

'They believe in Calvin, some old guy in Geneva, who told them what to do if they wanted to go to heaven. Which is, principally, ban everything. And wipe out the Catholics. We're the enemy. They hate us.'

'So these young people believe deeply and fundamentally that they are good and you are bad? What else do you know?'

'Don't need to know more. I want to fight back.'

'Then you need a strategy. Find out who you're fighting. Know more about them than they do themselves.'

Joe was intrigued, but baffled. 'And how do I do that?'

'This is the capital, Di Angelo. It will have a library. Get yourself some books. Throw yourself into their lives: get to know them or what makes them who they are. Who knows? Maybe they were sent to show you something. As Croker here will tell you, I'm a believer in angels.'

Joe was trying hard to keep control of his face; he jiggled

his shoulders as if they were, for a brief moment, little stumpy wings. 'I can't say I ever saw one, Father.'

Daintry did not smile. 'You never know them at first. They are unlikely creatures. A bit like you, Di Angelo – dark as sin. Smile, if you like. But look again. Sometimes they're all around you.'

Joe was incredulous. 'Angels? This lot?'

'I'm not talking of seraphim and cherubim . . . pretty putti with wings and haloes. No wings. No harps. Angels bring messages. They bring news – from some place not of ourselves.'

Joe put on his foxiest grin to show us he was humouring the Rector, and he spoke very slowly, as if to a child. 'OK, Father, let's say I hear these angels. Then what?'

'It is not that simple. They can't finds the words. So we have to divine it – d-i-v-i-n-e – that is the word, Di Angelo. Seek it out. Reach for it inside ourselves. Don't spurn them, learn from them. You don't want to go shooting angels.'

'And then?'

Father Daintry's eyes were flakes of ice. He folded his pale hands over his belly. '*Then* you may shoot them, if that's what you wish. But get the order right.'

In the next months Joe turned from a worm, a ferret, a sardonic masochist who let Lockett riddle him with darts, who existed only to humiliate himself if it got a laugh or a flash of admiration for his suicidal yet salty aptitude for self-destruction, into an obsessive, insatiable researcher.

Joe left Capone behind. He left Lockett behind. He survived the darts. He moved on, ever deeper into darkness and pain, with his cheerful frigid grin and his homicidal ambitions. He took a bus into town once a week and he came back with four big books from the public library, his full quota, about Calvin and Geneva.

He found books that dealt with Puritanism, Presbyterians and the reformed churches of Europe and Scotland, Switzerland

and Germany in particular. He tracked down maps of old Geneva, a plump little fortified town fit to bursting in its corset of walls, and he'd point out to me Lac Léman and the spire of Calvin's parish church, St Peter's Cathedral. He could walk me through the old town much as he once walked me through the Chicago of Al Capone's heyday.

He would say to me, apropos of nothing very much, as we walked to rugby practice or wandered down to serve Mass: 'Did you know, Charlie? Calvin's Geneva was run by a quintet: you had pastors, teachers, elders, deacons and, of course, terror – lots of terror. They called it order. What's interesting is how the guy controls things. In Calvin's Geneva the Church backs the State and the State guarantees the Church. Pastors were elected by other pastors. The council ran the city, and the Consistory – more pastors, of course, along with twelve elders – ran the spiritual show. Behind the council stood Calvin and behind Calvin stood God. Fucking brilliant, isn't it? What the Church wanted done, the city council of Geneva did. And vice versa. They closed the theatres; they picked the names you could give your kids. They passed a law in 1536 which said that butchers, bakers and pastry cooks better keep their traps shut on Sundays. You could not travel, talk loudly or be seen laughing. Singing was really bad news; you got your tongue skewered.'

It was not just the books he was reading, it was the sheer improbability of this ex-Sicilian, one-time cave-dweller turning himself into an expert on something so cerebral – yet of the very first importance to those who ran the country, and who had their hands around our windpipes and squeezed whenever we wished to breathe – that was so exhilaratingly perverse it made us laugh out loud. He was hearing angels, in Daintry's phrase. He was getting the message.

The enemy who ran our world might be foot soldiers in a faith inspired by Calvin, but as Joe liked to say, 'They know sweet fuck all. They don't read him. They wear him like a steel corset. For them reading is bad, thinking is bad, brains are bad, ideas are bad . . . I plan to blow them up.'

There appeared now on the steel door of the locker beside his bed a painting of a man wearing a flat black cap with earpieces; he had a hawk-like face, brooding eyes, a long thin nose, not unlike Joe's own, a black beard and a fur collar over a white shirt. Calvin had replaced Capone

The Rector was delighted. 'One down, how many to go, Di Angelo? This is real progress I see. The saint has taken over from Scarface. Next step: ask yourself why Calvin went one better than Capone?'

Joe said, 'I think I know. He was after the whole caboodle.'

'That's one way of putting it.'

Joe told me: 'Al Capone ran bootleg hooch, he ran the rackets, and he had lots of cops backing him. But Calvin, he ran the religious rackets, he ran the universe and he had God behind him. He went for broke.'

'You see, boys,' said Daintry, 'what you have encapsulated in this town is the great battle in miniature. Our beliefs and values against theirs. Rome versus Geneva. Go into the city, look around.'

We learned to look harder at the enemy, at his power, which pervaded every single aspect of our lives; at his exultant stupidity. It was infuriatingly impressive: it got along just fine on minimal brain in the cranial spaces. It had us every which way, and we knew it. It was Daintry who showed us loathing was no good and tactics beat curses hands down.

Daintry was a thinker and a strategist and he liked encouraging these qualities. To him this was natural. To those who learnt from him, his lessons were a liberation. Joe learnt from the Rector that in order to fight the enthusiastic worship of maximum force, muscle and lumpen stupidity, he needed to find unlikely weapons, because these did most damage. And reading became an act of pure rebellion.

Joe asked him: 'Does Calvin's view make more sense than the Catholic ideas he threw out?'

'Not really. He freed Geneva of popish superstition, the Mass, indulgences and holy relics. He was cooler and more logical than the Catholics he opposed. Let God make saints – the world made accountants. But do you know what his enemies called him?'

'The Pope of Geneva.'

'And the Pope is God's man on earth. Forget about the religious meaning of this. It does not matter whether you see God as an omnipotent being in the heavens, the engine of history, the perfect good of the people or the summation of natural law. It's about power. Calvin liked to call himself a poor and modest man. Did he say it with a straight face? A terrifying modesty it must have been, because either you did as he taught or you died. But he liked to imagine he was a quiet and retiring fellow with his heart in the right place. A man who really wanted to help others.'

'Like Capone did?'

'Yes, but better. Do you see, Di Angelo? He had God behind him. And that meant he got to run the world by his own rules. He was a monumental heretic and yet he burnt heretics. Where you commend absolute personal freedom but lock up those who oppose you. You hate murder and burn those you decide will be morally improved by their extinction. You invent a new moral order and it never stops you from getting what you want. You make your own rules and break them. There is about saints an insufferable pride, a self-love others are glad to die for.'

'Did Calvin point out that his initials were those of God himself – JC?'

'I'd be surprised if he wasn't tempted,' said the Rector, who had the alarming ability to answer frankly any questions he was asked. He was so far from what we had been taught to associate with religious belief that it was hard to remind ourselves he was a priest. 'What fanatical faith does is to make monsters of fairly decent people,' he said. 'It tells them they're right. When a saint reaches the stage of heroic virtue he is often at his most insufferable. It sanctifies thuggery.'

'That can't be helped. If you wanted to see the old world swept away.'

'Surely you don't wish to end up like the other side?'

Joe shrugged. ' If that's what it takes . . .'

It was then that Joe drew ahead of his teacher. Daintry was sensible, clever, but he assumed that there was at the heart of the world a functioning logic. What would Daintry have said had I told him what had happened to Joe one Sunday afternoon outside Polly's Hotel? He would have been properly horrified and he would have been thoroughly reasonable; he would have reported the crime to the school and to the police. He drew back from the ultimate horror; he assumed that the worst was still some way off. He did not see that it had been going on like this for years. When someone raped you, or threw six darts into your back, threw you out of a window, you did not think of calling the police. Things were too serious for that.

'That's what you get for walking like that . . .' the boy had said to me when he stabbed me with the sliver of glass.

It did no good to analyse the individual words. He didn't like me and he wished me dead . . . that was all.

I got the camera, and Joe got Calvin; and the Rector's gifts marked us for ever.

Joe would out-read the enemy, out-think him – he would do whatever it took. This made him deadly – to the enemy, yes, but also, ultimately, to himself.

CHAPTER 13

In the early hours of the following morning we were shaken out of sleep by an explosion that rattled the louvres of St Jude's and we all crowded the windows. Just up the street we saw Zwingli Hall spouting flames. Fire engines came screaming up Bonaventure, and pink lights danced on the brass helmets of the firefighters and the steam rose over the rooftops as hoses played water on the flames. Joe leaned forward on the window sill, his face expressionless in the firelight.

In the morning, flakes of ash floated in the dorm, the smell of burning was everywhere, and Joe's bed was empty. I was downstairs having breakfast when he came in carrying a book, as he always did now, sat down beside me, and pushed the porridge around his plate.

'Where've you been?'

He held up his book so I could see the cover, and for once he wasn't reading about Calvin or Knox or the great reformers. The title was *Fire Hazards in Water Boilers*.

'Good stuff?'

He turned on his vulpine smile. 'Gas-fired boilers work much like a burner on a gas stove. Put a big pan or pot over a naked flame. If you get enough pressure, and bring a spark to bear – bingo! It explodes. Second good point with gas: the pilot light is always on. You get even more bang for your buck if there's the right stuff around the boiler room. Flammable stuff. Lovely word, "flammable".'

'Where did you go last night?'

'Something bothered me. I needed to check it out. I saw the fire engines, but where were the ambulances?'

'You blew up Zwingli Hall?'

He nodded. 'The boiler room was stuffed with gas bottles, tins of paint, bottles of turps. It was a bomb waiting to go off. I needed to be back here in the Home for the show, so I took a guess at the build-up time. I calculated it would blow some time after midnight. In fact, it went up at 1.31. Not bad.'

I was suddenly terrified. 'But Joe, there were dozens of people inside.'

He shook his head ruefully, half-amused at himself. 'I fucked up. Didn't check my dates. Vacation began yesterday. Every bastard was gone.'

I didn't know what to say: the relief I felt was enormous, but it didn't banish the horror.

'You tried to kill them all?'

He looked modest. 'I'd have settled for lots of casualties.'

'But what if you'd got the wrong guys?'

He looked at me, his eyebrows dancing the way they did when he was really angry with himself. 'Back in the fourteenth century, the Crusaders in France were hunting down Cathar heretics, and they locked a whole bunch of suspects in the Cathedral of Béziers – and the idea was to kill them. Fair enough. But they had a problem. How to tell heretics from true Catholics? So they asked the bishop and he put them right: "Burn the lot. God will know his own." From where I stand, Charlie, there were no wrong guys in Zwingli Hall.'

He meant it. He was peeved. He had set out to kill them all, and he showed all the regret of a man who had just missed a bus. He felt he had let himself down.

Later he said: 'You're too damn sensitive, Charlie. It's the world. Get used to it. You're a thinking sort of guy. You like to mull things over, to read, to spend time inside your head. Right, here's the deal. One day I'll commit a really useful crime. Useful to me. And you'll own up to it, and go to jail. That will give you lots of free time. It will suit your personality, and I'll be happy too. We'll be partners in the perfect crime.'

A day or so after the fire that failed he took down the picture of John Calvin from his locker door. 'I'll have to find some other god, I reckon.'

'To serve?'

He shook his head. 'I'm done with serving. Being is what I'm after. What are you after, Charlie?'

I didn't know. I said I thought I'd sit my exams and go on to university. Joe was not impressed.

'Place is full of arseholes.'

Joe's failed attempt to wipe out a lot of people had a very odd sequel. Odd and painful. By way of a sharp lesson in how these things were done, our old adversary, the bony enemy, now took a hand, as if to remind us, again, what a real pro he was. And quite a show it was.

A week later, a Tuesday, just before the Latin lesson, as we were about to consider the use of the ablative case (never my strong point), the door of the classroom opened and in walked Trevor Lockett, who took a comb from his sock, slicked back his glossy, almost blue-black hair and put his arm around Joe's shoulders.

'Joe Angel,' said Lockett, 'your old man's croaked it.'

How and where and when it had happened no one seemed to know. Joe took the news as confirmation of something he had long suspected. When I tried to sympathize, he brushed me aside.

'Couldn't be helped,' he said, and then he added something that puzzled me still more. 'Pretty smart move. Under the circumstances.'

Joe vanished after that and there was some talk that he'd gone to take over his father's business. Weird! One minute he'd been trying to become a mass murderer, the next he had gone into the cement business. The question was (and it became more pressing), what did this ambition amount to? Disaster for me, certainly. And for him? His plan hadn't worked, but Joe got over it: saints always do, they simply ignore, forget or overcome their failures and press on regardless.

I should have remembered that.

Bethany's father, whom we had met now and then and who seemed a genial, rumpled fellow, went driving one night and ploughed into a van parked in the darkness of the road. He died instantly. The picture of this Oldsmobile was in the papers and the engine seemed to have been forced by the impact into the boot.

Bethany was crushed with grief, and her numbed suffering seemed entirely genuine. She loved the father she had lost. The St Jude boys did not understand it, but they gave her the benefit of the doubt. It was something, they supposed, that happened in the world over there, the one next to theirs, but from which they were separated by a wall sky-high and many universes wide.

These blows landed so fast we were shell-shocked.

The next one came from left-field.

Trevor Lockett, out riding his Harley not two days later, was hit by a beer truck and suddenly there we were, listening to a peroration from Father Daintry, which, though deeply impressive in the flow and its sincerity, was magnificently unrelated to the recently departed soul: 'Brave, bold and utterly honest – yet gentle with it . . . An upright Christian called to the Lord . . .'

This time the joke was on us: there was a boy in that box. At other times, I would follow Joe's mock-devout gaze as he knelt before Our Lady of Perpetual Succour. The Virgin's halo was tilted slightly over one eye, rather like the skeletal remains of a celestial straw boater.

What was it he always looked to me as if he was about to say?

'Please Miss, your little guy is about to lose his shoe . . .'

Not today; today Trevor Lockett was as quiet as the grave. Today he was in the box at the altar steps.

Death had done for Lockett, just as it had done for all the others. But what had he been thinking of? What did it mean? How could he have done this – to us? Thus were we pitched, time and again, without warning, from the familiar camaraderie of the classroom into the strained decorum of the graveside.

We looked at the bier and said to ourselves, 'But it can't be him, in there!'

It made me want to have a word with someone – but I knew, as the Requiem Mass began, that there was no one to have a word with. We sat remembering the darts as they buried their noses in Joe's white shirt, asking ourselves: 'Is this grief?' And facing the fact that it must be grief, because we missed him, cruel as he had been; we had been proud, in a terrible way, of Trevor Lockett and his silk dressing gown, and his style, his motorbike and his naked girl.

Julia came to the funeral, but she wasn't wearing her fur coat, which was just as well. She was buttoned up in a black tunic and skirt, and her long blonde hair was pulled tight in a severe bun.

A few days before term ended, Father Daintry had flown away to Italy for a short break. At assembly one morning a pale Mr Buttleby, the Australian housemaster, announced that the Rector had died of a heart attack.

It must be said that nothing raised the Rector higher in the opinion of the boys than the way he died, far away in a foreign land. It had a certain style, this extraordinary finale. Good for him, was the general feeling. And there was the customary half-holiday to come.

The Home fell apart after Daintry died. Our two-storey barracks across the road from the brick ship and the fortress walls of Holy Cross College shut its doors and everyone forgot it had ever been. 'For Sale' notices were up even before the last boy left, and the relief was as palpable among our Catholic allies as our Calvinist enemies.

Constanza and Bethany took their final exams and I did not see them again. Our deeply mortified housemasters went back to where they came from and to being what they had been: sensible fellows, expecting better, home to Holland and Melbourne, places that meant something. And the world we had made was gone.

I have the photograph, taken the day I left – it shows St Jude's around three on a hot afternoon, the sun laying a blinding light on the corrugated iron roof. I can almost feel the silence. Each time I look at the picture I'm reminded to my faint amazement that the place was painted a queasy green, and I ask myself: why did I never register that fact? I can see the window from which Lockett dropped me into the rose bed. I can see the big front door shut tight against the world. The end of the experiment. But nothing I can see says it is over, or that the Rector is dead and Joe and Bethany and Constanza have vanished. Like all photographs it fixes only an instant in the sea of time, but it has the look of eternity. Often it takes a long while before what you've seen becomes clear – until you understand what you're seeing.

Part Three
Out of the Frying Pan

'Truth begins as a fight with the police and ends
by relying on them.'
E. M. Cioran

CHAPTER 14

I went to a university that matched my profile, and there I studied physics, chemistry and genetics, with the vague idea of doing something in science research in what was laughingly called 'later life'. In truth, further education for me – no less than for the shaven-headed thugs who tormented us at St Jude's – was really a continuation of our low-grade civil war. It gave them the sense of their military might, their role as God's anointed, along with (it amounted to the same thing) their crushing political superiority. And in us it implanted the illusion that we constituted a resistance, and flattered our impotence by inflating our importance.

As one of our former, less asinine, presidents once put it: 'What counts here is what counts now.' Did he lead the reformers, the rebels, the rejectionists, the republicans, the royalists or the revolutionaries? Did the remark date from the time when the colonists held sway, or the settlers, or the indigenes – or was it made by one of the present incumbents? Hard to know because each cabal uncannily reproduced, with minor variations, the lamentable qualities of the gang it superseded, and each shaded into the next. Each called itself revolutionary, promised to deliver universal equity, by force if necessary; then, as it approached the apogee of its power, gave way either to stifling conformity or exultant sectarianism.

I took along to college my camera, and my pictures of those years show a varied cast: kids, cops, dogs, furious onlookers, water cannon, banners, rubber bullets, gas masks and police vans. It was hard to know what we were protesting about and, for the most part, it did not matter. It was action. It was fun. Everyone fell over a lot and I learnt to be quick and accurate. Photography was forbidden, of course, like most things, but I enjoyed the game. It was such fun for a while that I fell into it the way one might fall in love or come down with a fever or take to drink. We were eager to march, to confront the batons, the dogs, the birdshot, the tear gas and the prison cell, if it came to that, but it very seldom came to that. We rioted regularly, demonstrated dutifully, and got nowhere. But we did enjoy it. Our ruling band of dour puritans (now so faint a memory) were not simply deadly – they were prodigiously dull. Those they did not lock up or shoot, they bored into silence. What mattered was to enrage our leaders. Though quite why we did this, and for whom, we never thought about, except in terms so vacuous I have trouble even writing them down – justice, decency, fairness. All the nice nouns.

Somewhere inside we knew that our actions made – and would make – no difference, but we felt lighter, because we had done something.

The authorities played their part wonderfully, lashing out wildly like blind men swatting flies. We would run, jeer and run again; the cops would chase us and arrest just enough people to fill the six blue vans drawn up carefully outside Papa's Place, a café with red-leather booths in the backroom and a bank of pinball machines in the front shop, which stood close to the university gates, under the shadow of the great white wall of the brewery across the road, with an enormous clock displaying long luminous hands.

And that would be that for the day. Everyone still standing

then retired for lunch to Papa's Place. Next door, the student bookshop window displayed works that breathed a forlorn braggadocio: *Adventures in Anarchy*, *The Conspirator's Chapbook* – titles which failed to conceal the gap between the dissent they boasted and the despair they concealed.

In my four years on campus I was twice hit by water cannon, twice knocked unconscious by a truncheon, once bitten by a police dog, and spent twelve hours locked in a police cell. After one such incident I woke in hospital with seven stitches in my forehead, but I do not remember a police photographer. But then, I noticed very little; when you look through a viewfinder, you see only what you want to see and not who may be looking at you.

I remember a particularly strong picture I took of a police dog straining forward on its leash, while a girl cowers on the ground; the tension is in the juxtaposition of the jutting jaws of the young constable and his Alsatian. Man and dog bare their teeth, fangs mirror each other, and the leash holding the dog runs tight as a bowstring into his handler's tight fist. Only later did I see that I had made a record of a most elaborate, sometimes wild ballet, a history of carefully staged and expertly choreographed spectacles, from which each side derived predictable satisfaction. Only now, when I am to all intents and purposes extinct, do I see how laughably light-weight we were. We never amounted to more than a minor irritant, about as threatening as mild dandruff.

I was always behind the camera and never in the picture. Or so I believed. I thought I was recording what I saw, but, as it turned out, someone had been recording me. Another picture-taker was also shooting those years. It would have been in one of those theatrical riots that I ran across the man who really did change my life. Though I never saw him then. He wasn't the one on the business end of the truncheon that laid me low outside the library, spilling books from my satchel. But he saw it happen and, like everything else about my years in the college, he made sure he recorded it. In all that time I don't know that I was ever aware that someone was also shooting me.

In any event, my four years at college had the desired effect: I emerged far less informed about reality than I had been when I started my studies. Higher education, a terrible oxymoron, made me into a prig so hooked on outrage that I did not get over the addiction until life took over and kicked some sense into me. The mismatch between the heady years of student rebellion and the steady plod of the world beyond appalled me, and must have shown in my face.

I was unemployable, but I looked for a job. I was, briefly, a teacher, a banker, a copywriter, an insurance clerk, and found my university years had ruined me for all of them. I still believed that a job told you what you were, it defined your nature. Another mistake. I came to understand, slowly, that what you called yourself was nothing but a comfort or a fraud. Labels we hung around our necks to cheer ourselves up.

In a sealed universe you might claim to be a doctor, a street-sweeper or a housewife, but these were pathetic attempts to pretend you lived in a normal world, with something real to do and a job to your name. In fact, we were all elementary particles, assigned a value by those who observed and plotted our paths in an experiment they controlled. It was not whom, but where you were that mattered. Everything depended on your position and performance in the political spectrum. You might be reconstituted again as something new or vanish in a flash of spent energy. The only question, in a sealed universe of whizzing particles, was: 'If you run into an opposing force will you survive or cease to be?

It was by chance, then, that I drifted into a job on the weekly news sheet, the *Capital Post*. The *Post* was split by the inevitable contradictions of having to sound like a dissident paper, while carefully toeing the official line. It has served all our governors down the years to value the uses of a free press, just as they have all preferred to keep in reserve a small but harmless opposition. The difficult line the *Post* had to tread was to castigate, on its centre pages, the follies of our masters, while celebrating in the rest of the paper the easy life their policies guaranteed its privileged readers. The wailing tone on its prim editorials earned the *Post* its nickname of *Capital Punishment*.

It was we, though, who felt the strain of being fearless but very careful. My editor, a frayed man named Monty Nines, was terrified afresh each morning that, inadvertently, he'd print something which would succeed in offending the regime. He had a phrase which governed our editorial meetings – 'if in doubt, leave it out'. The trouble was, we never knew what was best left out. The administration's caprice was inexhaustible; a robust attack on death in police detention might pass unscathed; yet a bland item on brassières could bring in the security police and close down the paper. We could be rude but not rebellious; satirical but not unkind; angry but not unpatriotic. The authorities paid out the rope from which we might, one day, find we had hanged ourselves.

My beat was Municipal Affairs, a circle of hell reserved for those who dreamt of changing the world. It took me into panelled council chambers, carpeted and claustrophobic, where appointees of the ruling caste droned on about refuse collection and public tramways, residential rates, sewage disposal, sporting facilities and hawkers' licences. Might diesel-driven buses replace the present electric trams? Should the resurgence of street gambling, run by itinerant Romanian godfathers, be monitored more closely?

Every day I confronted the dismal truth that life was not elsewhere, waiting to happen, it was here now. It was like this and it would go on being like this: the smell of the green leather benches, the reek of respectability, the voices in my head that told me, 'Well, you may think this talk of refuse and rates and potholes does not count; you may kid yourself that there are more important things – justice and decency and truth – but, frankly, no! You are not merely ignorant, you are wrong. Indeed, you silly young man, observe these flunkeys, their bureaucratic drudges, these pathetic yes-men, and know they are kings. They dwell in their achingly dull, effortless way on the banal details of daily life and they regard it as right and proper. They decide what counts; true power oversees the humdrum, as well as the executions.'

I sat with my notebook and wrote down what they said, these loyal functionaries, and if I hated them, I hated myself even more. It was a job that skimmed the surface – not of life (because it was never that) but of a huge boredom, like some dead sea, in which we paddled away our lives, up to our necks in its salty absurdity, unable to strike out in some new direction, yet unwilling to drown.

To escape I'd get in my car and take a drive. One day, on a whim, I headed along Bonaventure Drive. St Jude's was firmly closed and deserted. Beyond was the burnt-out hulk of Zwingli Hall. Beside the front gate an artist's impression showed a tower of glass and steel. A new Zwingli Hall was to rise here. The blue and white contractors' board outside the chain-mail fence announced: *Di Angelo Conglomerate: Building the Future.*

When I saw his name, it felt as if someone had tweaked the line that ran between us, and then, of course, I decided that there was no longer the least connection. I felt a little angry, a little smug, and a little sad. Phrases like 'the future' had been appropriated by the ruling elite, along with words like ' freedom', 'choice', 'wisdom', and only collaborators or fellow-travellers would trade in this debased coinage. The future, everyone knew, would be as narrow and as cramped as those who controlled it. In this future, a marriage of brutality and stupidity, the gun, the whip, the boot, would prevail, and the iron certainties of the chosen few, cemented by the blood of their victims, would make a conglomerate more powerful than anything that ever came out of the Di Angelo factory.

I was looking at a success story. Across the capital, older buildings were being replaced by banks and hotels built to resemble bunkers, forts, glass-and-steel redoubts. Repression was very successful, and those in power were presiding over a bonanza. The worst of closed societies is the overwhelming sense that this is how it is – and will be – for ever. The regime would adapt and accommodate and survive; it faced no true enemies, and if any were to show themselves, they would be eliminated.

I photographed the site of the new Zwingli Hall so that I'd have proof one day, when I asked myself if this degree of treachery was possible. And, on an impulse, I drove next to Polly's Hotel. I found a hill of rubble covering the alley where our assailants had dragged Joe and I on that Corpus Christi Sunday. The piles of bricks, the fallen roof, the tall crane, the absence of every sign that said this was where Joe had been attacked, where I had watched, and the elegant woman with her gin and tonic, high on the wall, pointed her gloved finger at Joe as he was forced to bend. All gone.

But the contractors' boards were there, familiar now, navy-blue lettering on cream: Di Angelo Conglomerate was building the future, again . . . His desire had been to blow them and their world sky-high. And here he was, building sky-high hatcheries for future directors of our prison house.

I would escape the council chambers for an hour each day, sitting on a bench in a park beside a little stream that runs alongside the Municipal Offices. I'd eat my lunch and watch the water sliding past my feet, hearing the traffic at my back.

I did not hear her sit down next to me until she spoke.

'Don't turn to me. Look straight ahead. Do you want to be more than peripherally involved? If yes, nod your head.'

'Bethany?'

'Yes or no?'

I nodded.

'Saturday night. Sixty-seven, Bellevue Mansions. Do you know it?'

Did I know it? There was nothing 'Belle' about the view, and 'Mansions' was a wildly inaccurate way of describing a six-storey, cinder-grey tower of modest studios, rented by students and struggling teachers. But I said nothing and watched her go, her tumbling blonde hair as rich as I remembered it, and the set of her shoulders as solid.

CHAPTER 15

When I knocked just once at the door of Number 67
it opened instantly and she drew me inside with a quick glance
along the corridor.

'Hello Bethany.'

She put her finger to her lips. 'No names, please. We wondered if you'd come tonight, and now you're here I've lost the
bet. But there's someone who will be very happy to see you.'

I knew these small, nondescript studios inside out; each
had a single bedroom, with a kitchenette counter running
along the back wall and a small bathroom at the rear of the
building, where a fire escape zigzagged past the window down
into a dark well. The location – with Papa's Place on the corner,
across the road from my university, opposite the brewery with
an enormous clock high on its façade – had been a constant
reference point in picture after picture I had taken of demon-
strations and riots all through my time as a student.

I saw her sitting at a table piled with what looked like school
exercise books, wearing a blue kaftan, her feet bare, a glass of
wine in her hand. A man in a ill-fitting blond toupee was talking
to her. She looked, in her long-flowing blue shift, neither older
nor different, but a bit like a nurse, perhaps, or a nun.

'Constanza!'

'Hello, Charlie.'

From a single speaker, atop a wooden crate, Josh White was singing of John Henry, who died bravely: 'Now Lord, there lies a steel-driving man . . .'

'We can't call him that if he decides to join,' said Bethany.

'Do you think he'll join?'

Constanza looked at me. 'I'd like it if he did.'

I could hear my heartbeat, and I had trouble breathing. 'What am I going to join, Constanza?'

Her green eyes still had those lights in their corners. 'I'm Katya now.'

'And I'm Rosa,' said Bethany.

'Why these other names?'

'We're other people when we're here.'

'Here?'

'Together, in the group.'

'And what is the group?'

Again they looked at each other, but said nothing. It was like meeting members of some born-again sect, where you recognized old friends but they had converted and taken new names and you had to get to know them all over again.

I heard another knock at the door and 'Rosa' looked up, pleased. 'That will be him.'

'Now perhaps we'll find out what Charlie wants to do,' said 'Katya' with that clarity of tone and purpose I remembered, the sense that things were to be settled because she wanted them to be so, and I would understand if I was patient and trusted her. She waved now to the man who had just come in, put her arm around my shoulders and pressed me forward into his presence: I felt very much like some sort of initiate, or a novice being presented to the master.

His thin grin was the same, at once shy and secret, as if he tried to keep some joke to himself. The half-smile that said he was always faintly disappointed with himself, but that he'd

128

get over it, given the chance. It was the smile he had worn all the while Trevor Lockett's darts buried themselves in his back. It was the smile I thought he'd lost, finally, on the day of the Corpus Christi march and our kidnap. It was the sub-zero half-smile he showed when his plan to blow up Zwingli Hall did not achieve the massacre he had so devoutly wished.

Little else was as I remembered. He was square now, with a chunky look to him. Even his hair, which he wore in two plump dark locks over his ears, seemed to have put on weight. He wore a soft, slightly rumpled linen jacket, blue jeans and beige flying boots, and he knotted at his throat a flaming red neckerchief; he looked part-guerrilla, part-fairground barker. But his jowls did not hide entirely that vulpine quality. The furious Sicilian boy still peeped out of this thick-set man, his face still narrowed to a bony chin, and the teeth were sharp.

He wrapped his arms around me and pulled me into his soft self. 'Hell's bells, Charlie, it's good to see you.'

'He wants to know what we do,' said 'Rosa'. 'Will you tell him, Hugo?'

'If he can stand it,' said Joe. 'OK, pour us some wine and I'll fill him in. Let's step outside, Charlie.'

He led me out on to the wrought-iron balcony, suspended high above the dinky cars far below, and there we stood with two fat tumblers of red wine. The wind was soft, the luminous hands of the clock on the brewery wall shone like spears. Above us the stars flickered in a hazy sky, as if someone were having trouble with the lights and they were about to cut out any minute. I had the feeling of being in a theatre, on a set, at a show. The rumble of traffic below groaned and faltered. Sound effects.

'What's this about, Joe? Why the secret stuff? The new names?'

'You could say we're a pressure group.'

'Political?'

He looked solemn. 'We press for freedom.'

'We pressed for freedom, in this neck of the woods, all the time I was at college. Unhappy years, Joe, a total fucking waste of time. Why meet here?'

He raised his eyebrows. 'These are pretty average flats, filled with pretty average people. They don't attract attention. This is Katya's place.'

'Why is she called Katya?'

'It's a *nom de guerre*. We don't use real names in FIRE. She does the hard stuff.'

'What's FIRE? Are you having me on?'

'The Forum for Independence, Redistribution and Equity.'

'Now I know you're taking the piss. And what does it aim to do – this forum?'

'Same as always. To hit the one thing they've got: the feeling they can't fail; their one and only fucking big idea of themselves. You work, slowly and patiently and secretly towards wiping out their single most powerful weapon, which is stronger than guns and truncheons and jails – their belief that they are saints. Right now they reckon they're unassailable. Force and grace are theirs. Take away their belief in their divine election and they crumble. That's what we do.'

'It's a loser, Joe.'

'Hugo.'

'Whatever. But it's still a loser.'

He smiled. He was enjoying this. 'Maybe there is method in my madness.'

'Method? Cosying up to the Calvinist creeps. There is money, for sure. I see the work you're doing all over town. What is your line? *Building for Tomorrow*. Yeah, their tomorrow. You're the guy who blew up Zwingli Hall and now you're building it again.'

He laughed now and put his arm around my shoulders.

'That's my old Charlie, convinced what you see is what you get; mixing up the movie with the real thing. Yes, I build: I do concrete, contracts, plans . . . that's my day job. But my question is what it always was: how do I go for their throats?'

He gave his small smile, with its quick gleam of fangs. 'Why the surprise? I aim to bite the hand that feeds me, and I am very well placed to do that. How about you, Charlie, what are you doing on the *Post*? Every time it gets up off its knees and actually says something real, it falls over faint with fright. Nothing particularly noble about the *Post*. And they tell me you cover the municipal beat. Must be hell.'

I rose to the bait. 'Years ago you wanted to be Public Enemy Number One. Now it looks like you're the Number One Sell-Out.'

He sipped his wine. Across the way the minute hand on the big clock lurched forward, and stopped with a small quiver. Nine twenty-five.

'Seen my company boards, have you?'

'Outside what will be the new Polly's Hotel.'

'Bet that set you back, Charlie.'

'I was appalled.'

'You've always been easily appalled. What happened in the alley that day was done to me, not to you. Who says you can take a moral position on what happened to me?'

'That's rich. The purveyor of conglomerate to the creeps he wanted to wipe out talking about moral positions? Why did you sell out – Hugo?'

'Adaptation doesn't mean betrayal.' He gave a half-sneer, dark and malign, an angry goblin. 'I took over the business when my old man kicked it, and I found we were in deep shit. My dad was looking at a stretch in the slammer when he upped

131

and died. That's why I had to admire his timing. There'd been a series of cock-ups. Roads were crumbling. A couple of bridges fell down. Rumour had it he'd skimped on materials. Reinforced concrete has great compressive power, but too much sand in the mix undermines it. So I rebranded the old place. Changed the name to something more local. Sweet-talked the clients. And now we're bigger than ever.' He sipped his wine, the minute hand on the clock across the way lurched, then stopped, quivering, ready to spring again. 'Don't jump to conclusions, Charlie, about the building jobs I do. Just because I put them up doesn't mean I can't knock them down. They believe God loves and protects them. I want to shake that faith.'

'So you're playing with FIRE. What exactly do you do?'

'You'll have to ask Katya that. She handles the hard stuff. Now, here's the thing we all want to find out: will you stand with us?'

'No.'

'Then stay on the sidelines and watch. But I'm going the limit.'

'You went the limit when you bombed Zwingli. Next time they'll eat you alive.'

'Next time I won't miss.'

'You'll be dead, more likely.'

As soon as I said it I knew I'd made a mistake. I'd come round to that place where Joe was unassailable.

'That's a risk too small to count.'

He spoke with what I'd have to call, if I had been scripting it, magnificent disdain. But the script was his, and so was the role, and for the past thirty minutes we had been running through the balcony scene. I knew then that it wasn't me who couldn't tell the difference between the movies and reality. We were back in the darkness of the flick house in Jeweldeane, when we bunked out of the hostel to watch Lucky Luciano or

Pretty Boy Floyd pump someone full of lead. This was *The Fall of Zwingli Hall* – the remake . . .

I enjoyed, in a nervous way, the show he'd been putting on. Like the kill-flicks he so enjoyed, it was fatuous and frightening. The question was: could he play the part of lackey-in-chief to a regime he hated, while secretly directing a lethal plan of attack? Of course. Could he pull it off? Never. Since getting the job on the *Post*, I had seen close-up, daily, the forces he wanted to take on; I'd felt their dead weight, the ease with which they gloried in their shining ignorance, their mountainous power. It would take more to shift them than dreams of shapely carnage – or some explosive mix of Capone, Calvin and Lenin that Joe was eternally screening inside his head.

My face must have said it all, because he shrugged and walked back inside. When the door opened, I heard Josh White singing 'Waltzing Matilda': 'Up jumped a swagman and grabbed him with glee . . .' Then 'Katya' was beside me. I heard her skin ruffle the cotton kaftan when she leaned over the balcony, her lips caught the moonlight and turned silvery.

'Joe says you need convincing.'

'Are you really planning to blow things up?'

'The time for peaceful action is over.'

'You're crazy. This thing has disaster written all over it. Joe doesn't get these things right. He tried something like this and he fucked up. And now he's working hand in hand with the guys he once tried to destroy.'

She looked at me gravely. 'I don't need him to get it right. That's my job. He sees what has to be done, and he'll do whatever it takes, and that's wonderful. I take him as I find him, his failure – and his fire.'

'What is this "hard stuff" Joe talked about?'

'If I tell you that, you'll have to join.'

Maybe it was the fact that 'Rosa' had bet against me showing up that night; maybe it was feeling her standing close, but I didn't hesitate: 'Tell me.'

'I blow things up.'

The hands on the face of the shining clock on the brewery wall showed a quarter to ten.

'What if you kill someone?'

She gave me a look poised between pity and amused affection – as if she'd known I would say that.

'I choose our targets carefully. Won't you come in with us?'

I tried one last time to get out of where I'd got myself to. 'Why me? What can I do? You don't need me.'

'If you're right about Hugo, and he fucks up, then I'll need an ally. Someone who sees very carefully how things are.'

And that was how I became that night a member of FIRE. Even now I blush to remember it. They offered me a walk-on part and I took it. I'd like to think, at least at the start, that I was doing something useful, though I was simply at a loss to say what it was. I landed a bit part in this production that Joe was directing and in which 'Katya' was the star. That is what I told myself – but as it happens, I had landed nothing but trouble. If this was just a bit of theatrical business, then I had lost the plot.

FIRE numbered just the four of us, plus the man in the blond toupee, whom 'Katya' introduced as 'my Uncle Ernie'. He was not, strictly speaking, a member of FIRE. He told me he was 'on secondment', though from what he did not say. He was not her uncle and his name was not Ernie. He called himself a 'technical adviser' on 'matters of ordnance', and he wanted, he told me, 'to see the other side fry in hell'.

Deciding on the name I was to use in the Forum was a bit of a problem: they tried Louis and Terence and Max – eventually Joe came up with the one that stuck.

'Why don't we call him . . . Winston?'

'That's a ter-r-rible name,' Uncle Ernie said.

'It is what he came into the world being called. That was his real name, until I changed it to Charlie. Now I've changed it back again,' Joe said.

Once I had been named, everyone left, traipsed away into the night, and I had no idea what to do next. 'Katya', sitting on the small sofa, smiling at me, seemed to be really very pleased. When I told her that I'd better be going, she pulled me down beside her just as she'd done long ago, when she was Constanza and I was Charlie, and she had taught me how to make love under the picture of St Teresa with her arms full of lilies.

'Stay, if you like, Winston,' she said and kissed me.

And I did, though I could not help feeling that had I chosen to stay plain Charlie Croker, Municipal Affairs reporter for the *Capital Post*, she would not have given me the time of day. I moved in with her that night, and went back to my own place from time to time to pick up an iron, a TV, my computer. Small things, yet they seemed rank luxuries in Katya's spartan studio, with its scuffed parquet flooring, narrow kitchen counter, and a couple of pallid overhead lights in shades of rice paper, glued around wire frames, like the threadbare ribs of hungry children.

From the horsehair sofa of our first love-making, to her hard bed under the picture of St Teresa armed with lilies, to the skimpy foam-rubber mattress on the bed in Bellevue Mansions, all the locations of our love had been uncomfortable, yet the enchantment was so intense I would have slept with her on a bed of nails. I had the feeling that I had just stepped over a cliff and it was a long way down.

CHAPTER 16

It was at this time I took the only picture that shows us all together briefly; and that once stood, in a silver frame, on Constanza's dressing table. It was what we came to call the 'famous photo', though its fame had as much to do with our fear and insecurity as it did with a picture of friends at a dinner party. It was famous because never again were we so happily together. Or so numerous.

We had gone to supper at Dino's, an Italian restaurant not far from Bellevue Mansions, now long gone. That evening we did not bother to use our code names, we did not pretend to be revolutionaries, we were just friends out for dinner. We all seemed to be having a good time. How very young we looked, and how innocent. Clueless might be the better word. Stupidity is not something the camera registers and instead, because of the way the light reflects, we are shown up to be, quite literally, starry-eyed.

Joe is in the foreground, leaning back in his chair, holding a glass of Chianti, the straw-covered bottle is in front of him. Bethany is on his left, she leans forward, her arms bare, her dress low, her cleavage creamy. Constanza sits on Joe's right, her expression is dreamy, not unhappy, but reflective, a look I got to know, one that masked a capacity for concentrated action none of us could match. The photograph seizes an instant of time. There is no before or after, there is only the now. It is a miracle that stops time dead. Before the camera, there was no holding it, all was passing instants. Then suddenly the snap of the shutter, the hand on the collar of time, the instant arrest.

From that moment the Forum began to come apart.

Bethany's perfume company announced they were transferring her permanently to the coast, and she would be able to get to the capital only once in a while. It broke her up, having to decide. But she took the job. I remember her reasoning: 'Maybe I can be a country member. Eyes and ears in the provinces?'

Joe was virtually invisible. Building was booming and the Di Angelo Conglomerate prospered along with it. Our rulers simply could not get enough of the stuff they needed to throw up yet another broad-shouldered, low-browed steel and concrete bunker with tiny windows, thick walls and aluminium trimmings; and lots more dams, bridges and motorways.

Joe told me: 'The compressive power of concrete gets better all the time, and the mix lighter and stronger, and it means we can builder higher and higher. One day it will outperform steel.'

We lived in an age of concrete and Joe was making a fortune. At the same time we were expected to believe that he was subtly undermining the compressive qualities of the power he helped to enhance with the great building projects in which he collaborated; he was going to be the subversive sand in their mix and, one day, their seemingly rock-solid world would fall down, like the bridges his dad had built. That was the plan, the line, the fatuity. Joe was perfectly in sync with the age.

I remember saying to 'Katya': 'It might be an idea if the convenor of FIRE started turning up for meetings.'

She seemed unfazed. 'Hugo's job is tactical oversight.

Someone has to have an overarching view of what we're doing.'

But she must have said something to him, because he came round one night and asked me if I had a problem.

'You're hardly ever here, and you're the convenor.'

'Think of me as the conductor of an orchestra; as long as the players know what they're doing, I am really just a figurehead.'

But the Forum wasn't an orchestra. It wasn't even a small band. With 'Rosa' gone, and 'Hugo' busy elsewhere, we were down to just 'Katya' and me; though now and then our duo became a trio.

This tended to happen well after midnight, when we were in bed and I'd hear someone in the bathroom, and I'd know that Uncle Ernie had just climbed six floors up the rickety iron fire escape, and hopped through the open window. 'Katya' would slip on her old dressing gown, blue silk embroidered with daisies, and Uncle Ernie, in his charcoal suit, black shoes and Rotarian tie, looking more like a bank manager than a demolition expert, would sit down at her work table, take from his pocket a child's school slate and a piece of chalk, accept the brandy and Coke she poured him, and the lesson began.

'Let's hear-r-r our-r-r catechism, gir-r-r-l.' Uncle Ernie rattled his 'r's. 'What takes the for-r-r-rm of pale yellow cr-r-r-ystals?'

'Trinitrotoluene, otherwise known as TNT.'

'Stable?'

'Fairly. When a detonator is not present. It has a low melting point, which makes it useful for pouring into artillery shells.'

'Yes. And somewhat old-fashioned these days. Now, tell your Uncle Er-r-rnie, what is the base of most common militar-r-ry explosives?'

'Cyclonite, also called hexogen. Good because stable when stored.'

'Would that we were all like that, eh, my gir-r-rlll? Stable when stor-r-red. What exactly is the mix of mater-r-rials in military dynamite?'

'About 70 per cent cyclonite – or RDX – to about 15 per cent TNT.'

'What's best for Pr-r-rimacor-r-rd fuses, when used to detonate a good char-r-rge?'

'Pentaerythritol tetranitrate.'

'Other-r-rwise known as PETN, which we mix, of cour-r-rse, with dear old TNT. Ver-r-ry good on demolition jobs. Now, for your pr-r-roject, what have we decided for a tar-r-rget?'

'Katya' said, 'Something in steel, tall, isolated, embedded in concrete.'

Uncle Ernie would quiz her on detonation rates and speed of burning: his chalk would rasp on slate and there I see, in his angular scrawl, the three main forces of an explosion: combustion, deflagration and detonation.

'The blast pr-r-ressure wave has how many phases, and what are they called?'

'Two. Positive pressure stage and suction phase.'

'What is the effect of the two for-r-rces?'

'Together they ensure that high explosive delivers a double-whammy to anything that stands in its path.'

'R-r-right again! And that includes you, my gir-r-rllll, if you don't do things r-r-right. What I am telling you is a matter of life and death . . . yours, quite possibly.' He drew out the words 'lifah and dethah'.

Uncle Ernie taught her about the uses of cordex, safety fuses, timers, detonator caps, margins of safety, and about how many legs or supports you needed to knock out a tall steel target – at least two of the four, and three if the legs were sunk in reinforced concrete.

At some point, when he was satisfied, Uncle Ernie would

retreat into the bathroom, step out on to the fire escape, and vanish into the night, and 'Katya' would return her equipment to wherever she hid it. She did not see the point of telling me much.

My aim was to stay close to her in every way possible. Her aim was professional perfection. When she came home from school, she had forty books to mark. When she finished her marking she began what she called her 'homework'. She would cover the table with old batteries, alarm clocks, dismembered mobile phones, fuses, nitroglycerine wrappers (the waxed and coloured papers in which high explosives are packed), and study spidery diagrams showing the construction of grenades, booby traps and a variety of improvised explosive devices.

'Can I help?'

'Thank you. But this is a game only one can play.'

I saw her utter concentration, how surely she learnt to judge and balance these things, to make and master the devices. It was her talent, her brilliance, her unshakeable determination that got things done. I was happily hypnotized, helplessly absorbed by seeing what she could do: she didn't merely point in the direction we should be going, she *was* the direction, and she brought to the business of sabotage all the deftness and subtlety she brought to sex.

Though she was now living a long way from the capital, 'Rosa' kept sending us a stream of messages urging us to be watchful. The security police were everywhere, sniffing around. *Keep nothing in writing. No accounts, letters, maps, dates, numbers . . .* Her notes invariably ended: *Burn this now!*

We set out on reconnaissance trips in my old Renault, scouting for targets. Identification was meticulous; the right ones had to be far enough from centres of habitation or late-night walkers or curious kids, but near enough to allow us to be back in the city before the blast occurred. Once a week or so she would report to Hugo, and list potential sites. But when and how we hit the targets was her decision, and she would tell me nothing.

Did she love me? I'm not sure. I think rather that I provided some useful back-up to an adventure that was hers alone. I didn't mind, and our time together was too busy to think much, and, as it turned out, too brief. But I was an available, fairly useful partner, until, suddenly, I wasn't.

I noticed that she was leaving open day and night the glass door which led on to the small balcony, even though it was autumn and the nights were cool. A steady current of cold air passed between the open bathroom window and the open glass door.

I asked, half-seriously, 'Are you a fresh-air fiend?'

She gave her slow, delectable smile. 'I can't sleep if I'm too warm.' Then she suddenly rolled over and turned on the bed-side light. 'Look under the bed.'

I got on my knees and squinted into the darkness and I made out three boxes made of blond wood, pine perhaps, with rope handles. Suddenly I knew why we had not seen Uncle Ernie for a while.

'God almighty. Are those what I think they are?'

She nodded. 'Probably.'

'Where do you find it?'

'Some of Uncle Ernie's engineering pals had the job of blasting tunnels for a new road in rough country. They were storing the stuff in a locked wooden cabin in the hills. We had a copy of the keys made, nipped along there a few nights ago, and helped ourselves.

I remembered enough from Uncle Ernie's lessons: 'That's why all the fr-r-resh air. You have to keep the stuff cool.'

She nodded. 'If it sweats it may go up.'

For several nights that week she and I had made vigorous

love on a skimpy mattress, inches above a cache of high explosive that would have demolished the entire block of flats and quite probably most of the buildings in the street. It was difficult to assess the risk. I knew from Uncle Ernie's lessons that all dynamite, conventional or military, was packed in identical cartridges of coloured wax, marked M1, 2 or 3. Even had I opened one of the wooden boxes I should not have been able to tell which was which. Military dynamite does not contain nitroglycerine and is safer to store, and it is more or less impervious to friction, heat and bullets. That was not a lot of comfort because I knew, too, that when it exploded the blast wave moved at around twenty thousand feet per second.

The next day when I got back from work I took a look under the bed and the wooden cases were gone. Was there also, perhaps, still an oily whiff of something sugary? I knew from Uncle Ernie's lessons that true dynamite, as opposed to the military variety, besides being unstable, has a strong sweet smell – that's the nitroglycerine in it. But it was almost certainly my imagination at work. The rope-handled boxes that she'd hidden under the bed had been sealed.

'Where did you take it?'

She shook her head firmly. 'You don't want to know.'

'I slept above it for nights on end – why not tell me?'

She looked at me with her immense green eyes. 'Don't look so sad. It's nothing personal. It's simply good tactics. We're up against serious people. Let's say they get you, haul you in, ask you where the dynamite is kept . . .'

'What makes you so sure I'll tell them?'

'Because we all do. I suppose there must be some rare souls who hold out. But sooner or later – you, me, most of us will crack. And if you gave us away? Then what?' She came close and pressed her lips to my cheek with a tenderness that made my eyes water. 'I know you. You'd never forgive yourself. And

I don't want to risk that. I've cleared away every last thing that might incriminate us. Every note, clock, diagram. This flat is clean. Now, shall we head on out to the night's business?'

'We're taking my old jalopy? The springs are gone.'

She picked up the rucksack from the table. 'We're not carrying raw stuff now.'

We rode into the rough country north of the city. I had only a vague recollection of having been this way before on one of our expeditions to identify targets. She must have kept every site we'd visited clearly in her memory. I told myself I was pleased to be driving, I had more control as we bumped over the dirt roads, the rucksack visible in my rear-view mirror humped darkly on the back seat. It was a comforting illusion. I knew my life turned now on how well she had absorbed Uncle Ernie's lessons.

She told me to stop about fifty metres away from the pylon, a silhouette on the hilltop. I killed the engine, doused the lights, and watched. She picked up the rucksack and headed up the hill, a small figure casting a long shadow, rising and falling, as she made her way over the stony ground. I saw her stoop at the base of the pylon, kneel beside it for a few moments, then turn and start running back to the car. She was panting when she climbed in beside me, and looked at her watch.

'What's the delay?'

'About five minutes.'

It seemed shorter. Suddenly, a jagged flash opened the sky, I saw the great stanchions of the pylon flex and the whole thing jumped like a big metal grasshopper. The sound of the explosion came hard behind the light show, and in the dark that followed I heard splintered metal thudding to earth.

'Wonderful!' Her look was one of utter peace.

The exhilaration lingered for the next couple of days. We

looked at the papers, at the TV, expecting some sort of reaction. None came and we were disappointed. After all, we had performed well. Why had no one noticed? Why wasn't there a review or two? I was as proud as she was. I wished I'd been able to take a picture, just to remind ourselves it had really happened.

CHAPTER 17

In the small hours of a wet Wednesday, one week after we hit the target, we had a late-night visitor. She had got into the flat using Uncle Ernie's route: climbing up the fire escape, and coming through the open bathroom window. The first I knew of it, she was sitting on my bed, shaking me awake and calling my name – my *real* name – 'Charlie! Charlie!' – and for a moment I wasn't sure who she was talking to.

I reached over and switched on the light.

'Rosa?'

She was sitting there like some bright garden gnome, but without the grin. In a yellow plastic mac over a cherry-red blouse. There was, to my sleepy eyes, a gleam about her I found worrying and which turned out to be water. It was pouring with rain. There were streaks on her cheeks that looked like tears.

'Bethany will do for now, Charlie.'

The rain battered the window panes and suddenly I wanted to stay with all the false names; somehow they were safer. Beside me, Constanza lifted herself on her elbows, yawned, stretched and sat up, not bothering to pull the sheets up over her breasts, her long hair rippling over her bare shoulders.

Bethany, in her mac, dripping water, was very pale, very serious.

'Have you guys gone and hit something?'

'It's not something we talk about,' said Constanza.

'Obviously then you have hit something. Well, we're blown,' said Bethany.

Constanza said, 'Would you get us some tea, Charlie?'

I said, 'Do we have time?'

'He's got no clothes on and he's shy,' Constanza said. 'Bless his heart.'

'Go on, Charlie,' said Bethany, 'I won't look. I'm right, aren't I? You have been out and done something?'

In the bathroom I pulled on my clothes, feeling the curtains stirring and smelling the rain on the breeze from the open window. I heard Constanza saying, 'We set off the stuff the other night. The first test. It worked well. I wondered why there was nothing about it on the news. They must have known.'

'They knew all right,' said Bethany. 'They just kept quiet. And now they're coming for us.'

I went out to the tiny kitchen counter, put on the kettle, made the tray up carefully with milk, sugar and biscuits, and carried it over to them. I poured the tea, offered around the milk, and heard myself asking, in a surprisingly calm way, who would like a biscuit.

'What do mean they're coming for us?' Constanza asked.

Bethany folded her hands in her lap and I could see they trembled.

'It happened yesterday, Tuesday, when I was at a sales conference. My neighbour phoned. She's a retired vet and has the flat opposite mine. She's OK, that woman. She sympathizes and she told me there were cops in my flat.'

'"What sort of cops?" I asked her. "Plain clothes," she says. "Special Branch – you can tell by the look." I knew then we were in deep shit. I left the meeting, filled the car and headed for the capital. Six hours hard on the road. When I got here, I went straight to Joe's place. Not to his house – they might have been watching – I drove to the factory and Di Angelo Conglomerate was just closing for the day. I told them I was a customer with an urgent order for ready-mix and I needed to see the boss.'

"'Ah, yes," they said, "the Boss . . . he's not here. He had to go somewhere." I knew from their faces – Joe had been picked up.'

Constanza was worried now. 'But why Joe? No one knew about him. He was the best hidden of us all.'

Bethany shrugged. 'Who can say? I got the hell out. My fear was they'd got you too, so I drove here. I didn't know that Charlie was here with you. I was parked along the road, where I could see your lights. I couldn't make up my mind whether to wait or go. I worried it was a trap. In the end I climbed up the fire escape and came through the bathroom window.'

'You were really brave,' Constanza said. 'But you shouldn't have taken the chance.'

Bethany was shaking. She took a sip of tea and I heard her teeth on the cup. 'I couldn't not tell you. Now, grab some things and let's hit the road. I'm heading for the border.'

Constanza said, 'We don't have passports.'

'We'll head east. That stretch is wild. No patrols, and not much of a fence. I'll dump the car when we get close and we can walk across. But let's hurry, please!'

'Give me a few minutes.' Constanza got out of bed and walked calmly to the bathroom.

I remember how straight she stood, her breasts high and pointed, and she didn't look back.

I began shoving clothes into a bag. Bethany was pacing around the flat, her plastic mac creaking.

'Anything here you don't want left? Papers, notes, stuff the cops might find?'

'Nothing. Not now. We cleared out everything.'

I told myself we had been lucky. I thought of the boxes with their rope handles, under our bed, Constanza's fuses and timers, her 'homework' for Uncle Ernie.

Bethany stood in front of the dressing table and she had in her hands the 'famous' photo I'd taken of the group of us at Dino's.

'You can't leave this! Jesus!' She pulled the photo from its frame and, taking the box of matches from beside the gas stove, she set it alight, fanning it to make it burn faster.

'There will be no more of us.'

I got a glimpse of Joe's foxy smile and his raised glass, and then the flames took over.

Constanza was still in the bathroom, and Bethany was more and more anxious. 'For God's sake, Charlie, what is she doing in there? We've got to move. It's a good three hours' drive to the border.'

I knocked on the bathroom door and, when I got no answer, I tried the handle. The door opened and the night breeze from the window stirred the curtain, carrying on it the fresh smell of the rain. I looked down into the dark well; the rain shone on the stippled steel of the fire-escape steps.

Bethany was right behind me, swinging her car keys.

'Well? Where is she?'

I waved towards the open window. 'Gone. The same way you came in. She dressed and went down the fire escape.'

'But why, Charlie?'

'Who knows? Maybe she thinks if she splits from me, I won't get hauled in.'

I didn't really believe that. Joe was out of it, and if Bethany and I made it across the border, that left just her to keep the show on the road, and that was fine. Constanza had decided I was no longer an asset. The raid on Bethany's flat and the taking of Joe might have finished off the Forum – poor, stupid thing that it was – but nothing was going to stop Constanza. She'd put in too much work; the next device was ready and she was seeing it through. As she'd said, this was a game only one could play.

'Well, that's her affair. Let's get out of here, Charlie.'

I shook my head.

'I can't wait, Charlie.'

I knew that I had very little time. Those hunting us would be on their way. Constanza was gone, I had to think of myself.

'I can't go.'

Bethany didn't argue and didn't say I was making a big mistake, though she wanted to, I could see that, and I was grateful for her silence. She stepped out on to the fire escape. 'If I can hit the border, I'll be OK. Good luck, Charlie.'

Leaning out of the window, I watched her clambering down the steel steps and when she got to the ground she looked up, a solid figure in her yellow mac at the bottom of the fire escape, and she waved as if she were off somewhere nice and this was all perfectly normal.

This was the thing: I knew that things were far from normal, but I simply could not feel what I was sure must be some appropriate level of anxiety. I felt drained but relieved, not because Bethany had gone and I had decided to stay, but at being left alone with myself, because that self seemed a very light and airy husk. A shadow.

It is from that moment that I date my feeling of extinction. I simply could not grasp the self I was supposed to be. I knew that it was just a matter of time before they came for me. But knowing something doesn't mean you believe it. The 'me' whom they were after felt wispy and unreal. I kept seeing myself as someone 'over there', the solid, accommodating Charlie Croker, sitting at Constanza's table where she had, night after night, taught herself to build the device which had set the immense steel pylon rocking and then tumbling to earth. I sat in the flat that night and watched myself, my double; he walked over to the kitchen counter and made himself more tea.

In the morning I watched him getting ready for work, searching for his car keys, locking the front door. Who was real – him over there, or me over here? Well, we would see. When the cops caught up with one of us they'd have to take hold of someone, wouldn't they? And then I'd know.

I got into my office around eight, as I usually did. Everything for the next few hours was, in an eerie way, appallingly normal. Monty Nines came out of his office, looking more frayed than usual, and rubbed his pale hands in his thin hair as he tried to remember my name, gave up and settled for 'mmm', in his low, not unattractive, voice: 'Today – mmm – yours is the joy of roadworks . . . Shall we say five hundred words by mid-morning? Suit you? Hardly pulsating stuff, I know. Never mind, it can only get worse.'

He always said that. It was his way of saying sorry.

'Someone has to do it,' I said.

'That's the spirit, mmm.' And he went off, rubbing his hands.

I made a cup of coffee and began to write up a piece on road-widening: how it heightened noise levels when the surfacing was badly done; the price of yellow loading-zone paint; and the life-expectancy of roadside reflectors. If I had been chronicling a particularly bloody murder, or the torture of children, I would not have felt so wretched. I was terribly aware of my own inconsequence, of how, when measured beside such terrible facts as the estimated costs of culverts or the purchase of a new steamroller, human life is a laughable thing; of how we lie to ourselves all the time.

At around nine, two men walked into my office without knocking. They stood over me, oddly wrapped in beige rain-coats on what had turned into a lovely sunny morning, though I knew it meant they had probably been on the job all night. One of them was tall and had a full head of chestnut brown hair, which he wore long. The other was squat with a boxer's nose and wheat-blond hair, which, together with his sallow complexion, yellow tinged with orange, made me think of cheddar cheese. My editor was in the doorway of my office now, alarmed, and doing what he could to hide it, trying to be imposing, and failing. Clearly these men had walked into the newspaper as if they owned the place and he felt some small protest was obligatory.

'Is there some trouble? Can I help you?'

The cops didn't look at him: they only had eyes for me. It was the tall chestnut guy who spoke.

'Croker, Winston?'

I said yes.

'Get your jacket . . . And come wuthus . . .'

Monty Nines said, 'Croker, what the hell is going on?'

He knew what was going on. He knew who they were, even if he found it hard to believe what he was seeing. The baggy trousers, the suede shoes, the curious air of boredom and menace. As Bethany's neighbour had said: you always knew when it was the Branch, even if you'd never seen them before. It was the look. His vexation and fear were entirely to be expected.

Besides being afraid, he was hopping mad – at me. Monty Nines would not have gone so far as wishing to be arrested in my place – he had spent his professional life avoiding just such a fate – yet he wanted at least some of the prestige that went with being raided to be attributed to him. His paper had been raided. Some young guy whose name he struggled to remember was to blame. It was appalling that someone so far off the radar could, apparently, bring down upon his newspaper the weight of the State.

'Let's go,' the chestnut cop said, and took my arm.

'I'll see you later,' I said to Monty Nines, wanting to feel less frightened. Wanting to hear my own voice. Wanting him to say something reassuring.

'Forget it,' said Cheesy, and took my other arm. 'You won't be back for a long time.'

They took me downstairs and put me into the back of a powder-blue Ford. I never knew their names; to me they were just Chestnut and Cheesy, and I saw a lot of them over the next hours.

Chapter 18

They took me to Pinnacle Point, a tower of concrete ribs and dirty glass – quite probably a place Di Angelo *père* had helped to build. It is long gone now, but in that era it had a fearsome reputation: principal police station, barracks and interrogation centre. I was marched into an office which might have belonged to a bank teller or an insurance clerk. Those were the days when the office of a high-ranking police officer could be kitted out with a government-issue, varnished box-wood desk. Splintered at the corners, its pitted surface carried an ink-stained green blotter, beside which stood a water jug. The rug was grey with black chevrons and a chintz curtain hung over the large picture window looking out on the city.

My interrogator sat with his back to the view, and mentioned it only once – when he jerked a thumb behind him, just as the setting sun sidled down the sky in all its streaming glory, gilding the concrete bunkers where bankers and civil servants were cloistered, and church spires were crowned with weathercocks clasping in their steel claws a parcel of spears – and he said softly, referring to the ten storeys between us and the ground – 'There but for the grace of God – go you.'

But I'm getting ahead of myself. That came much later, when our interviews, our conversations, our connections, were nearing the end . . .

Behind a desk sat a man wearing a salt-and-pepper sports coat. He was around forty, I guessed, an earnest face with high cheekbones, and his fringe of dark hair was marked by an ice-white arrow or wedge in the middle of his forehead.

Cheesy pushed me forward. 'This here is Major le Moerr.'

The man behind the desk pointed me to the swivel chair opposite him and told my minders they could leave. He smiled at me across the desk, as if he were a doctor or a bank manager, and this was a slightly formal but perfectly normal interview. Though what he said was not really much like a doctor or banker – it was the unexpectedness of his words, delivered in a warm, gravelly tone, or their lack of tact, or, if you like, their appalling directness, which I have not forgotten.

'So then, Mr Croker, please begin by telling me – *who* is Katya? Better still – *where* is Katya? We know where everyone else is, even Rosa. She crossed the border some hours ago and I really wonder why you didn't go with her. I grew up in a small town called Excalibur, very near that far edge of our country, and I know that all it takes to leave is to step over some barbed wire, and you're out. Would you like a smoke?'

He pushed a pack of cigarettes across the desk – the pack showed tobacco and mint leaves entwined in a kind of Roman wreath, and a line in spiky script said: *Mentholyptus Kings – for the man who smokes a lot and loves it!*

'I don't smoke.'

He flipped back the box top and with a quick movement sent a cigarette spinning into the air and caught it between his lips. He picked up a box of matches and, leaning back in his chair, struck the match on the sole of his shoe and the room filled with the aroma of minty smoke.

'It's an old trick.' He said this almost apologetically. 'It is also a childish wish to show off. I apologize. We are all susceptible to repeating old habits, aren't we? Mine are particularly awful. How are yours?'

I could think of nothing to say.

'Never mind. We'll come to your habits soon enough. Now, tell me, Mr Croker – do you mind if I stick to your surname? I know some call you "Winston", but for me your nom de guerre holds no charms. Tell me, please, why are you the only one in your, what shall we say – association? – to keep his real name?'

I thought if I could spin things out, I might buy some time.

'Actually, it's a joke.'

'A joke? You and I must be well suited. I do tricks with cigarettes and you tell jokes. But you also belong to an organization that plants bombs. I am impressed. Please, tell me more.'

'My real name is Winston, but no one ever called me that. Everyone calls me Charlie, so when it came to the business of choosing a – new name – I got my old one back.'

He nodded. 'Names. A serious business. It's something I understand very well. I am the son of a classicist and he named me Scipio Africanus after a famous Roman general. Imagine growing up where I did, carrying that handle around, in a rough town where the boys' idea of fun was bunking school and throwing bricks at passing trucks. I got rid of the name fast. Scipio became Skippy, then just plain Skip. The rather portentous Africanus went away altogether and was never heard of again. When I joined the force I picked up a nickname, owing to this here' – he touched his little sharp arrow of white hair – 'my friends called me Lightning le Moerr.' He sighed and shook his head. 'Names. What a trial. Get saddled with the wrong one and they can kill – don't you reckon, Mr Winston Charlie Croker?'

I didn't trust my voice, so I nodded.

'You're now one of the few to know my real name, Mr

Croker. I like to be direct with people, in the hope and wish – seldom granted – that they will do the same for me. Take another name – the so-called Forum for Independence, Freedom and Equity. What sort of name is that? As the son of a classical scholar I know "forum" is a Roman word and it meant a talking shop. Why not go for a name with a bit of muscle – the Liberation Front . . . the Revolutionary Faction? Something to get the heart pumping. Not this wishy-washy rubbish.'

'It wasn't my idea.'

'No?' He smiled happily. 'Who dreamt it up then? Maybe the same person who had the idea of blowing up electric pylons?' He looked at me with concern. 'I want you to know something, Mr Croker. I am not a religious man but my life is shaped by my beliefs. My faith, as you'd guess, is Calvinist, and to me Calvin was great precisely because he was honest. What did some old Pope say of him? "If I had men as honest as this heretic I'd have no need of reformers." John Calvin freed us from superstition. He believed in probity. So do I. This is the calling deep inside me – though I cannot guarantee this calling will save me. Do you know why?'

I found my voice. 'I do, actually. We can be saved only by irresistible grace.'

When something pleased him, Le Moerr had this way of waggling his ears, rather fleshy ears, covered, I noticed, with soft white down.

'Hell's teeth! I've found another Calvin man! What a fine thing to happen to me. Yes, exactly. We cannot ever know if we are among the few souls saved by God's grace. That is up to the Lord. But we can behave as if we have been saved, isn't that it? So, here's my promise: I will treat you with probity. I don't believe in violent action, which is more than can be said for you and your colleagues, who wilfully place the lives of others in peril by detonating high explosives in public places. Isn't it so?'

When I said nothing, he went on in his slightly rusty, even voice. 'Let's go back to the principal members of your so-called Forum. So we have Winston, Hugo, Katya and Rosa . . . your assumed names, your noms de guerre. The main thrust of my investigation is to find out which of these actors is likely to do something serious. No – let me rephrase that. I need to know which, if any of them, is competent enough to do any-thing. Given what we have seen of your organization, we appear to have a gang that would have difficulty running a bath or lighting a firework, never mind committing a sophis-ticated act of sabotage designed to impress and bewilder the authorities. Which, then, of the members of your so-called committee would have been remotely qualified to blow up an electric pylon, on a hill just outside the city, four nights ago?'

I said, clearly and calmly, 'That was me.'

Why did I offer? I've often asked myself that question in the decades that followed. An answer is that I wanted to keep attention away from Constanza, at least until it was forced out of me, because I did not believe his assurance about violent action. I expected that eventually, if he had to, he would beat the information out of me. I hoped I was buying time. But I don't think that is why I answered as I did. Maybe it was vanity. Le Moerr's contempt for our group and our plans angered me.

'You did it? Now that is spellbinding. If a little unlikely. Would you describe the effects of the blast caused by one of these devices you've made?'

That was no problem. I had listened carefully to Uncle Ernie's tutorials.

'Steel casing is wrapped around the explosive. When the blast is triggered the hot gases expand very fast and the casing grows to about one and a half times its original size, then fractures and throws out fragments.'

'Speed?'

'Around two thousand five hundred feet a second. These bits of hardened steel travel in straight lines until gravity pulls them down.'

'Or they hit someone?'

'Correct.'

He was slightly perplexed. 'This is almost intriguing, Mr Croker. I am leaning towards believing you. But a word of caution. What you say had better be true or you will have wasted my precious time and that could have consequences. As I said, I will use no force: no fist, no boots, no cigarette burns and no electric shocks. The same does not go for some of my colleagues. They lack – probity. They would see you as . . . pet food.'

He got up, went to the door and called in Chestnut and Cheesy, who must have been waiting in the corridor.

'Take him over to Central and lock him up – on his own. I don't want him near anyone. He might be a principal per-petrator, or he could be a liar. Either way he is a Potential Political – and I want no one in the cell with him. Good night, Mr Croker, we will speak soon.'

At the Central Police Station – a barn of a place near the square from which Joe and I had been kidnapped – the com-mander was a big beefy fellow in olive-green fatigues with lots of stripes on his shoulders, and he didn't look pleased to see us.

'He's a Potential Political . . . a PP,' said Chestnut. 'The Major wants him in solitary.'

The beefy guy shook his head. 'No can do. For fuck's sake. Where d'you expect me to find a cell? I can't just conjure them out of thin air – I'm not God – I may look like him but I am not him. This is not a jail, this is a cop shop. In the cells I got drunks, pervs, con-artists and killers. To your Major he's a PP. To me he is a problem of space. I got just twelve fucking cells and detainees fucking coming out of my fucking ears. And you want me to give some ponce a private room?'

But he found me an empty cell with a neon strip on the ceiling, and a filthy brown blanket. I was very tired. I lay down on the bunk and pulled the blanket over me. It smelt of sweat and old socks. Some time later the light went off and I could hear the jailer still complaining.

'Fucking Special Branch cunts – walking in here and asking for the moon . . .'

I hadn't slept for a long time, and as I lay down gratefully and closed my eyes, the words going through my head were 'probity', 'pet food' and 'a problem of space' . . .

CHAPTER 19

I had not been asleep long when Chestnut and Cheesy were back in my cell and tipped me off the bunk on to the floor.

'Get up,' said Cheesy. When I struggled onto my feet he pushed me over again. 'You bastard . . .'

In the queasy glare of the neon strip overhead I saw at my cell door the warder in his drab green, looking unhappier than ever.

'Stick him in solo, you say. He's a PP and "not to associate". So I find him my one free cell and next fucking thing you want him out.'

Chestnut and Cheesy didn't reply; working together they rolled me on to the floor; one of them kicked me several times in the kidneys, and when I managed to turn over, someone stood on my face. They yanked me upright and leaned me against the cell bars. My mouth was numb and, with my tongue, I found I could move my front teeth.

'He's bleeding again!' The warder pushed them aside and rubbed my face with his sleeve. I smelt tobacco and brandy. 'Stop the drip! I'm the damn idiot left to deal with the mess, hey!'

The cops half-carried me out of the cell and the warder followed us into the night: 'Look at my fucking corridor. Special Branch bastards!'

He was still shouting when they loaded me into the back of the Ford. I didn't ask where we were going; I didn't need to.

When we got to Pinnacle Point they marched me into a bathroom, gave me a towel and told me to clean up. The mirror showed my mouth was a mess of caked blood and I had trouble opening my right eye. I stripped off my shirt and used the towel to wash away as much of the blood as I could. They brought me a clean shirt – navy blue, standard police issue, and it made me angry that I should wear anything that belonged to them, but I pulled it on. I had trouble walking, and they had to half-carry me into the lift to the tenth floor.

The Major was sitting at his desk, patiently, as if I had left him just minutes before. His men held me up, as if displaying a painting or an item for auction, then, at a nod from Le Moerr, they dropped me into the chair facing him.

'I specifically asked you not to do this! Bring him back in one piece. That was my order.'

His forehead wrinkled, his lips turned down. We had all let him down. He let us feel the depth of his disappointment.

'What a mess! I'm sorry, Mr Croker. I hate this stupid muscularity. If they can't hit or kick something they don't know what to do with themselves. But to them you represent everything that is most repulsive.'

He waved them out of the office and they cleared off with an embarrassed shuffle, hanging their heads like kids who've been told off by the teacher.

Le Moerr came around to where I sat, patted me on the shoulder, poured me a glass of water, then lit a cigarette.

'It's as well you're in my charge, Mr Croker. Had others taken you in hand, you might by now have come seriously unstuck. My officers, to be frank, overestimate your importance, as they have shown. But believe me, a few cuts and bruises are a small price to pay –'

'To pay for what?'

'For being in my charge. Things sometimes happen in Pinnacle Point, things I do not like. Someone's head hits the cell wall, someone slips in the showers or takes flight from a window, like the one behind me. Remember that. Next time, I may not be here to protect you from your own mistakes. You lied to me when you said you had set that explosion.'

'But I did have a hand in it.'

'I've told my officers that the real enemy is not you. Not by a long chalk. Your immensely silly group is barely worth bothering with. The true enemy is not here – yet; and when he is, they won't know him. Now I know you lied to me and I think you did so because you were taking the blame for someone else. I admire that. It shows probity.'

I said nothing. My lips were too sore, and when I touched them flecks of congealed blood came away on my fingertips.

'Now, let's be moving. We have an appointment.'

He must have pressed a buzzer or a bell because Cheesy and Chestnut were back, shuffling nervously, as if they expected to be bawled out by their chief. But all he said was, 'Put him in the car and let's go.'

Downstairs, the Ford was waiting, and I could see someone already in the back seat. Cheesy opened the door, shoved me inside, and handcuffed me to the silent man, who sighed deeply, as if he were asleep or overcome with sadness. Le Moerr got behind the wheel and Cheesy took the passenger seat beside him. A grey pickup kicked into life behind us as we pulled out of the parking lot. The man to whom I was handcuffed inclined his head a fraction, just enough to acknowledge me. I saw the half-moon curve of his nose, the long, thin chin – his face, though in shadow, looked rumpled. It was Joe, and they'd also had a go at him.

Le Moerr looked back at us in the driver's mirror. 'You two

are old friends, isn't that right? And it's as old friends that I want you both to see what happens tonight.'

Le Moerr drove with a sureness that said he knew where he was headed. The grey pickup sat on our tail as we headed out of the city. It would be Chestnut, I guessed, providing back-up.

We were moving in open country. Every now and then the headlights raked the wooden ribs of a fence and lit the roadside grass, bowing low as the car's slipstream pushed it aside. Joe and I sat shoulder to shoulder, the handcuffs tight. I could feel him breathing and he was so quiet he might have been asleep.

An hour or so out of town, we turned off the tarmac on to gravel and ran along a dirt road, the coupé juddering on the deep corrugations, and behind us the lights from the pickup turned yellow in the dust. We slowed and began threading our way between boulders the size of houses. It was in the shadowy lee of one of those that we pulled up and Le Moerr killed the engine. In the steely moonlight, over the hill and down into a flat ground ahead of us, there marched a line of tall electric pylons, arms up in the air, like surrendering troops.

'This is where you will sit and watch,' said Le Moerr. 'What will happen, exactly, I'm not entirely sure myself. It all depends. But we'll know soon enough.'

He turned to Cheesy. 'One peep out of either and you shoot, OK?' And then he vanished.

Cheesy swung round and smiled. He pointed his gun at Joe and then at me, as if he really didn't know which of us he'd be happier to shoot first. Here was something he was made for.

'That's what faith does for Calvin's palookas,' Joe had once told me. 'It gives them a crusading belief in their own perfection. It makes it OK to kill. It sanctifies stupidity. They answer to a higher order.'

'They're in God's hands?'

He shook his head and smiled at me. 'They *are* God's hands.'

Cheesy's revolver swung between us like a pendulum. Instinctively I jerked away from the ugly snout of his gun, but my left wrist was locked to Joe's and he moved with me. Otherwise he might have been dead, he sat so stiff and still. Joe, who had been able to dive down so deep you thought he was drowned, only to see him bob up again, had hit rock bottom.

Moonlight lay in a cold wash on the saucer-shaped swathe of grass and stone where the pylons marched. The vantage point had been carefully chosen: Le Moerr wanted us to have ringside seats, and we saw her make her appearance, rather as one might enter a stage, from the right-hand wings, with the rucksack on her back. She was heading for the pylon at the lowest point of the slope, where the shadows were deeper – but even there enough moonlight reached to show her plainly enough.

It was now that Joe came alive, he began whistling very softly and it seemed to rattle Cheesy, who swung his gun away from my face and pushed it into Joe's forehead.

'Shut it, Di Angelo!'

Joe kept up his tuneless whistle and ignored the gun: his eyes were on the figure kneeling beside one of the stanchions, slipping off and then unclasping her rucksack. I had been at enough run-throughs to know what came next. She would have prepared two charges; her gloves would give off the faintly sweet smell of nitroglycerine. In the moonlight the detonator cap would appear almost orange, and beneath it snaked the chemical long-delay fuse – she would be using mercury.

I began to raise my left hand, the hand cuffed tightly to Joe's; or maybe it levitated all of its own accord, I could not say, but up it went into the air, taking Joe's right hand with it and Cheesy wasn't happy and hissed at me to put it down, but once I started I could not stop. I had a question. I hadn't got it right in my head, but there was something I wanted to know and this seemed as good a time as any to ask. My hand stayed up and Joe's flat whistling went on. Cheesy swung the gun back at Joe. He was rattled, he was aching to shoot us and what confused him was that we were ready and willing.

'What the fuck's your case?'

The gun came back my way. I closed my eyes and felt the crusts of blood on my eyelashes. I'd forgotten the beating the cops had given me in the cell. Cheesy pressed the muzzle of his revolver against my forehead and my flesh shrank from the cold metal kiss. I was going to die.

Do it then!

Who moved first I never knew, but our raised arms came down on the gun like a club and a shot tore through the seat between us. Joe gripped Cheesy by the hair, and I heard from far away – his wheezy rattle and the thump of bone – as our two arms repeatedly slammed his head against the dashboard. I was doing it, but I was not really involved. I was watching the moonlit bowl where the pylons marched, where Constanza was on her feet, looking up at the sky, as if that was where the shot had come. She took off like a buck and someone shouted something. I heard two flat cracks, whiplash quick, and I could not see Constanza any more. There were men reaching into the car and they dragged us out, threw us down on the grass. We kept such a tight hold of Cheesy they had to prize our hands from his windpipe.

Then I heard Le Moerr, very quiet and calm. 'Take the cuffs off them.'

I heard one of the cops ask, 'Are you sure, sir?'

'Do as I say!' Le Moerr climbed into the car and started

the engine. 'Get Di Angelo and Croker back in the car – now!'

Someone unlocked the cuffed hands that had tried so hard to kill Cheesy.

We were pushed into the back seat and the door slammed, and I sat there rubbing my skinned wrists. Le Moerr put his foot down and we skidded away fast, bumping over the uneven ground in silence. Joe now and then sniffed, or wiped blood from his face. I kept seeing Constanza, suddenly on her feet, half-turning, and running. Then came the two flat cracks. A rifle. She would have been in the sights from the moment she stepped up to the pylon.

I assumed we were heading back to Pinnacle Point or to the police cells, where the warder so lamented my spilt blood. The car stopped and I saw the tall wall of the brewery building, the entrance arch to my old college across the road and Papa's Place, with its red banquettes and students playing the pinball machines, and I realized we were back at Bellevue Mansions.

Le Moerr reached across, threw open the passenger door and snapped back the passenger seat.

'End of the line.'

Joe spoke thickly through swollen lips, he sounded mad. 'What are you doing with us?'

'Get out of the car.'

I said, 'Are you leaving us here?'

'It's where you live, isn't it?'

I was still confused. 'Why are we here?'

Le Moerr sighed. 'I could charge you both as accessories – to sabotage. No problem. You would go to jail for – oh, I guess – say, seven to ten. And then what? You'd come out as brave guys who risked their lives. All that sort of baloney. Sentimental rubbish. That would be too good for you. You don't deserve it.'

I said, 'You shot her.'

'I've played this by the book, up until now. You were witnesses to something done correctly. In fact, I was neither here nor there. She would have understood. I hope you think about that in the time ahead of you. Now get out.'

Joe said, 'You can't do this.'

Le Moerr nodded. 'There will be questions, but I'll deal with them. We got the perpetrator, not so? And we'll have no more bombed pylons for a while. Case closed. Not that I think this is the end of the war. I try sometimes to tell my colleagues that, but they keep looking in the wrong direction. As you have shown, the danger isn't from disconsolate amateurs. I wouldn't waste cell space on you two. Goodbye.'

We climbed out and stood there. Le Moerr made a screeching U-turn, lifted a derisive thumb, and was gone. In the uneasy glow of the sodium streetlights I could see Joe's face was smeared with blood, and I could feel the freezing heat he seemed to give off, as he had done after the business in the alley beside Polly's Hotel. He was sinking down deep into himself, where he boiled in his own acids. A volcano smothered in ice.

'Why did you go for the cop, Joe?'

'Come again?'

'If you hadn't done that maybe she wouldn't be dead.'

'Why did you put up your hand? What did you want to say? That guy was ready to shoot you, Charlie. Sure as hell I'd say you owe me one.'

He took my breath away. 'Owe you? We're so useless we're not even worth arresting. We're washed up and you say I owe you. Constanza's dead.'

'But I'm not. Wait till next time.'

'There'll be no next time.'

'I'll find a cab. See you, Charlie.'

And he walked away. He was like a man who has hit a bad patch, but he would come through. As if all that we had seen had been a test, specially prepared for him, and he had the luck and the guile and the inner strength to survive it. This was his war. No one else came into it. This was what he spent his life training for.

Dawn was breaking in streaks of pink and gold over the rooftops when I took the lift up to the sixth floor and let myself into the flat. It was awfully empty. I sat by the window and stared at the clock on the brewery wall which showed just after five. I went into the bathroom. The window through which she climbed when she had vanished into the night was still open, the curtain billowing in the breeze. I closed the window, sat on the side of the bath and began to cry.

Part Four
Funeral Games

'And if I must take part, where is the Director? I have
something to say to him . . .'
Kierkegaard

Chapter 20

I had only the vaguest memory of St George's-in-the-Dell; perhaps I'd been in the church for a christening, or the wedding of some friend, back in the days when I lived in the capital. A noticeboard near the gate gave – in golden script, still bright, on a rich red background that had always reminded me of a Nestlé chocolate wrapper – the hours of Sunday services and Evensong, as well as the vicar's name, improbable and convincing all at once: the Reverend James Peebles, MA (Oxon).

The flowers in the churchyard had been watered and someone had repaired with duct tape the cracked baptismal font in the porch. St George's had faded. But then many places of worship – dating from the old days and dedicated to what seemed, to anyone under thirty, rather outlandish creeds – looked increasingly forlorn, overwhelmed by a new faith, a kind of cargo cult, preached by portly prophets in designer gear, who rode large limousines and promised the patient poor riches: running water, and jobs for all, just as soon as the flying boat came in.

Long lines of glistening ministerial conveyances waited in the street outside the church, chauffeurs dozing behind their sunglasses. An honour guard in party khakis, black berets and gloves stood ready. An immense hearse loaded with floral tributes – the largest, a yacht made of lilies, complete with anchor, sailing upon the roof of the car. Why the nautical note I did not know, though Joe had, of course, owned several racing sloops. As I watched, an orange Lamborghini was waved into an official parking spot in the line of ministerial limos. Out of the car stepped a tall woman wearing a mantilla over her thick, straw-coloured hair, chopped square above her shoulders. I knew her: she was Cameron di Angelo, Joe's last wife, looking even younger than she had done in the pictures I'd seen of their very glitzy wedding, and, later, of their separation. She had looked frightened then, and she looked nervous now as she slammed the door and hurried into the church. The fancy cars, the honour guard, the buzz and the glitter gave the occasion the feel of some incipient party or a military parade or even, strangely enough, of a society wedding.

In the church porch two girls in baseball caps, their blonde hair springing in thick ponytails from the little Velcro windows above the napes of their necks, were handing out T-shirts from cardboard boxes that had once held Benny's Bananas, *As Fresh as the Day is Long!* . . . The T-shirts, which were somewhat wrinkled, carried a photograph of Joe's face and the lines

Joe Angel
1956–2006
Son of the Soil, Pride of the Nation

Even now, in its heavier version with its rumpled jowls, I made out the hand-axe shape, the sharp chin, the bruised look about his dark eyes, under a fringe of black wiry hair.

But if the picture of his face brought him back to me, the lines below it were ridiculous. Joe had never been much of a 'son' and 'soil', in the sense of earth or dirt, was not something he knew about. Cement, concrete, aggregate . . . yes. As to 'pride', his pride had rested in triumphant survival; in being prepared to go down before his enemies, only to bob up again. Mephistopheles would have had a hard time with Joe – he began with his soul and worked back from there. You played the game till you were called and if you lost you made icily clear just how little you cared. 'I'll raise you a life – mine . . .' And he meant it. He'd get ready to lay it down like a poker chip. The whole thrill, the point, was dicing with death.

But he'd never been called. Until now. As for 'nation', that was a word he had hated. 'An excuse for killing someone,' he said to me once.

But then, of course, the lines on the shirts were intended to help to set the mood and encourage the right sort of thinking. Joe, it was clear, had become incidental to his funeral. It did not matter who he might have been. This was a party show. A day of solidarity. No matter how bleak the circumstances of his death, we were not there to dwell on them but to overcome them: we were there to celebrate, not to sigh.

The choice of an Anglican church for the funeral of a cradle Catholic who might otherwise have seemed pretty wild, if you knew where he came from, now took on a more calculated aspect. Our British connection had been a shotgun marriage between now extinct indigenes and a pale wavelet of invaders, who washed up on our shores, brandished their beliefs like battleaxes, prevailed briefly, and vanished. For reasons no one understood, there was something still about the Church of England which allowed it to escape the anger directed towards other faiths more closely identified with cruelty and repression, and which had been the hallmark of most regimes, especially the boorish, brutal and lethally boring gang so recently departed.

St George's had been chosen by someone who wished to draw a firm and final veil over any lingering Italian links:

forgetting for ever the cave where the Di Angelo family had huddled in Sicilian penury, gnawing their single stick of salami, and preferred to remember instead an Anglican called Angel: banker, patriot and political mainstay of the ruling party. It was a clever choice; an air of liberal Anglican gentility befitted the leave-taking of a man whom the arrangers wished to portray as a rebel, a freedom fighter, a resister.

Photographers darted and pointed: a couple of TV cameras from the state broadcaster were trained on the altar, the technicians standing by patiently. The role of the state broadcaster was to flatter the administration, and scenes from Joe's funeral would be turning up again and again, sandwiched between sporting triumphs and presidential visits to a sports complex or a pork-processing plant.

'Commemorative garment?' the girls with the boxes of T-shirts murmured to mourners entering the church. 'They're free.'

Ahead of me, a large guy in a silvery suit and salmon-pink tie was chatting to a short, bulky fellow with a scoop of red hair. They accepted T-shirts. The organ unfolded Bach's 'Air on G string', and everyone talked in slightly embarrassed whispers.

I declined the offer of a commemorative garment, and waited as the two guys ahead of me struggled into the T-shirts, pulled on their jackets and, with Joe's face framed between the lapels of their expensive suits like a man on a wanted poster, they walked into the cool gloom of St George's.

'He was a prince, was Joe Angel,' said the man in the silver suit.

With emphatic flicks of his coppery hair, like someone drying a paintbrush, his companion agreed. 'But when he fucked up, he fucked up big time.'

'Right. I don't give one fuck who says otherwise.'

'And I don't give six fucks who says otherwise.'

I chose a pew towards the back of the church, something I was glad of later. St George, a shining figure with abundant chestnut hair, mounted on a creamy stallion, his silver lance thrust deep into the dragon's scarlet throat, gleamed proudly in the stained-glass window above the altar. He was flanked by St Peter, carrying the keys to the Kingdom of Heaven, and the Venerable Bede, with quill and parchment.

The walls were hung with fraying regimental battle standards, adorned with coronets, escutcheons, fleurs-de-lis, unicorns, gryphons and marmosets. Brass plaques on the walls listed the regiments and ranks of troopers, hussars and fusiliers who had perished in faintly remembered conflicts. Here and there I saw ugly oblong patches, as if something had hung there once but had been roughly stripped away.

In the front pews, to the right of the aisle, sat four women, and because the woman nearest the aisle was Cameron di Angelo I guessed the pew held all of Joe's ex-wives. They made up his entire family. The front pews to the left of the aisle were taken by business bigwigs and political bosses, their spouses and bodyguards. At three on a hot summer's afternoon most would have been in parliament or cutting business deals or playing golf. The soft light from the stained-glass windows overhead speckled their heads and shoulders with flecks of blue and pink, like confetti. They eyed each other awkwardly, looking for cues to the proper deportment: what to say, where to put their hands, what to do with hymn books and prayer cushions. They had the look of men who knew they had little option but to grin and bear it, because this was evidently a carefully choreographed command performance.

Filling the body of the church, seated under identifying banners, were coveys of young kids from Joe's charities and good causes. There were the Angel AIDS orphans, in neat collars and ties; behind them were rows of students in blue blazers and grey shorts from the Angel Academy for Intellectual Excellence; next came performers from Angel Opera; ballerinas from Ballet Angel: and, in robes embroidered with intricate country scenes of villages and cows and goats, a pew containing seamstresses from the Angel Tapestry Project.

I looked again at the patches of wall where something had been stripped away, and it came back to me. These old traditional temples had dated badly and it was common to see razor-wire ringing deserted synagogues; or roofless Quaker meeting houses, their smashed windows plugged with newspaper; and shuttered cathedrals crumbling in the chilly shadow of enormous casinos. I remembered reading somewhere that churches like St George's-in-the-Dell were increasingly the targets of temple thieves, stripping off flags and memorials, the brass plaques and the regimental colours.

'First, make blood run in the streets and rout the enemy.'

That had been Joe's take on Calvin's method. He had been thinking of the despoliation of Catholic churches by zealous puritans.

'What Calvin did was to break utterly with the past,' Joe would say. 'It's wrong to call it a Reformation. It was bloody revolution. Blot out the blasphemies. Get back to basics.'

The copes and albs, heavy with gold thread, would turn up in street markets and be hawked from door to door, and sold as heavy tablecloths and good solid curtains. Not so much robbery as recycling.

The organ, with 'Jerusalem', brought us to our feet. Led by a man in a very good suit, the pall-bearers of the Party Youth League came slowly down the aisle, the casket on their shoulders. They set it before the altar steps, saluted, and solemnly draped it in the national flag. The man who had led the honour parade went up into the pulpit to faint applause, quickly muted when he waved for silence. He had a considerable nose and hair slicked down so tightly it showed every tooth-groove of his comb, and he introduced himself as the Secretary General of the New Democrats.

'We say farewell to Joe Angel, our brother in action and in ideology . . . a great egalitarian with no sense whatever of rank or station. I knew Joe as a leader of all seasons: brave, true, stalwart, dedicated. As General Secretary in the Presidency, and later, Secretary General in the Senate, I am honoured to count as my comrade a man who felt as I did about our country. Joe Angel was among the greatest of our native sons. A man with no time for elitists. Go well, old friend.'

That was how it went from then on. Speaker after speaker preached the Gospel of Joe Angel – of Comrade J., 'Our Native Son' and 'Our Dear Cadre'. He was the 'Driving Force Behind Party Structures' and 'Loyal Ally of the Lumpen Proletariat'. He was a paragon of patriotism, a national treasure; he had secretly run soup kitchens for the poor, and he baked a great cherry tart. The congregation, revved up on the good news of Joe's patriotism, energy, acumen and wealth interrupted the panegyrics with cries of 'Yeah man!' and bursts of clapping and stamping.

I noticed that money featured everywhere in the eulogies, and Joe's role in what seemed to have been a single-handed funding of the liberation of the country was condensed to a single slogan, clearly very familiar to the congregation, because when one speaker declared 'The revolution banked on Joe Angel,' the entire church responded with 'And Joe Angel banked the revolution!'

It was hard to come to terms with the man they praised. Until Joe showed up in McLeod I had more or less expunged from my mind the memories of that rather preposterous figure, the convenor of FIRE in the red bandanna and the creased khakis. What mattered, what was real, was that Constanza died where she had fallen. And so in a way had I. Only for me it had not been final. My life was over, but I kept on breathing, moving and remembering what he had once said to me.

'The crazies always win, if they're crazy enough. Just you wait.'

I hadn't waited to see whatever it was Joe wished to show me. Ever since that night, when we had been unceremoniously thrown out of his car by Le Moerr, I had no wish to see Joe again. I tried hard never to remember the furious figure stalking off into the dawn, made beautiful by the pastel pinks and gilded grey tones so characteristic of early morning light in the capital. The only really consistent emotion I felt about that time was rage.

Was this what he meant by winning?

I was angry, even now. I wanted to ask him how he got from the boy I knew at St Jude's, to builder-in-chief to the last regime, then to revolutionary hero, without ever having to explain or apologize. How on earth had he got away with it?

Yet there was also a strangely defensive tone to many of the speeches from the pulpit. I had the impression that his new comrades might have shared some of my confusion. As if, somewhere, there were suspicions of another Joe, more way-ward and rebellious, which his funeral was intended to dispel. Speaker after speaker praised the way Joe had allowed himself to be 'posted', ' directed', 'recalled' as the Party ordered. The idea was to position him correctly and to get right in all our heads exactly how we were to remember Joe, and to portray even his death as a further act of loyal service – contrary to 'unfounded' and 'sensationalist' media reports, to the 'lies' and 'slander' of liberal forces of reaction. Joe's demise was not a setback for the forces of freedom and democracy. If anything it was to be seen as another patriotic victory. In fact, someone who did not know that the man in the coffin had been shot eight times on a dark night by unknown assassins might have assumed that he had not died at all, but had merely been deployed by the Party in some new and useful direction.

What were these lies and rumours? I had read the papers and while it was true there had been questions about Joe's last hours, the press had for the most part been unrestrained in its adulation. There had been no hostile reports but rather almost universal sadness and shock.

A woman with orange hair was in the pulpit now. Describing herself as 'a sister in solidarity with the deceased', she racked up the tension and delighted the congregation with a slashing attack on 'the jackals of the press'.

'I say to those who deal in lies and rumours and slanders – I say shame on you! I say to all our friends in the media – take care!' Jabbing a finger at the roof of the church, which was painted a deep indigo to resemble the heavens and freckled with small golden stars, she spoke through her furious tears. 'On the grave of our departed comrade, I swear that if you fail to keep your house in order, the administration may be forced to do so for you. Long live Comrade Angel!'

She brought the crowd to its feet, punching the air and giving the party salute, a rather curious lateral movement of the left elbow, followed by an upward jerk of the right knee: a ritual which was reckoned to mimic how our new rulers had elbowed the old guard from power, and booted them out for ever.

The organ started up windily. We rose for the national anthem and sang loudly, glad of the song sheets because hardly anyone knew the words. The service was over, the relief was palpable, and I headed for the door.

That was when I saw her. She wore her long fair hair in

a chignon and I could make out what looked like a silver necklace threading through tendrils of hair on her neck. It was Bethany. I'd not seen her in over thirty years, but it could be no one else. A small waist and strong thighs, a dancer's body, and a lean profile. But she was well ahead of me and when I got out of the church she was nowhere to be seen.

I felt a slight stab of regret. Gone now, and perhaps for ever. But then, what would she have had to say to me? Too many years had passed since the rainy night when she climbed the fire escape to Constanza's flat and warned us to get out. She had fled, we had stayed, and everything had changed.

People were hurrying for their cars and I could feel their relief. They had been present at the show, they had acquiesced in the canonization of Joe Angel, son of the soil, banker to the revolution, but it was over now and they wished to leave it at that.

For some reason, I could not leave it at that. I stood watching the mourners coming out of the church and milling around the steps, the bigwigs and the tycoons talking shop, the girls in baseball caps packing away the spare Joe Angel T-shirts, and the AIDS orphans getting into their bus.

I saw the ex-wives now, spilling out into the sunshine: they hugged and consoled each other and it was a rare human show of grief that afternoon. For most of those in the church this had been a cross between a party rally and a display of solidarity, a highly political show funeral.

I reckoned tall, blonde Cameron di Angelo had been married to Joe for no more than about six months. She had been the last person to see him alive. For some reason he had gone to see her after the opera, and Cameron had prepared the meal that the newspapers had analysed in such detail. I remembered reports that the divorce settlement had been enormous. Her car was the orange Lamborghini that brightened the line of official ministerial limos at the kerb.

She glanced up at the sky where flossy clouds moved in tumbling mountains across the blue, as if she might find an answer there, then shook her head as none was to be found in that quarter, and headed for her car. She had the engine going when I tapped on her window and she looked up, as if seeing me there was no surprise at all. Her window sighed as it sank into the door.

'Charlie Winston Croker!'

I didn't know what to make of her smile, full of recognition, even relief.

'I don't think we've met.'

'No, we haven't.' She reached over for her handbag and took out a photograph. 'Look.' Her eyes were green and amused. 'My husband gave this to me. Or should I say my former husband?'

It was a shot of me, walking out of the school in McLeod. The stencilled figure of the gunman was clearly visible on the gatepost.

'When did he give this to you?'

'The last time I saw him.'

'The night he was hijacked?'

She said very quietly and firmly, 'Joe wasn't hijacked. He was shot, very deliberately. No more than twenty minutes after giving me your photograph. You're confused? Well, so am I, Mr Croker.' She nodded solemnly at my perplexity. 'Am I saying you had a hand in shooting him? No. But are you involved? You bet. Which is your real name? Charlie or Winston?'

'Both, actually.'

'When Joe turned up that night, he said I could expect to see you. He left you a message.' She took a pencil and notebook from her bag and wrote down an address on the back of my photograph. 'We need to talk, Charlie Winston Croker. But somewhere more private than this place. Over there, on the church steps, a man has been watching you ever since you stopped to talk to me.'

When I turned, he seemed quite unconcerned as to whether we saw him or not. His hair, though speckled with white, was still a mass of springy curls, and the wedge of silver-grey over his forehead was as distinctive as ever. He would have been watching in church, contemplating with his surgeon's eyes Bethany's slender neck, her collarbones clear under her dress. Estimating where the knife should go in. Without taking his eyes off us, he pulled from his shirt pocket a box of cigarettes, and I had no doubt they were his old brand, Mentholyptus Kings, lit one and flicked away the match.

'Do you know him?'

'I'm afraid I do.'

She turned the key in the ignition. 'I've shocked you, haven't I? Well, join the club. These last few days have surprised all the surprise out of me.'

I put the photograph in my pocket and watched her accelerate into the traffic. When I turned again, Le Moerr was nowhere to be seen.

CHAPTER 21

The funeral was no sooner over than the tide of opinion began to turn. There was no shortage of coverage, and it remained as wild and angry, but the consensus collapsed. When news of his assassination had first broken, the mood had been one of shock and grief, but now people were not sure what to feel any longer. Indeed, no one talked of death at all. Instead, people chose sides, and stuck to them. Those who had spoken for Joe in St George's must have known that it was not going to be easy to hold the line. To echo what the man in the silver suit had told his carrot-haired companion, prince of men though he may have been, it seemed Joe Angel had indeed seriously fucked up.

His friends and supporters still talked of 'the unfortunate incident' or the 'blow to the construction industry'. But to his critics, and they multiplied by the day, he was no longer the near-godlike figure of a week before, tragically struck down near the golf course. Instead he became, once again, Giuseppe Roberto di Angelo, and his murder was blamed on the Sicilian Camorra, on Nigerian drug lords, and the Chinese triads.

Every facet of his legacy was under assault. It was alleged his business empire was a gigantic fraud. In his share dealings he had swapped bad paper for good paper, skimmed profits, talked up the value of his stocks, sold mines and mineral rights at vastly inflated prices. His art collection was full of fakes, his charitable work was a con trick; and some went so far as to assert he could not even play the flute. Joe's reputation had not just fallen, it had gone over a cliff.

His supporters didn't take this lying down. They hit back using state-controlled media. The rumours about Joe's finances were rejected with 'scorn and contempt'. State television repeated daily an official statement of support that we soon knew by heart: 'To all structures, formations, cadres and stakeholders; let us salute the memory of comrade Dr Joe Angel by pledging ourselves anew to the success of the national democratic revolution.' Budding tycoons took ads in the papers testifying to Joe's generosity, his ebullient embrace of the new political dispensation and his many soft loans and outright gifts to first-time entrepreneurs finding their feet in the cruel world. Fund managers, orchestra conductors and educationalists came forward to confirm that Joe had been a financial colossus; a great musician, a tremendous philanthropist. Economists warned of a conspiracy by 'a hidden hand', 'a third force' and a 'fifth column' intent on derailing 'the democratic revolution'. The Finance Ministry foresaw falling investment and speculative runs on the currency. The press was told again and again 'to put its house in order', several journalists were detained, and the ruling party tabled legislation making it an offence to release information likely to harm the country.

The hole Joe's death had torn in the body politic became a contested space, a battleground into which competing forces projected their prejudices; a pantomime where the villain is unmasked and his misdeeds are revealed to the happy jeers of half the audience, who cry out on cue 'Oh yes he did!' only to be corrected by the other half, who love this endearing rogue, with 'Oh no he didn't!' As if to make up for an embarrassing early reverence felt now to have been mistaken, the press and television laid into Joe, who was skewered in mocking head-lines: BILLIONAIRE'S DODGY DEALS and GIUSEPPE'S TAKEAWAY. Canonization, once so apparently certain, was put on hold. The love affair had turned into a lynching party. The national schizophrenia was neatly summed up in a headline in one of the more strident tabloids: SON OF THE SOIL . . . OR S.O.B?

The drinkers in the bar at my hotel stayed loyal, probably because it was a team thing: they had stood by Joe when he was struck down and they cheered for him now that he was under attack. They played his murder the way they played the sporting fixtures eternally unfolding on the big TV between the vodka bottles.

I took no side. I felt lost and abandoned, and trapped. At night I lay in the bed under the hideous purple cover. I could smell the dusty carpet and the furniture polish on the sagging easy chair and boxwood bedside tables. I had, increasingly, the feeling that somehow I had been set up. I was playing a role in a piece of theatre that someone else was directing. Even Joe's death seemed somehow to have been orchestrated. I told myself that this was absurd, that no one could have organized and carried off the series of astonishments which I had felt since my plane touched down. Yet I had the photographs: of Joe and me when we were at school; of the later version of myself, the remedial teacher, coming out of McLeod High, which Cameron di Angelo had given me. Someone had fol-lowed me, known all about me, and had probably supplied Joe with the photo and my address and my movements. Then Le Moerr had shown up at the funeral.

If I was somehow implicate in all of this, then perhaps it was time to resign and withdraw. I didn't want to know what message Joe had left me. I didn't care why Le Moerr was around once again. I had done what I could for Joe and a fat lot of help I had been. Why shouldn't I simply turn back, leave the capital, head home to McLeod?

The next morning I packed what was left of the cash in the false drawer in the cupboard, threw my clothes into my bag, conscious as I did so of the intense and mocking theatricality of my actions, and I went downstairs with a firm tread, planning to tell Gregoire I was leaving. I found him behind his desk, holding a flat square package, waiting to hand it to me with a smile, right on cue.

'For you. In the post. Me, I get only bills, summonses, traffic fines. Or someone write to say he kill a girl. Nothing neat, like this.' He ran an admiring finger around the crisp edges of the square parcel.

It was infuriating, this sense of being overseen, tempted and taunted by someone determined to destabilize my sense of myself every time I made up my mind to do something. As if I had no self worth speaking of, no mind worth making up and no more freedom of movement than a snooker ball, to be sent careering around the table, or sunk, at the whim of whoever was in charge of the game.

'This did not come in the post, Gregoire. There are no stamps. Did you see who brought this?'

But of course it was pointless asking him. He shook his head and handed me the parcel.

'Charlie Croker,' Gregoire traced the letters with his finger. 'Your name is very clearly writ.'

'Yes. One whose name is writ on water.'

'Oh yes?'

'That is what the poet Keats, dead at twenty-five, wanted on his tombstone.'

'Mugged?'

'TB.'

'We get a lot of that. Aren't you going to open it?' Gregoire handed me a pair of scissors. 'Try these.'

I sliced away the brown paper and found, tucked inside a sleeve of bubble wrap, an unlabelled DVD.

'All that wrapping for just a movie.' Gregoire was disappointed.

'Do you have a DVD player?'

'Of course. In the bar. He is a battery job. I keep him for power cuts when we have no TV. I show movies then.'

The usual mix of sales reps, drifters, desultory girls and muscled guys with earrings sat around the horseshoe bar. Up on the TV screen a team of tag wrestlers smacked and thudded together, their palms striking flesh as they dug into each other with excited grunts. Gregoire introduced me to a brunette in lime-green slacks, sipping tea. It was Krystell, the recipient of the death-threats he had told me about. Her pimp was wearing a Superman T-shirt, and sat hunched over a bag of crisps and a lager.

Gregoire pulled out the DVD player from under the bar and plugged the leads into the TV. A wrestler, catapulting himself off the ropes, landed heels first on the chest of a man lying on the canvas, and the screen faded to fuzz. There were groans from the drinkers as the silence surged.

Gregoire waved his hand apologetically. 'Short movie coming up. Thanks for patience. Normal service soon resume.'

He needn't have worried. From the first frame, the bar liked what it saw. A crowd of angry men and women was shoving and shouting and throwing things. The camera pulled back to show a crowd milling about in front of a large building, with smoke spouting from the second floor. It was clearly a school because the camera peered through a broken window, picking out charred desks, and blackboards were cracked and splintered, as if someone had taken an axe to them.

The crowd now appeared to be torching the school library, and the bar enjoyed the spectacle. Someone cried 'Hey, look at that baby burn!' As they fell, the burning books flapped their pages like dying birds, and when they hit the ground papery embers danced on the updrafts. Through the smoke, inscribed in spiky silver letters high on the sleek façade: *Angel Academy for Intellectual Excellence.*

And suddenly there he was, face florid, hair wild, coming out of the front door of the burning school, holding a handkerchief to his mouth. He lifted his hand to call for attention. 'Comrades, colleagues . . . !' The smoke was making him cough.

But the crowd shook their fists and shouted him down. Placards were hoisted and waved: TO HELL WITH ANGEL and GO TO HELL, UNHOLY JOE.

'Please, a little patience . . . a few more days.'

The whistles and jeers were wild now: 'No! No! No!'

'Give me a little time.'

'Give us our money!'

The bar was in no doubt about what they were looking at. A voice said, 'Hey, that's the fancy college of the guy who got drilled in the Beamer.'

Krystell's pimp turned to her. 'The billionaire hijacked by the golf course?'

'Hit eight times, but kept moving,' said Krystell. 'Quite a guy. Why are they burning down his school?'

The building aflame behind him, we saw Joe throw away the handkerchief, and he began shouting through cupped hands at the milling demonstrators. 'I trained you. Gave you jobs. Where's your conscience? Where's your fucking loyalty?'

The answer came, loud and clear, from somewhere in the crowd: 'You want loyalty? Buy a dog!'

The camera moved in close on Joe's face, his eyes swollen, with anger or grief, I didn't know, the vein in his left temple beating like a tom-tom, his mouth working, but no sound, no words.

Then the screen flickered into cold grey, and that was it.

Gregoire said: 'Who is the poor bastard?'

'That was Joe Angel.'

'Just shows,' said Krystell's pimp. 'You give your all – and what d'you get? You get your arse kicked from here to next week.'

Krystell said, 'When I think of that beautiful school I want to weep. Those people there, they got everything that opens and shuts, and what they do? They trash it!'

'Teachers, that's for sure,' said a salesman, nursing a brandy and Coke. 'Either drunk, AWOL, on leave or on strike.'

'Or sleeping with their students,' said Krystell.

Gregoire said, 'You want I run it again?'

Joe had looked utterly alone. I remembered the words of the cop on the phone at the airport. *You don't go in without back-up. You never know what the fuck hits you, do you?*

'I've seen enough.'

Gregoire switched on the TV once again. A cricket match was underway: a man ran up to bowl, the ball hit the batsman just below his helmet, and he fell down; the camera homed in and feasted on the blood streaking the batsman's chin. The guys around the bar perked up; this was reasonable stuff: blood, balls and concussion. But what they'd seen of Joe, a man pilloried, a man pleading, that was hard. The call went up for fresh drinks all round. Normal service had been resumed.

CHAPTER 22

I was having breakfast the next morning when Gregoire appeared in the doorway and crooked a finger.

'Lady downstairs who is in need, she says, of yourself.'

Bethany was sitting on the little plastic sofa, opposite the reception desk, with its tatty red-leather trimmings, its 'No Firearms' notice, and the kilted piper on the mirror, touting Black Watch Scotch. She jumped up and hugged me hard. When she put her arms around me she smelt of jasmine.

'Dear, dear Charlie! You do still know me, don't you?'

I was cornered: no matter which way I turned a ghost of the past was waiting. Gregoire took up a position behind the desk where he could lean comfortably on his elbows and pretend to be leafing through the hotel register.

'How did you find me, Bethany?'

She laughed gently. Her tawny hair was tinged here and there with grey, but her eyes were as blue and as wide as ever.

'That's a fine way to say hello. I'll come to that. Are you surprised to see me? You knew I was here?'

'I spotted you in church, at Joe's funeral, and I missed you. When I got outside you were gone.'

'I fled. I couldn't bear it. That sad church, all those angry people wearing Joe's face on their chests. It was like a party pep talk or a revivalist meeting.' She took my hand and pulled me down beside her on the sofa. 'It's been ages, Charlie. I've lived in Geneva ever since.'

'Ever since?'

'You know what I mean. That's where I went when I left, and there I stayed. Some people join the Foreign Legion, their old lives are cancelled, and they start again. I fetched up in Geneva, stayed, and made a whole new me. I've never been back.'

'Married, and all that?'

She nodded. 'Absolutely. To a Swiss, of course. I wasn't doing things by halves. After about ten years of a new life, I said to my husband, "I think I'm an honorary Swiss now," and he said, "*All* Swiss are honorary Swiss." Thomas and I run a gallery. We specialize in what you might call second-eleven Impressionists. It's a good business. Our gallery is in the old town, off the rue de la Fontaine.'

'Not far from the English gardens, close to St Peter's Cathedral?'

'Then you know Geneva!'

I shook my head. 'Joe had maps and pictures of the old city. He'd walk me through the streets, just as he did with Chicago, in the days of Capone.'

Joe had even found, somewhere, a shaky little tourist movie of St Peter's Cathedral. He pointed out the chair where Calvin sat, the pulpit from where he preached. I remembered Joe's satisfaction with the aggressively plain walls, the angry absence of ornament, the shrivelling disapproval of spiritual fripperies. It had been the sparseness Joe liked; it spoke to him of utter clarity. It was 'all of a piece' (high praise). As opposed to 'all over the place' (bad). Single-mindedness of the sort given only to saints and terrorists: the consolations of the chosen ones.

'Surely you didn't hear about Joe in Switzerland?' I asked.

'Even in Switzerland the papers carried stories about Joe.

When I read about the shooting, I got on the first plane.' She blinked. 'I just had to come back. Tell me about you – where are you living now, Charlie?'

'Tucked myself away in a place so small I hoped no one had heard of it. I'm in a school there.'

Bethany smiled. 'A teacher?'

'Not really. I give lessons.'

'Are you married? Family?'

'Somehow, I never got round to it.'

'Is there someone else?'

'In a way.'

'What does that mean?'

'She runs the English department in the little school where I give lessons. If you're asking if we sleep together – yes, now and then. She deserves better.'

'Better than?'

'Than a living fossil. She once called me a man of some extinction. She gets her English a bit mixed, but she was right. I'm a relic, lost in time.'

'Then why are you here, now?'

'Joe asked me.'

She raised her eyebrows. 'What? To his funeral?'

'In a way. A few nights back he turned up on my doorstep and practically begged me to come to town. I came, only to find he was gone, and now I don't seem to be able to leave.'

She nodded. 'I was supposed to fly back straight after his funeral, but there is something I need to get off my chest first. If I can find the words. Something very hard to say. Is it true that you owed Joe? Because of what happened that night Constanza died?'

I was astonished. 'Who told you that?'

'Joe did.'

'But I thought you'd never been back.'

She nodded. 'It was a couple of years after – that night. He turned up at my gallery one day and we had coffee. Of course, I knew Constanza had died, but I never knew the background. Joe told me she had walked into a trap and the police shot her. They would have shot you too, but he got in the way and saved your life. Is that true?'

'No. It's what Joe believed. What was he doing in Geneva?'

She looked at me steadily before she answered. 'He said he was getting to know the city where John Calvin lived and worked.'

'And what did you think?'

'Geneva is a small place, and the word around town was rather different. They said he was shifting cash to secret accounts for government people back home.'

I thought I must have misheard her. 'But at that time the old lot were still running things.'

'Think about it, Charlie. They were finished and they knew it. It was time to consider retirement and pensions.'

'You're saying he turned bagman for the guys we tried to bomb?'

Bethany was remorseless. 'The best way I have of explaining it to myself is to think that he was playing some sort of deep game. Joe always used to say that being one thing does not rule out being something else. He always had a thing about what he called "good cover". You're shocked, aren't you?'

'Yes, though I don't know why. The only consistent thing about my connection to Joe has been my utter misunderstanding of everything to do with him. One of the newspapers put it well: son of the soil – or son of a bitch?'

'Is there a version you prefer?'

'Neither. Or maybe both.'

'Why does it matter so much to you still?'

'Because not knowing what he was up to means I never got myself right, either.'

'Were you and he that close?'

'Too close for comfort. But then, so were you – did you ever work him out?'

She turned her blazing blue gaze on me. 'Joe was my first boyfriend, my first sexual partner. What we had was flesh. The gangster movies and then the Calvin obsession, those were things – over there, away from the daily stuff. I thought it was interesting but not vital – like showjumping or sky diving. I didn't care about his beliefs, I was after his body.'

'And later?'

'Later?'

'When he got you to join the Committee.'

'We weren't lovers any more. Joe saw his role as some sort of high priest, I think. That's why we changed our names. It was almost a baptism. New names, new life.'

'It was a disaster, wasn't it?'

She nodded. 'We didn't do well, I know that.'

'We were totally fucking useless. We set out to fight the enemy and we ended up in jail or dead or, in your case, decamped. The Forum of Independence, Resistance and Equity died of embarrassment. It was a balls-up.'

She thought about this. 'Maybe everything Joe did was a balls-up. But I'll say this – nothing ever happened to Joe that he didn't make something happen back.'

'What he did left Constanza dead.'

'I've always wished you had come with me that night.'

'I couldn't leave her behind.'

'Why not? She'd left you behind.' Bethany put her hand out and rested it on the back of mine. 'I'm sorry to be so fierce. What did happen that night, exactly ? Or does it hurt too much to say?'

'It hurts whether I talk about it or not. Like you, I have trouble finding the words.'

'Are you really extinct, Charlie?'

'Halfway, perhaps. Not properly. I thought I was, but I was bluffing myself. I realized that when Joe pitched up. Deep retreat is the best I've managed. Then my dreams find me out and I wake up.'

She took away her hand and uncovered the half-moon scar. It was small and insignificant and had healed long ago. But there it was, along with the questions I had asked myself, still without answers. How and why were such things done? Joe had said because it was what people did. Was it possible, then, to kill, easily and often? Of course. Just as it was possible for Calvin to find that some were saved and some were damned and – here was the real kicker – either way we had only ourselves to blame. As one of Joe's favourite passages from Calvin's *Institutes* – the *decretum horribile* – put it: 'God ordains eternal salvation for some and hell for others.' Son of the soil or son of a bitch? Bagman for the old bastards, and banker to the revolution.

From behind the desk, where he sat pretending to be examining the register, Gregoire spoke now. 'Tell her about the DVD.'

I said, 'Do you mind? This is a private talk. Please leave us alone.'

'OK, I go.' Gregoire closed the register and smiled at Bethany. 'Ask him about the parcel.'

Bethany looked as if she wanted to know more, but Gregoire, to my relief, walked off with a backward wink at me.

'What kind of place is this, Charlie?'

'It's a home from home.'

She laughed gently. 'Tell me about the parcel.'

'One of Joe's pet projects was his school: the Academy of Excellence. Rigorous selection of kids from very poor families, maximum discipline, best teachers money can buy. Well, a DVD turned up here on Gregoire's desk. Addressed to me. It showed those teachers at the Academy torching the school library. They were furious because he couldn't pay them. I saw Joe begging for patience and understanding and being told, "If you want loyalty, buy a dog."'

'Someone wanted you to see Joe suffer?'

'On Joe's scale of things teachers' salaries would have been piffling. Yet he couldn't find the money to pay them. The man I knew would have said, "If you want loyalty, buy a big weapon." Friendship follows firepower. Terror wins every time. Joe didn't just talk tough. He really lived it. Whoever sent me the DVD wanted to drive home how far short he'd fallen. Someone has been taking a close interest in how I perceive things.'

'Same goes for me.'

She pulled a white envelope from her suede bag. She wore no rings, and when she gave me the envelope I noticed that her fingernails were bitten.

'This was waiting for me at my hotel this morning.'

The envelope was addressed to *Ms Bethany Greene* in the clear looping hand I knew all too well. Inside was a photograph showing the members of the Forum at Dino's restaurant, those many years ago. Joe sat forward, glass in hand; the straw-covered bottle of Chianti got in the way of Bethany who had her chin resting on her hand. Constanza leaned back, dreamy, half-turned to me, the candlelight on her face. I was smiling at something she had just said. I turned over the photograph and there on the back was my name and the address of the Summerland Hotel.

Bethany was looking at me with intense concentration. 'That's how I knew where to find you. I came straight over. So you can tell me I'm not dreaming.'

I remembered the night we had waited for Constanza to dress in the bathroom, Bethany had ripped the picture from its frame and struck a match.

'There will be no more of us,' had been the way she put it.

'You think it's the "famous" photo.'

'It can't be, Charlie. There was only one copy.'

'Of course, and you burnt it.' I handed the picture back to her. 'It's not the same.'

She shook her head. 'It is! We're all there.'

'That's my point. *All* of us. But I wasn't in the original, because I was behind the camera. Someone else took this photo that night. Someone we didn't see.'

'It's Joe's writing on the envelope. I knew it at once.'

She put the photo back in the envelope only to pull it out again, as if by staring at it long enough, she'd find out what it was supposed to be telling her. She did remember, and she was frightened, just as someone had intended she should be. But it wasn't just fear; there was also a kind of awkwardness about her, she looked almost embarrassed, and that bothered me.

She began to cry then. 'Charlie, do you think Joe really is dead?'

'Yes, I do.'

She turned on me her unwavering gaze. 'It doesn't seem to have got through to him, does it?'

She was right. That Joe was dead was neither here nor there. Or rather, he was both here and there. Joe was unkillable. Kick him, punch him, fill him full of darts, rape him – shoot him with eight bullets, and what did he do? He kept right on coming.

If what he had been was open to interpretation, so was the way he died. If Cameron di Angelo was right, then it had not been a hijack that went wrong, just another unfortunate

197

murder. It had been premeditated. But why would anyone wish to kill Joe?

'I met his wife, his ex-wife, Cameron, at the funeral,' I said. 'She thinks he was deliberately targeted. She says she can prove it. The question is why?'

Bethany gave that half-smile again, not mocking but rueful. 'I'm not sure that's the fundamental question. If you listened to his fans at his funeral, Joe was a saint. Now others are calling him a villain.'

'To the people at the funeral he was a super hero. Read the papers today and he's some kind of super crook. The adulation in church was weird enough – too over the top. But this wish to crucify him, that's just as odd. Why this strange moral fervour? Joe was very rich and the way he got rich is absolutely unexceptional. Did he talk up his share prices, swap bad paper for good paper, skim profits? Well, who doesn't? Did he flip sham deals into share deals, strip, loot and finagle? Did he gamble with other people's money – well, isn't that what other people's money is for? He dealt in shares and mineral rights, gemstones, precious metals – chicanery is the default position, and those he dealt with wouldn't have recognized a moral scruple if one was abandoned on their doorstep with a note pleading for it to be given a good home.'

'Yes, Charlie, but something else happened, something so big it buried him.'

'When are you planning to go home to Geneva?'

'I told you – there is something I have to get off my chest first.'

'Is it a confession? Because if it is, maybe we can fix that. I'm going to take a ride. Would you like to come?'

CHAPTER 23

The drive across town took no more than half an hour, but it carried us back decades. Bethany sat very still and at one point she closed her eyes. Her eyebrows were stark against her pale skin and ran very straight from the bridge of her nose, then flexed sharply like miniature flails.

'Where are we headed?'

'The scene of the crime.'

'The place where Joe was shot?'

'Further back than that. Back to where Joe died and was reborn.'

'That sounds more like a religious experience than a crime scene.'

'It was a bit of both.'

We were in the city centre now, with its squares and statues, its bunker-like buildings of green-brown sandstone, a dappled and depressing shade akin to military camouflage.

Bethany opened her eyes and shook her head. 'God, it's weird. What's changed?'

'Nothing!'

Without turning around she said, 'Do you know someone is following us?'

'I do. Red car. Opel, maybe? About half a block behind? He wants to see where we're heading. But it won't tell him much.'

'Who is he, do you know?'

'I have a pretty good idea, and I think I know a way of checking on it. But he can wait.'

As we got closer to Central Square she said, 'It still looks like the dead centre of town.' Her voice was low and amused, but slightly shaky.

The old joke had made us laugh as kids.

The buildings beyond the square had altered somewhat. Once they were cinemas and department stores, but these had given way to office blocks and parking garages, as squat and as ugly as the buildings they had replaced.

When I had been growing up in the capital, I had thought of those who ruled as dinosaurs or dragons, implacable in their overwhelming being, and to venture into the city centre was to see close up the armoured power of those who ran our world – and it was a frighteningly impressive vision. No matter that the regime showed very little brain in its cranial spaces – it was the yards of bone which impressed me.

We parked across the road from the Central Square. As we stepped on to the concrete path that led to the tall statues, she took my hand, almost as a child would do. This tall, elegant woman, who seemed so much in control of herself, was now the kid she had been when the centre of town represented to us a forbidden zone we rarely visited.

I walked Bethany over the grass to the spot where Joe and I had been sitting.

'We'd marched in the Corpus Christi procession that morning. Togged out in full regalia, following priests and bishops displaying the body of the Lord. Joe was swinging a thurible, and I was his boat boy, carrying the incense, and as usual the people watching were giving us a hard time. Swearing, laughing, all the usual stuff. Suddenly, Joe gave the finger to the bastards who think it's amusing to spit on people of another faith. Pretty good, I thought.'

Bethany gave a blazing smile. 'That was brave.'

'We didn't really give it another thought. The march ended and we were exactly on this spot, eating our sandwiches, still wearing our cassocks and surplices. Next thing we knew, these guys came running across the grass, grabbed us and ran off.'

'And no one said anything?'

'It looked like kids messing around.'

'Where did they take you?'

'We'll go there.'

I found the street fairly easily, but it had been very much developed, a line of office blocks and a new Polly's Hotel, all glass and steel and a long way from the old colonial building it had replaced. This had been Joe's work: a monument to a time when he had been martyred, erecting in concrete the power and money of a cabal he was working to undermine. Good cover? Pragmatism?

Only the narrow alley running alongside the hotel was as it had been. I walked Bethany past rubbish bins stuffed with cardboard and paper, all now so utterly without menace. I told her about the elegant woman in white gloves in the advertisement, huge on the back wall, with her gin and tonic and her cigarette holder – *in a class by itself, in a glass by itself.*

'They dragged us in here, beyond where the dustbins are. If you wanted to do something bad, this dead-end alley was perfect. No one about and it was Sunday, remember, and the town was double-dead. Two guys held me – the others took Joe.

'They asked him if he thought he was funny, giving them the finger. They asked him if he was a girl because he was wearing a dress. They asked him why he had such a big nose.

Was he Jewish? I knew we going to be beaten up. They pushed him against the wall over there and one of them raped him.'

She shook her head, but said nothing.

'Then they ran.'

'They just – went?'

'We're talking thick as pigshit and proud of it. We're talking guys who believed that neuron activity was best left to females, fags, foreigners. They took off and didn't look back.'

'What did you do?'

'Walked back to the square. Took the bus back to St Jude's.'

'You never told anyone?'

'Joe asked me to say nothing. It was at that moment he changed. Until then, it was Calvin over Capone, because Calvin ran a universe. After that Corpus Christi Sunday he went off in a new direction. Joe found out these guys lived in Zwingli Hall, just up the road from St Jude's, and he blew the place up.'

'It was the least he could do.'

I was amazed at how calmly she spoke.

'As it turned out, he missed. The student hall had closed for the holidays. It was empty. But he might have killed dozens of people. I asked him about that and he was only sorry that it didn't work.'

'And if he'd killed them, how would he have felt?'

'Pleased. No doubt about it. He was ready to do whatever it took. And if it meant killing, then God wanted it that way.'

She shivered. 'It's hard to think of him as a murderer.'

'Then think of him as being on the road to salvation. When we were at St Jude's we used to read *Lives of the Saints*. It often took something appallingly bad to push the apprentice saint over the edge into serious sanctity. From then on he could do what he liked. At the same time as he recruited us to the Forum and Constanza was learning how to blow up pylons,

Joe was actually rebuilding Zwingli Hall. He was reconstructing the future – for them. How do you figure that out?'

She shook her head. 'I'm not sure. But if he was saved and chosen, then, as you said, he could do anything.'

She was right. It was what Joe had told the Rector when he baulked at the thought that he might turn out as badly as those he hated. Joe was going for 'the whole caboodle', and if selling himself to the enemy got him some advantage, then that was what he would do. This the angels had explained to him: and once he'd got the message he was ready to shoot the messengers.

When we got back to our car, the Opel was parked across the street and the driver held a newspaper to his face.

'Will you tell me who he is, Charlie?'

'I'd say that he is almost certainly the man who shot Constanza.'

She stopped dead. 'My God, and now he's following us.'

'He was at Joe's funeral, too. Watching me.'

'But why?'

'I think he needs to know what we're up to. You said to me some time back that you wanted to own up to something. Me too. Why not a full confession? Shall we go and do that now?'

I don't think either of us was prepared for what we found when we drove into what had been the old Catholic quarter. Bethany gave a running commentary: 'St Jude's is now called the Orange Haven. Holy Cross College is Calvinia. The nunnery is the Swedenborg Sports complex. Weird, weird, weird!' It was like going into some long-deserted buried city, hidden under mounds of desert sand. The small, slow acquisitions of land over the years had ended in a full-scale takeover. It was like putting on a pair of special bifocals that let you see the world as it had been, and the world as it now was.

I parked outside Orange Haven, the two storeys of unremarkable yellow face-brick utterly and achingly the same as they had been when I lived there. There was an AIDS counselling unit on the ground floor where the prep room had been, and a pizzeria in the library. The chapel where Joe and I had served at Mass had rather cleverly been converted into a squash court. It was possible to trace with my hand the indentations left by the altar and tabernacle, just below the red service line of the back wall. The dormitory, from whose window I had been dropped into the rose bed, was a recreation room, with table football and computer screens.

We skirted what had been the parish gardens, a mass of cypresses and firs and rough grass. The parish hall had become a cafeteria where notices warned diners to produce their student cards or they would be refused service. Beyond the hall, the Church of the Holy Redeemer, its freshly whitened spire shining in the afternoon sun, stood exactly as I had left it, the clock stopped at three minutes after six. We walked into the church porch and for old times' sake I dipped my hand in the dry stoop, which once carried holy water, and crossed myself. While it was just possible to ignore the Roman Catholic trappings of the buildings that had once made up school and convent, the Church of the Redeemer allowed no such blindness. We walked down the central aisle, watched from stained-glass windows of emerald green and royal blue by evangelists, saints, angels and popes. Lining the side walls were tablets of carved marble depicting the twelve Stations of the Cross, from the arrest of Jesus in the Garden of Gethsemane, to the trial before Pontius Pilate, and the Crucifixion between the two thieves on the hill of Calvary. Gory – and gaudy – portraits of blood and pain: the scourging shown in livid stripes, the spiny crown of thorns raising drops of blood, fat as rubies across the forehead of the condemned man.

'It's nothing but a painted barn.'

I put my arm around her – it was a spontaneous thing. Two lapsed Catholics – the only ones able to read the codes in the windows, the statues, the paintings. Alone in our useless, saddening knowledge.

'What do you think they use it for?'

'Some sort of social centre. Concerts, meetings. Even weddings, perhaps. For couples looking for something more than a magistrate's office, but who don't want a proper church wedding.'

We turned from the altar and walked slowly down the aisle, and she put her arm through mine. Near the doors that led out of the church we drew level with the confessionals on the left and right: discreet little wooden stalls for the exchange of sins and secrets. A blank piece of white cardboard was slotted into the brass holder above each of the doors. Bethany let go of my arm and turned the cards around so that they read CONFESSIONS, and then she moved away.

I opened the door and stepped into the darkness, just as I had done hundreds of times when I'd been a boy at St Jude's, and we'd marched down on Friday mornings and the class waited in the pew. Would I get Father Fergus, who demanded details of your sins and tended to lecture, and might impose entire novenas you had to make before you could consider your sins forgiven? Or Father Johnson, who leaned forward encouragingly and heard you out, passing lightly over even the most mortal of sins with the whisper: 'I want you to say three Hail Mary's and now make a good act of contrition, and do not sin again.'

I knelt down in the box and the door swung closed behind me. As my eyes got used to the darkness, I saw through the grill that separated me from my shadowy confessor the outlines of a head, turned sideways so that I might whisper into the ear close to my lips.

'Bless me Father, for I have sinned.' I had to clear my throat; my voice was rusty in the dark. 'It is many years since my last confession.'

'Tell me what troubles you.'

'Long ago, I caused the death of a person I loved.'

'Did you mean to do that?'

'I would have given my life for her.'

'But your sacrifice was turned down?'

'I never got the chance to make it. Someone else ruined things – he wouldn't wait.'

'Why wouldn't he wait?'

'I don't know.'

'Well, then – ask him.'

'I can't do that. He's dead.'

From the other side of the grille came a short sharp exhalation, a sigh perhaps, or a very small laugh. 'That doesn't mean you can't ask him. It just makes what he has to say a bit harder to hear.'

Shades of Father Daintry and the advice he gave Joe about angels. They want to tell you something vital, but it's up to you to work out the message. Later, if you must, shoot the messenger.

I knew I could never shoot anyone: as Joe had pointed out to me over and over again in the foyer of the Monte Carlo Cinema in Jeweldeane: I took these things much too seriously – the whole point of this sort of blood-letting, in Joe's view, was that it should be enjoyed for what it was – terrific fun.

I didn't need to know any more, and acting on an instinct instilled in me those many years before, in the hours I'd spent in this confessional, absorbed in the same ritual, pretending not to know who was behind the gauzy curtain while he did me the same favour, I now bowed my head, closed my eyes and began for the first time in many years to recite the act of contrition: 'I confess to Almighty God, to the Blessed Mary ever Virgin, to blessed Michael the Archangel, to blessed John the Baptist, to the holy apostles Peter and Paul, to all the Saints, that I have sinned exceedingly in thought word and deed . . .'

What I was confessing to, and repenting of, did not matter. The words came tumbling out, and I felt my heart lifting. There was consolation and happiness in the old familiar spell. Of course, I knew the relief would not last and the really hard test lay ahead: the penance, the necessity of finding out who killed Joe di Angelo.

When I opened my eyes, the figure on the other side of the wire mesh had gone. I got up off my knees, closed the door and Bethany was waiting. Like me, she was free. She had found the words she had been looking for. She took my arm and we didn't say anything; there was nothing to say. We walked out of church like old believers who had returned to the faith. We'd visited the altars, observed the Stations of the Cross, and I had been newly shriven. And now we strolled into the sunshine like a newly married couple. It was a wild joke, and it was shadow play – the painted barn was empty and the old enemy was reduced now to several thousand less than interesting lukewarm Protestants who knew less about their faith than we did. Yet we had struck a blow. We had returned to a pile of stone and painted plaster a brief dignity.

The sun was going down when I dropped Bethany at her hotel high on the Ridge. A doorman in dove-grey topper and morning suit directed me to a parking space beside the garden. The lobby sparkled with shards of preposterously pricey jewellery in brilliant glass boxes. Bethany had a suite on the fifth floor. The heavy door swung fast, the air-conditioning sighed in the rich hush; it was a sumptuous foxhole, painted white and gold. But looking down on an avenue of jacarandas where traffic crawled silently beyond the double glazing, there, beside my rented Toyota, sat the red Opel, ready and waiting.

'Persistent bastard,' said Bethany. 'Why doesn't he just go home?'

'I don't think he can. That's the strange thing. He's as caught up in this as we are. It's as if he can't move until someone asks the right questions.'

Back at the Summerland I returned the cash to its drawer and unpacked my few things. I was going nowhere. I looked again at the photograph Cameron di Angelo had given me. Who would bother to track and photograph a supplementary teacher of remedial English from McLeod High? Who would film the torching of a library, and the humiliation of Joe Angel ? Who would leave a good copy of the 'famous' photo with Bethany? Maybe there was a way, as my confessor had suggested, of asking the man who was dead. After all, Joe had apparently left me a message.

CHAPTER 24

The address she had given me was on South Ridge. I knew it so well it made me ache. On the one hand I was utterly confused. I knew where I was, and yet where I was kept adding new dimensions. South Ridge was where Joe and I walked the streets after school each Wednesday, beside Bethany and Constanza. It was green and cool and catered still, as it had done then, to diplomats and business people, its broad avenues planted with jacarandas and pines. At the foot of the Ridge, to the left of the traffic circle, stood the house where Bethany had lived, and where we all went swimming that summer. I was tempted to walk up the driveway and knock on the door. But I kept going. The feeling of being back was so strong that several times my eyes began to water with what emotion I couldn't tell – sadness, joy, longing, nostalgia? It was all too much, and too close. In McLeod I had trained myself to go hunting for vanished lives; now it was myself I was looking for, and I kept catching sight of someone who looked a bit like me, only to lose him again.

Cameron di Angelo's house was on the crest of the Ridge, looking north to the city and beyond to the squat, flat-headed hills of the rough country, now faintly mauve in the distant haze of heat. We sat in a glassed-in patio, furnished in shades of russet and beige, with a tea tray between us. Through the window I saw how the garden descended in a series of granite steps, between hedges of lavender, to an olive-dark swimming pool. She wore jeans and an apricot bolero blouse in a slim sheath around her ribs. She kept clenching and unclenching her hands.

I passed her the photo of myself, 'Who took this, do you know?'

'I told you. I've haven't the faintest idea. But Joe wanted to be sure I knew you. His oldest, his only – friend.'

Being identified like that made me uncomfortable. It was a uniqueness I did not want. 'Surely there were others?'

'He had minions, colleagues, ex-wives, enemies, admirers, rivals. But no family, and no friends.' She held up two fingers pressed tightly together. 'He told me you and he were once like this. Will you tell me about that time?'

'Did Joe ever talk to you about something we were caught up in when we were young? It was a political group he started. It called itself FIRE?'

Cameron shook her head. 'He never spoke about the past. Fire what?'

'The letters stood for Forum for Independence, Redistribution, Equity.'

'Sounds pretty silly.'

'It was. And ended badly. The police got us.'

'Did someone go to jail?'

'Someone was killed. Shot.'

'Like Joe.'

'Tell me why you believe someone set out to kill Joe. The police theory was he'd been shot in a highjack that went wrong.'

'I sat here for days thinking about the order of things that night. Running it through my mind. Joe drives by the golf course, but in the dark he stops and rolls down the window. Nobody sane in this town would do that.'

She looked out of the patio glass where stone stairs led down to a pool. Two bay trees, cropped into perfect ovals, standing in terracotta pots, were etched against the white garden wall. 'So I paid for a new post-mortem by an independent pathologist. It turned up some very strange things and it gave a context to the police autopsy. Those eight bullets, for instance – they had been fired quickly. Six missed major organs, three careered off various bones and three never exited the body. The last two did the damage. But here's the thing – it turns out that these two were fired from such close range that they left gunpowder burns on the neck.'

'Do you think he knew whoever shot him?'

'I'll come to that. The second post-mortem also identified the kind of bullets used. They were full metal jacket. I understand that you need a specially adapted gun for them, because they travel a bit more slowly than ordinary bullets. They're professional ammo. The sort hired killers use, or special forces.'

'Well?'

She shrugged. 'This was no hijack. Joe stopped for someone.'

'And that someone shot him?'

She looked at me. 'How else do you explain the open window? And the powder burns? Whoever it was got close enough to practically hold a gun to his head.'

'The car kept moving though.'

She nodded. 'He was perhaps still conscious when the car hit the stanchion at the entrance ramp to the motorway.'

'Where is the car now?'

She smiled. 'The police told me it was in the police pound. Material evidence. They wouldn't let me see it. So I spent some more money and paid a private investigator to find it. It turned out it wasn't in the police pound. It was at a joint called Harry's Valet and Vroom-Vroom, covered in a big tarpaulin, and when my guy asked Harry what he planned to do with it,

Harry said he was sitting on it until word came through to vacuum, wash and valet it. Joe was dead and gone and someone wanted the car wiped clean. Maybe that's why you're here.'

'I don't understand.'

'I want to know who did this. You were his best friend. Will you help me?'

I shook my head. 'Mrs Di Angelo. I came to the capital because Joe asked for help, and I walked right into this – mess. The person I need to help is myself.'

'It might be different when you hear what I have to say. You might feel obliged, like I do.'

'I'm sorry to be rough, Mrs Di Angelo, but you were . . . what? Wife number four? I saw you all in the same pew. Why should you feel obliged?'

'Ah yes, the former wives' pew. The protocol took some sorting out. We were all Joe's exes, but some of us had been that way longer than others. And some of us had been married to him longer than others. So who should sit where? We decided that the more recently you'd been married – the closer you got.'

'Closer?'

'To where – Joe was. I was last in the marriage stakes, so I got the aisle seat.'

'But Joe dumped you, just as he dumped the others.'

'With the others the pattern was predictable. He married you, he met someone else, and he dumped you. This time there was no one else. He swore it.'

'Did you believe him?'

'To be honest, no, I didn't. I thought, "He's divorced me, hasn't he? So where's the difference?" I was sure there was someone else. I was bitter. But the divorce settlement was huge. Far more than I asked. He told me I was lucky, and if I didn't believe him I should believe my bank balance. "You'll thank

me," he said. And then suddenly he was gone. So I had to – rethink. Maybe he really did know what was going to happen and he wanted to protect me – from the storm to come . . . That's why I feel obliged.'

'What message did he leave me?'

'It was pretty straightforward: "When you see Charlie, tell him I couldn't wait." You know what he meant, don't you?' She was watching me so intently, it made a mask of her pretty round face. But her upper lip trembled slightly, as if under her impassive stillness there ran a rivulet of delight – everything, for her, was falling into place. 'He was waiting and you didn't show up.'

'No, that isn't it. I wasn't late. I got here on the day he fixed.'

'Then what did he mean about not being able to wait?'

'I've spent a lifetime trying to work out why Joe couldn't wait, Mrs Di Angelo. But he never could, and it had very bad effects. A long time ago, a girl I loved died because he couldn't wait.'

She gave a half-laugh, half-sob. 'No, he never could wait. The last shot probably killed him. It severed the artery carrying blood to the brain. But the car was automatic, still in drive, and it moved on until it hit the bridge. There was something else – my guy went over the car and found this under the driver's seat, wedged between the metal runner and the car mat.' From the pocket of her blouse she took a cellphone, a slim wafer of chocolate-brown metal, banded with silver. 'It's typical of Joe. Always had to have the latest ridiculously expensive designer stuff. This phone was either brand new or wiped clean. It has no addresses, no messages, no voicemail.

'Any calls?'

She opened up the call register and showed me. 'One. To another mobile, a few minutes after one in the morning. Ten minutes after he left me. He would have been very close to

the golf course by then. It's almost as if he panicked about something – he dialled a number he knew by heart. My guess is he had this in his hand when he was shot.'

I reached out and took the phone from her. It was a nice weight, and sat beautifully in the hand. By letting her give it to me I had taken over what it meant, what it signified; it was tacit acceptance that I was in this, right to the end. I looked at the log.

'The call lasted sixteen seconds.'

'Time for just a few words. As if he were checking something.'

'Did you try the number?'

She shook her head. 'I was scared. Whoever owns that number knows what happened to Joe.'

I put the number on the screen and dialled. On the fourth ring someone answered and said, quietly and repeatedly, 'Hullo . . . hullo . . . hullo . . . ?'

I waited. I was, perhaps for the first time since arriving in the capital, beginning, very faintly, to enjoy myself. When he said 'Hullo?' for the fifth time, I hung up.

She was appalled. ' Whoever it is you called will know you've got Joe's phone.'

'I think so, yes.'

'Are you sure that's wise?'

'Maybe not. But it's a relief.'

'A relief?'

'I know the man who answered.'

'But you didn't speak to him.'

'No need to. He'll see Joe's number and he'll know he's just had a call from a dead man.'

I slipped the phone into my pocket and headed for the door. I thought again about Joe's message and why he couldn't wait. It seemed almost certain that when he asked me to come to

the capital he fully expected to be there to meet me. Yet, by the time he stopped at his ex-wife's home, just hours before I was due to fly in, things had changed. Cameron was right – Joe almost certainly knew whoever waited for him in the shadows of the golf course. But there was something else, far more alarming, about that brief call. Perhaps when he stopped in the dark, opened his window and waited, he also knew he was at the end of the line.

Chapter 25

He sat tight on my tail and I led him out of town, feeling my way, trusting the vibrations, and soon we were in the rough high country, north of the city. The hills, spiky mounds of red sand and horsegrass, looked as if a half-blind child-god playing at sandcastles had dumped them there, lopped off their heads and forgotten them for a couple of aeons. Even so, there had been plenty of development since I'd been there last; walled citadels sprouted from ridges nearest the city: stolid, face-brick villas with an apron of scruffy lawns out front and scrawny dahlias crowding the razor-wire fences, wash lines spinning in the sharp hill breezes.

We used to head up that way to smoke, to booze, to make love, because, in the rough country, you forgot the city and its angry adults, who disapproved in principle of just about everything remotely light or warming. Not that the hills did not have their share of dangers: there were said to be crazy drunks who hid in the bushes and spied on couples in parked cars; there were stone-vipers; and hyped-up knife-men sometimes attacked picnickers or lovers who dallied in the stony clefts and small stands of timber. But such dangers were small beer by comparison with the low-browed vicars presiding over what passed for life in the capital, and when they came across anything like joy or energy they called the police or throttled it to death.

The grim armies of puritans were long gone, of course, and with such finality that you wanted to call them back for a moment to explain how they could have ruined so many lives and slipped away without explanation. But they had vanished, leaving barely a trace of their former preposterous self-importance, and it made no sense to remember them. But I did remember. They remained presences; for me they were still unfinished business.

Higher still, where once you bounced over trackless, rocky ground, the road was tarred now, and the man in the Opel sat close on my tail. We were travelling in convoy, and I could feel him saying, 'Well, I know you know the way, so lead me there.'

It had been a long time. I had only ever seen the place by moonlight, and I wondered if I could get the location exactly right. But I'd been on these blind searches in the desert country outside McLeod, looking for what was no longer there, and I knew I was close to what I was looking for when the ghostly gravity, cold and clear, began tugging at me, my skin crawled and I followed the feeling until I hit the place. I had lived and died here, in another existence. All was much the same at three in the afternoon, only less dramatic: a shallow depression of grass and rock of about fifty metres, side to side. Across this saucer of land, from the nearer edge on my left, down into the dip, then up over ridge and out of sight, marched the tall steel pylons, carrying the power cables balanced on their outstretched weightlifters' arms.

I parked, walked over to the edge of the scoop of land, and sat down.

The Opel came slowly over the hard ground and pulled up beside my car. A stocky figure waved, and I knew what the wave meant. Until then we had been playing an interesting game of move and counter-move. This was reality time. He came and sat down next to me and looked around him, as if seeing it all for the first time: the small hills on the horizon, the pylon in the centre of a saucer of land. A stippling of grey in his sandy hair, and fewer wrinkles than you'd expect in a guy past fifty. He nodded, as if I'd made a good choice, pulled a box of Mentholyptus Kings from his shirt pocket and proffered the packet. When I shook my head, he did something I hadn't seen in years, he snapped open the flip-top and, with a flick of his wrist, sent a cigarette somersaulting into the air and caught it between his lips. He remembered, I was sure of it, that I did not smoke, but this was the opening gambit in a little trip down memory lane.

I said, 'Very impressive. Do you still strike matches on your sole of your shoe?'

'When I had your call, I thought, "This man is catching on. At last."' He smiled and lit his cigarette with a pink and gold lighter in the shape of a mermaid. She had very blonde hair and very pink lips, and I saw his thumb pressed firmly between her pert, pointed little breasts. 'As to my little habits – these things make us what we are – no matter how we think we change.'

His voice was a little rustier, from all those menthol cigarettes over the years. The last time we'd met, he'd been wearing a brown and rather hairy sports jacket with leather-covered buttons and fawn corduroy trousers. The colour of his tie at our first meeting had never left me: it had been a startling egg-yolk yellow. Now, he had on a good blue suit, dark-blue shirt and polished black brogues. He'd progressed from young country-bred, plain-clothes Special Branch man to smooth city gent. Though the old trapeze-artist cigarette trick showed he was still a mixture of many styles.

'You've given me a good run, Croker. I should not be surprised. After all, you and I have had our little games in the past, and you've shown me how – adroit – you can be when you try.'

He stretched out three-quarter length, leaning on an elbow, as if he were on a manicured lawn, and not a patch of stubbly grass so sharp it could draw blood if you weren't careful where you put your hands.

'You make it sound like you knew I was coming to town.'

'I had a good idea you'd fly in. What I didn't know was whether you'd stay, or turn right around and head back the way you'd come. Back to school and the arms of Beatrice Tromp.' He gave me a quizzical smile. 'To think you're a teacher now – remedial, part-time, perhaps, but still – who would have thought it?'

I realized he was winding me up, but I could not stop myself. 'Any reason why I wouldn't make a teacher?'

'I wasn't sure if you'd ever make anything, Croker. Going on what I knew from our last meeting – and I am sorry if this sounds harsh – you were one of the most foolish, childish, naive individuals I ever had the misfortune to arrest. I marked you down for failure. I despaired of you. A snap judgement, and probably unfair.' He looked at the grass waving in the breeze. He blew out smoke, and visibly relaxed. 'Though I doubt it. I remember saying to myself when we first met that here was one very sick bunny. Call it a policeman's instinct.'

'What sort of cop are you now? Colonel? General? Commissioner?'

He had a shy, rather soft smile, as if he were really and truly moved and refreshed by the utter perversity of other people's thinking, or the lack of it.

'You've been out of things for a very long time, or you wouldn't ask that question. I gave up the force ages ago. When the new lot came in. They wouldn't have had me, would they? Fascist collaborator, servant of the old regime, right-wing weirdo, foot-soldier for the Puritan catastrophe, etcetera, etcetera . . . People like me were spat out. I moved over into the security business. These days I am plain Skip le Moerr.'

'You knew where I was, didn't you?'

'Eventually. My instructions were straightforward: spend whatever it takes, but find him. Shades of Stanley, sent to discover where Livingstone was tucked away.'

'Did you take that photograph of me coming out of my school gate?'

He nodded in his thoughtful way. 'It had to do with this very question: were you really still with us? I was asked to confirm the fact.'

'It was well done. I never knew the first thing about it.'

He inclined his head again. 'That's praise – coming from a fellow professional. Surveillance photography is an art and needs constant practice. It's years since I did any work of that sort.'

'And you've been trailing me ever since.'

'I was paid to find you by a client. Once I'd done so, I never expected to see you again. Nor did I very much wish to.'

'Then what's all this about? You've been behind me since I flew into town.'

'Because things did not go as my client planned. Something happened and he was forced to think again. So he came back to me, for further consultation.'

I nearly laughed. 'What do you consult in? Or for?'

'Security. I am in that field, and I consult a great deal.'

'I'm sure there's a lot of call for it.'

'Absolutely. In this city, and all over the country, hundreds of folks, week in, week out, are knifed, shot, bludgeoned, burnt . . . etcetera. Wham, bam – another corpse. We're talking here about haphazard, common or garden homicides. The sort of thing that happens to your neighbour, your granny, your kid.

Wrong place, wrong time, and you're just another statistic. But it's also no big deal. Right? Regrettable, but nothing special. It's a growth industry – but it's not yet a service industry! D'you follow me, Croker?'

'No, I don't.'

'Let me spell it out for you. Dying to order, when you want it, the way you want it, that's much harder to fix. It takes' – he searched for the word he wanted, mouthing the options silently; he tried 'organization', but rejected it with a flick of his cigarette, then 'forethought' – he didn't like that either, and he settled for – 'assistance'. My clients come to me for something very specific. It's not protection against the usual terror and trauma. Of being, say, burgled or shot. For that you buy armed guards, psychotherapy and counselling. My service is proactive. I help people who have a special sense of their approaching end. Who have special needs. I specialize. I deal principally in fear. I advise people who are, quite literally, scared to death. I talk them through their requirements.'

'You look after them?'

Le Moerr shook his head. 'No, that would not be the right description. I try to ensure they are well served.'

'How do they know they are going to die?'

He looked around him and sighed happily, as if everything he looked at pleased him, as if he was a contented man.

'That was a fine woman you spent the day with, wandering the city.'

'She's Bethany Greene. And she's been living in Geneva.'

'Ah yes. Rosa – by another name . . . the only member of your committee I never met. The one that got away.'

'You sent her the photo of all of us having dinner that night, at Dino's.'

'A little reminder.'

'Why are you here, Le Moerr?'

He blew smoke at the perfect heavens. 'The real question is: why are you here? Answer that and a lot of other things fall into place.'

'You know why I'm here. Joe turned up in my town and asked me to come.'

'According to him you couldn't say no.'

'We differ on that.'

'Di Angelo's take on things was this: you came to the capital at his request because you owed him. When you and he were in the back of my squad car that night, in this very spot, and my guy was ready to drill you, he saved your bacon.'

'That's balls. Joe made his move, and your guy fired a shot. But does it really matter now?'

Le Moerr nodded. 'It matters, believe me. What happened at that time, with the girl dying as she did, and the rich guy blown away a few nights ago are so tightly locked together you couldn't drive a blade between them. By the way, do you have any idea who killed Di Angelo?'

'I know this. It wasn't some botched hijack. His wife had another post-mortem done. Whoever shot him was a pro; someone who knew what he was doing, and someone who almost certainly knew Joe.'

'She got a private detective on the job, didn't she?'

'That's right. He found the car.'

'Sensible woman. Better than waiting on the cops. They're truly useless. I guess it was this private guy who found Joe's phone?'

'It was, and I hope it scared you shitless when I called.'

He nodded, as if I had made a rare, sensible suggestion; a gentle inclination of his head, the arrow of grey white hair over his forehead still crisply pointed. 'It worried me, yes. What if the cops had done a proper job, as I would have done in the bad old days, taken the car to pieces, and found the phone and the number? It was damn silly to let it slip. Then again, there was a lot going on at the time.'

'Why did Joe phone you just before he died?'

Le Moerr was looking at me now the way he'd looked at me the night he had thrown us out of the police car and told us we were free. His expression mixed scorn and incredulity, tinged with a not entirely convincing regret that anyone could be so utterly clueless.

'To say he was close to the drop zone.'

'I don't follow. What was being dropped?'

'He was.'

'You're telling me that Joe set out to have himself killed?'

Le Moerr's smile broadened and deepened. 'Three times, as a matter of fact.'

'And you helped?'

He laughed now, an easy, happy laugh. 'You're getting ahead of yourself. We'll come to me in a moment. Let's start with the first try. As I told you, once I'd located your hidey-hole and sent Di Angelo the evidence, I was out of it. He had his own plans. He had found a couple of palookas who said they'd do the job. He paid them big bucks and he told me they had good references. But he had his doubts, I know that because he drew them a map of the drop-zone, three blocks from Angelo Plaza, just off the seventeenth hole of the City Golf Club. X marks the spot, a clump of bluegum trees, which were good cover. He also insisted they all synchronize their watches. He even asked if maybe they'd like a dry run? But the palookas said no – they were pros, weren't they? Leave it to them.

'Anyway, Di Angelo rocks up as arranged, dead on time. The two guys are waiting – at least they got that bit right. Di Angelo rolls down his window. The shooter walks up and levels the piece. Joe braces himself. Imagine, you're on the point of extinction, looking into the face of your own death, right? And what happens? The gun jams. And what does the gunman do? He starts slagging off his sidekick. "Who bought this fucking piece of shit?" he wants to know. "It wasn't my fault," says his mate, "they said it was A1." "How can it be A fucking 1 if it fucking jams?" says the shooter. And Joe says, "Listen, are you going to do it?" And the shooter says, "Hell, man, how can I do it? This fucking gun is fucking useless." Then his mate says, "Give it here." And he tries, but it's still no go. So what do they do? They start heading off, and when Joe sees this he gets out of the car. He shouts, "Listen, I paid you good money! You can't just walk off the job!" And they say, "Tough titty, chief!" Joe's really breaking up now – he runs after them. They say, "We're out of here. You want to die? Go jump off a cliff!"'

Poor Joe. Story of his life. That's what he must have got, with variations, from everyone he turned to for help. 'You want loyalty, buy a dog!' He was fated to be hit, again and again. Not just by bad luck but by something he had spent so much effort and ingenuity trying to dodge – terminal incompetence, life-destroying absence of style. Never finding anyone who did it like Capone or Calvin.

I could see Le Moerr was truly angry.

'How do you explain the – demeanour – of those bozos? Lack of in-job training? Skills flight from the country? Anyway, that's how it is today. Just hang a sign on your door – call yourself a hotshot, rocket scientist, big cheese, brain surgeon, hit man, whatever. Talk it up, shout the odds. Until you got to do the stuff, and the piece jams. My God, what a lot of arseholes we truly are!'

I understood now. It wasn't that he advised people who knew they were going to be killed how to avoid that fate. As he had told me, his was a very specialized form of consultancy. Le Moerr had found a niche market, people who wished to end it all, and he made sure it happened the way they wanted.

'So you did it . . . you shot Joe?'

Le Moerr raised his eyebrows. Modest, self-deprecating. 'I'd like to think I was of some help. Joe di Angelo took his own life.'

'Your finger on the trigger.'

'It was his call.'

'Whichever way you play it, you killed him.'

With his pocket knife, a Swiss army job, he began to dig a small hole in the earth, flicking away the soil from its rim like a man sweeping crumbs off a tablecloth.

'You're with me now, Croker. I can see that. Very good! You're waiting to hear why he wanted it to happen, isn't that right? I think, I really hope, I've given you some signs in the past few days just how very deep in the shit your friend was. For years and years he's been king of the castle, then suddenly he's sunk. What triggers the collapse? Maybe he bought some-thing or sold something, or his gold or his diamond mines looked a bit iffy, or his derivatives went sour, or the shares he flogged were based on wishes and prayers. For some reason we need not go into, his fortune, fame, arts projects, were going down the tubes. So what? All this stuff is utterly illusory anyway, it all hangs on the willingness of other people to believe. While they believed, he was Jesus. But now they no longer believe in Joe di Angelo. God is dead, right? The banks were asking questions, the stock exchange was hopping up and down; the bloody government was having hot flushes. Joe kept playing one against the other, selling and buying and faking it. He still had the mines, the casinos, the yachts, the limos, the jets – but everything was on the skids. He couldn't even pay his teachers at his school. Such a shame – them burning down the library. What good did it do to man or boy? But that's how we are. Stupidity followed by cruelty, relieved by a bit of book burning. Very local, very characteristic. But he's a broke billionaire – basically he's fucked. He needs cash, mountains of cash; he's leveraged everything until there are no more levers to pull; he has begged but no one listens. However, there is a fallback – he has insurance. Big fat life policies. Lots and lots of them. Enough to settle any outstandings. To see things right. To restore the faith of those who once worshipped him. Are you with me, Croker?'

'Why do think you can cover it all up? Why did Joe think so? You've heard what people are saying. The truth will get out.'

Le Moerr was slightly agitated now. 'What will get out, I can't say. But I know this – it won't be the truth – or it will be the truth as someone wishes it to be. There is a lot of gossip right now. It will fade. It is in nobody's interests for Joe di Angelo to fail to be what everyone, himself included, believed him to be. He has done too much good to let it all go down the tubes. He knew he could save the legend only if he sacrificed himself. He did the right thing.'

'He arranged to have himself murdered so he could claim on his life insurance. And you say he did the right thing?'

'It is in everyone's interest that the picture painted at his funeral is the one that lasts. It is my belief, Croker, that most people will prefer the earlier version.'

'A version built on lies from start to finish?'

'We love our lies, all of us. Where would we be without them? It annoys me to hear how lies get bad-mouthed. A long career as a policeman has shown me that when they think it will help, just about everyone lies like there is no tomorrow. Everyone except me, that is. I tell the truth and I'm hated for it. Don't underestimate the capacity of people to forgive and forget, as long as the story stays strong. I see Joe di Angelo rising from the ashes. After all, what did he do wrong? He overreached, that's all.'

It was a great game Le Moerr was having, and he loved every second of it. He sat up and wrapped both arms around his shoulders and hugged himself, he was that pleased. It was a congratulatory embrace of the one who had made it all possible, Scipio Africanus le Moerr. It was as if he took into himself all the scene: the rocky hills with their fuzz of tawny grass, the marching pylons, the scoop of land where Constanza had died – also by his hand – as if this was the world he had made, and he looked on his handiwork and was pleased. He curled his right hand into a fist, stretched his other hand flat like a roof above his clenched fingers.

'You live your life. You hold to yourself like a rock, and over you thunderclouds form. The weather gets worse, the storm breaks and pours down on your head. But you hold fast, the storm slackens and passes. And you're still there. This will blow over. Let's not say Joe di Angelo was up to no good. He was up to lots of good. This bad stuff going on now, it'll fade away and he'll be back, bigger than ever. But to do that, he had to be fixed.'

'What do you mean – fixed?'

'Fixed in purpose. Fixed in place. With probity.'

'Yes, fixed with eight bullets.'

But Le Moerr was immune to sarcasm. For him, what he'd done was an act of kindness. Even by his steely standards, this final act was a signal triumph. First, he'd destroyed us as revolutionaries; he'd shown us up as rank amateurs not worth the cost of locking up. Later, he had been called upon to deliver the *coup de grâce* to a condemned man, whose time and luck and faith in himself had run out. It was quite a record: and yet all through this terrible and violent farce he had done nothing but the proper thing.

'Why did he phone you when he was close to the golf course? He knew you were waiting, and if you were such a pro, why the call?'

'Once bitten . . . He was badly shaken up by the bozos who ran out on him. I think he panicked. He wanted reassurance.'

'Did Joe say anything, at the end?'

'Just a word: he said "America". Like a prayer. I thought, afterwards, that he maybe aspired, you know, to the American way of life, or that America summed up for him all that was best and most perfect. Then again, it all happened quickly. One minute he was looking up at me, and the next – he was moving away, the damn car was in drive and he kind of sailed away. No stopping him. I didn't wait around. I saw him sailing away and I got the hell out. It wasn't till you called that I remembered his damn phone. That was careless. I'm ashamed of that. I guessed they'd taken the car to the police pound, because that's what you do with a suspect vehicle, keep it in the pound and run all the tests. But it turned out the cops had shipped it off to Harry's Vroom-Vroom and Valet, and Harry was going to scrub it clean of anything that might contradict the authorized version – that Joe had been shot in a hijack. A great man cruelly cut down, etcetera . . . By the time I found the car, his wife's detective had beaten me to the phone.'

There it was. Joe's last word for – not the American way of life, not at all – it was the way of death he had in mind. The way people got killed in movies, with style, with elegance, a world where killing wasn't bad or good or anything. The terms did not apply. He'd dreamed always of doing someone in. He wanted it to be stylish and shapely and smooth. And he did it, in the end. He had called in an expert.

CHAPTER 26

Le Moerr lit a cigarette, leaned back on his elbow, blew smoke at the sky and regarded the tall electric pylon that all those years ago Constanza had tried, and failed, to blow up.

'I believe you were once a fine shot. Bullseyes every time, Di Angelo told me.'

I remembered the rifle range at St Jude's and what Joe had said about calling on me, if ever he needed a hit man. Suddenly, I knew where Le Moerr was going.

'I told you Di Angelo tried three times to do what he had to do. Right? Let me help you through this, Croker. It's beginning to feel like I have a vocation. I'm always helping you over tricky jumps. But if it gets too much just stop me. Anyway, Joe tried it with the palookas who could barely cross the road. But he didn't start with them. He went to them because things got out of hand and he ran out of time.'

So that was why Joe had come looking for me. And that was why he had left the message with Cameron di Angelo: 'Tell him I couldn't wait . . .'

'I know what you're thinking, Croker. Maybe I am lying. Let's dispose of that escape route. Never have I lied to you. Di Angelo tracked you down because he knew he could rely on you to do what he needed.'

'I wouldn't have done it. I have a problem with killing people. Joe knew that. I couldn't adapt to the idea.'

Le Moerr nodded. 'I'm sure you believe that, Croker, and generally speaking I am prepared to accept it as the truth, but this time you would have made an exception. Di Angelo was sure – and I reckon he was right – you'd do the decent thing. He would have told you what he needed you to know, as soon as you flew into town. But he isn't here, so I'm going to tell you. It all goes back to that night we were all here together. You and Di Angelo were in the back of my squad car, and your girl was there.' Le Moerr pointed to the towering electric pylon. 'She had just put her rucksack at the base of the target, and was ready to blow it to hell. Now, ask yourself how it came to be that we were all here together that night?'

'I don't know.'

Le Moerr gave me his appallingly kind look. 'All right. That's hard to answer. Let me ask you another question. When I had you under my wing, as it were, in Pinnacle Point, you told me that you were the man who placed the bombs. I believed you. Until I found out you were lying. How do you imagine I got to the truth?'

I had nothing to say, I just shook my head.

Le Moerr dug in his pocket and took out his Swiss Army knife again, unclasped it and began deepening the hole he'd scratched in the stony earth.

'You know what, Croker? You're a sucker for punishment.' He looked hard at the end of his cigarette and then, very deliberately, he stubbed it into the hole. 'Your little group – what did you call yourselves? Yes, that's it, the Forum for Independence, Resistance and Equity – and it was, to put it mildly, completely fucking useless. Inept, silly, never remotely national, and it represented no one but your silly selves. But one of you was placing high explosive in public places and we couldn't have that. So when you came clean and confessed, I did something unprofessional – I felt relieved and I gave way to a fit of decency.'

'I don't understand, what did feeling decent have to do with it?'

'A lot. In a decent world people tell the truth. In a decent world they don't kill each other and they don't place bombs in public places. Against my instinct, I wanted to believe you. Your technical knowledge of explosives was convincing. You were clued up about what went bang, the how and the why. If you were what you said you were then the nonsense would stop. If not, there'd be blood before bedtime. That's usually the way: criminal ineptitude at the kick-off, then some inno- cent gets blasted. Story of our lives. And our country. I knew I had to fix this thing fast. What to do?

'I had Di Angelo brought to me and I told him both of you were going to jail. And he said, "That would be a terrible waste." "Of prison space?" I asked. "No," he said, "of me." He wanted to know how much time he'd get, and I said seven to ten. Twice that for you. It was a rough guess, going on similar cases when young people of sentimental liberal persuasion – and next to no brains – pissed about with high-explosives without – more by luck than judgement – killing someone in the process. Why twice as long for you? Di Angelo wanted to know. Because you were the explosives man, the brains behind the bombs, and you had confirmed as much. Frankly, his reaction disappointed me.

'You know what he did, Croker? He laughed. Of course, that was enough; it got you out of the way. That left the girl, but she was nowhere to be found. Then Di Angelo said maybe he could be of some help in that regard. Providing we saw eye to eye. I thought, "Fucking hell. This is one very cocky guy. He's up shit creek but he's talking deals." You with me?'

I could only nod. I felt myself drowning. I'd known it before, sinking below the waves of terminal shame. Le Moerr appreciated this, he nodded encouragingly as I went down for the third time.

'Of course, I could have told him to piss off. Except that I was not in a good place myself. Everyone in your group was accounted for – except the girl with the dynamite, and if another pylon went down I'd look stupid. I needed the girl.'

It was clear now, as these things often horribly are when it is much too late. After each sortie to identify a possible target, Joe had been kept up to date by Constanza. She'd told him about every one of our recces. He'd had to approve the targets. Even after Constanza vanished through the bathroom window the night Bethany came to warn us, she must have gone on telling Joe what she planned. After all, he was the Director.

'Joe told you where to look?'

'Di Angelo had a number for the girl, and he was very forthcoming with all the details. What do you say, Croker? About your monumental blindness? Do you, possibly, take any responsibility for it?'

Once again, as he had been at the ineptitude of Joe's first, would-be assassins, Le Moerr was angry. His mouth twitched at the corners, his right eyelid flickered, and a faint wave of wrinkles rifled up over his broad forehead and ebbed at his hairline, below the sharp arrow point of silver-grey hair, the way the sea will surge below a spur of rock when the tide comes in.

'You're saying Joe shopped us. He switched sides?'

'He made a tactical decision. A trade.'

'A trade? We were living, breathing people, his friends, and you talk as if he saw us as not much better than shares in some business deal . . .'

Le Moerr nodded. 'And your value was tumbling. You were dodgy stock and he cut his losses.'

'So when Joe and I sat here, on this hillside, watching Constanza moving to that pylon right there, you had it all sewn up?'

'A lot of it. But by no means all. There were things no one had control over, that could not be foreseen.'

I saw Joe and I in the back of seat of the coupé. My hand going up and up in the air, like a schoolboy wanting to ask a question, my mouth and Cheesy swinging his pistol from Joe to point it at my forehead. Then Joe yelling and flinging himself at Cheesy. The flat bark as the bullet went tearing through the roof of the car. In the moonlight, Constanza raising her head, ready to bolt.

When he spoke again Le Moerr was relaxed, his anger drowned in fond derision.

'You're wondering, aren't you, Croker, exactly why the girl was killed? Was it deliberate? Was it necessary? No, to the first question. Yes, to the second. Was it inevitable? Not at all. It could have gone either way. As it turned out, she took off like a hare. I called out to her to stop. She might have listened, but she didn't. And even that doesn't exhaust the possibilities. You have to ask *why* she ran.'

'Because I put my hand up and your guy panicked.'

'My guy wanted to kill you. He told me later he was very keen on that.'

'I was ready. But Joe went for him. He should have waited. If he'd waited maybe I would have been dead but she might have lived.'

'I'm guessing here, but I'd say he couldn't afford to wait.'

'Why not?' I was the angry one now. 'I was the one with the gun pointed at my head – I didn't ask for his help. What the hell was it to do with him?'

Le Moerr rubbed his chin slowly, he seemed to be having a struggle with his face, which looked like it was breaking up

233

again. I think he was finding it really hard having to deal with someone whose naivety bordered on the lunatic.

'I'd say Di Angelo suddenly had second thoughts.'

'About giving Constanza away?'

Le Moerr seemed to be debating with himself, turning my question this way and that – how to navigate around my fatuous ignorance. Should he answer me? Could he bear to make things worse? And then, with a sad shake of his head, he did just that.

'No, that was over. She didn't bother him. He was slightly more interested in you. I think the person who really worried him was me.'

'But why? He sold us out and you cut a deal to set him free.'

'Right. But it relied on certain assumptions. That the girl would run and I would not miss.' Le Moerr's voice was soft and inexorable. 'What if it didn't play out this way? What if she heard the shot and did not run? What if she did run and I only winged her? Alive, she's a problem. Conversely, what if I nailed her and my guy had killed you? That could also screw up our deal.'

I saw it then. 'Too many dead?'

'You're getting it, Croker. If Joe was the only one left standing, then maybe I'd have to charge him, after all. And so he found himself saving your life. Whether you wanted it or not. That's why he couldn't wait.'

'And Constanza paid the price.'

'You can see it that way. Betrayal. Then, again, it was a masterstroke. I'm talking of the logic of what he did. Not the morality. Was he going on to glory – or was he heading to jail? It was one hell of a gamble.'

'Does it please you, Le Moerr?'

'Not at all. I'm not a cynical fellow, Croker. I treated you with – restraint. When Di Angelo pulled off his trick – the way he fixed things – that was horrible, seen from where you sit. And I certainly don't think it was pretty. I'd never met anyone so' – again he looked for the word – 'so elsewhere. I also have to say – brace yourself for this – that what happened that night did the two of us no end of good. Di Angelo escaped a dead-end spell in jail. He got over his stupid fight he couldn't win. Now he could plan the greater war, the real crusade. The miracle was made. Giuseppe Roberto di Angelo the arsehole was dead, and Joe the Angel was born. It had taken time, cunning and cruelty. From then on he couldn't miss: billion-aire, do-gooder, fucking son of the fucking soil, Saint Joe, banker to the revolution. It is awful, or it is very impressive. Choose your version. I want to laugh till I weep. His side is in, his beliefs are gospel now. Those I stood for are finished and forgotten. He won.'

'That depends where you see it from.'

'When doesn't it? Looked at his way, his life was a triumph.'

It was hard now to get the words out, but I made myself do it. 'Constanza dies. And he walks free.'

Le Moerr assented with a grave nod. 'He covered his positions, as the speculators say.'

'And this is what Joe would have told me?'

He drew hard on the last of his cigarette and stubbed it out. Five or six cork-tipped filter stubs lay before him.

'He'd have told you all this. And that's why you would have done what he wanted. Stepped right up, real fast. You would have been waiting there on the seventeenth hole, just *dying* to do it, Croker. You would have shot him with pleasure. Because you owed it – not just to him, but to her!'

'Yes.'

Le Moerr looked pleased. His slow pupil was sharpening up.

'And then, being as you are unable to adapt, you would have suffered. Really Croker, you are a case! When I watched you go into that church of yours with the girl, that painted brothel with its heathen statues and its Eyetalian gewgaws, its smells and bells, I wondered what you thought you were doing. I'm of the opposing faith. Well, let me say after years as a policeman, I'm of no faith whatever. An old poet of ours who will be forgotten soon – like the rest of us – put it like this: 'I slice my bread and pour my wine, steer clear of God, and that's just fine.' But you're a believer, and it has caused a lot of grief.'

'I'm a believer, but I don't have faith.'

'Then why go into that church?'

'Because it's where I left a lot of me, long ago, and I wanted to see how it was doing.'

'And how was it doing?'

'Same as I left it. Stupid, guilty, angry, helpless.'

'What did you do inside there?'

I was going to say it was a silly question – but something stopped me. If this was his game, I'd play along.

'I told my sins. I confessed to killing a girl.'

'And now you know you didn't. Does that feel better?'

'Worse.'

'Oh heck, there's no pleasing you Holy Romans.' Le Moerr gave a great shout of laughter. 'But for the grace of God and my kind heart you'd be back in that broom cupboard confessing to having killed your old friend as well.' He looked over to the saucer of land where the pylon reared on its stick-insect legs and lifted its arms like some demented warrior doing a victory dance.

'Croker, I've eased your heart. I've been straight with you. I reckon now it's me you owe and I want something.'

'Will you ask for my soul? That's the classic way.'

He laughed now, fully, a gurgling bubble of laughter. 'I

wouldn't have your soul for all the tea in China. Reciprocity is what I want. A record. As it all happened.'

He took from his jacket pocket a manila envelope, opened it and let fall a steady stream of photographs, a few dozen of them, all black-and-white prints. He spread them in front of us, propping them up on the coarse grass. I was there, taking the picture of the policeman, the dog and the girl on the ground, and here was a picture of me taking my picture. Here was Constanza, her eyes wide, laughing at something someone had said the night all the members of FIRE had dinner at Dino's. Just one of the many pictures Le Moerr must have fired off while we sat eating. Here was Bethany, in what I took to be her apartment at the coast, writing something at a table covered with papers. Here was Joe, on the construction site of the new Polly's Hotel. Here he was in a café with Constanza, and I'd have said, judging by their ages and their manner, that it was taken around the time that she and I were picking targets. Here were our lives in pictures. All the time I had been photographing my world, Le Moerr or his people had been doing the same.

'Keep them. They may be useful when you think about these things. They'll remind you how close we were. And how much you missed seeing.'

He savoured my embarrassment, the way I had to stiffen my fingers even to touch his pictures.

'I was watching you long before you became, let's say – professionally interesting – to my bosses, back in the Branch. I saw you as someone who looks hard at things, runs around making sure he records it all, and never thinks for a moment that someone may be doing the same to him. Someone who has very good eyesight, but deliberately shuts his eyes. I was so close I could have reached out and touched you. Like your guardian angel.'

It was a terrible thought, his closeness.

Le Moerr pushed a last cigarette butt into the hole he'd made and buried it. Then he closed his knife, slipped it into his pocket. 'Now, perhaps for once, your kind of bone-headed blindness might be useful.'

'It hasn't been up till now.'

'I want only what you can give me.'

'And what's that?'

'I want you to write it.'

'Write what, exactly?'

'About you and Di Angelo and what happened to the girl, and my part in all this. There should be some sort of record. Of my story. Every last word of it. Just the way it is! That would be fair.'

'You do what you've done and then you want fairness?'

'Reciprocity.'

'But if I put it down, exactly as it happened, then people will know who Joe really was.'

Le Moerr leaned back and smiled, shook his head, and very gently punched me on the shoulder. 'There is no beating you, Croker. You are the limit. Tell the story with absolute . . . probity – and it is safe to assume that no one will believe you. Di Angelo's story will win through because he is on the up. But me, I am finished. Di Angelo told me he'd found you in that backwoods place, where you went round remembering and recording things everyone had forgotten. You photographed fossils, you chased after ghosts. You were speaking for the dead, and he thought you were crazy. Well, Croker, I'm dead. Speak for me.'

I tried to keep my voice steady, but it went up and down like a bad song. 'Have you any idea how much I hate you? The servant, the slave of the people who wrecked us.'

He nodded. 'I can see you're the one to do this right. Maybe not straight away. But sooner or later you will want to put all this down. And me along with it.'

'I won't do it.'

'I think you will. You're made that way. The photographs will help.'

'I don't want them.'

'Too late for that. They're yours now, Croker. Look hard at them. Try to see me as I was.'

I wanted to say something, I had my mouth open but no words came. This pleased him.

'You're getting there. Good! Find the right words, Croker.' He held up his hands in – what – mock surrender? Amused encouragement? 'And when you're ready . . . shoot.'

I shook my head and we walked to our cars in silence. I knew that when we left behind the place, with its blood, embarrassment, treachery, that it would return to being nowhere particularly special; a stretch of grass beneath some striding electric pylons. You would never believe something had happened here; unless you knew where to look.

Chapter 27

Bethany was wearing a royal-blue skirt of heavy wool that looked vaguely German or Swiss, a pink top and a gold necklace carrying a small diamond cross. We were sitting in her hotel room, a silver tray between us, drinking coffee. The light caught the hallmark on the teaspoon with which I stirred my tea, and embossed in the shaft was the silversmith's name: Sidgewick and Sons, Sheffield.

'If he's telling the truth, I think it's rather wonderful.'

A sense of the unutterable strangeness of other people came over me.

'He is a machine made for telling the truth. But that doesn't make the truth he tells any better.'

'At least you know where you are, Charlie. Now you see.'

'See? I see lies and betrayal.'

The way she bit her lip, her buoyancy, depressed me. She kept lifting the cross to her lips, in what might have been a kiss or a prayer, and I felt I was watching some sort of religious ceremony, a baptism, an initiation into mysteries that excited and overwhelmed her but left me cold.

'What will you do now?'

'If Le Moerr is on the level, it means Joe did himself in. If that were to be known then his heavy life insurance goes out the window.'

'You won't give him – them – away, will you, Charlie?'

Him – them . . . Joe Angel and Skip le Moerr had merged in her mind, indissolubly joined, crook and cop, holy man and hitman, guru and gunman – and she was right. To understand where Joe was, you had to know Le Moerr's position. Same the other way round. But what I found intolerable was that I was entangled too, caught up in the leaden coils of a brutal arrangement that I had nothing – and everything – to do with.

'All the witnesses are guilty.'

'At least you know the truth.'

'It's not my truth.'

'Maybe we can't choose the truth we have to live with. This is the living world, not a dream world. I never know about truth. It's slippery. Once there was Joe Angel: billionaire, philanthropist, patriot, visionary, son of the soil . . . ? True or not? Then he gets shot and he's Giuseppe di Angelo, a crook who pillaged his companies, cooked the books. Maybe that's true, too. This man, Le Moerr, has a point: if Joe Angel goes down, then whole worlds go down with him. Joe came up with a way to save things – why shouldn't he? Le Moerr made sure it happened. I have to say I think it is really rather wonderful, and I'm sorry if that disappoints you. What it gets down to is that it's better for everyone if Joe stays firmly murdered. And canonized.'

'He shopped us, Bethany. Joe cut a deal and Constanza died.'

'Constanza made her choice. She was unstoppable. She died, yes. We lost, yes. But it happens. That's living.'

'To give everything to the fight, and then just walk away?'

She stared at me. 'We were finished, anyway. We were a joke. Le Moerr had it right: we couldn't have run a bath. This is the living world, Charlie, wake up to it.' She gave me a long quizzical look.

'You'll be telling me next that Skip le Moerr was the good Samaritan.'

She nodded. 'You could say that. Didn't he cross the road to help a lonely, desperate man? That's charity.'

'Yeah. First he shoots Constanza, and later he kills Joe. The man is a saint.'

'He did what he could. Cleanly and professionally. Who of us can say the same? None of us is pure. Joe needed help. Le Moerr did him a favour. Call it assisted suicide. Don't be too hard on him – them – Charlie. You've done what you needed to do: you found out who killed Joe. It makes you unhappy and I'm sorry. I know this is hard for you – but if there is anyone who comes out of this with honour it's this ex-cop. Look at you – buried in some godforsaken hamlet at the back end of nowhere for years and years, because you believe you did not save Constanza. Now you know what really happened and it leaves you as unhappy as ever.'

'Yes, now I know it all. And it doesn't help.'

She got up and walked to the window. The sky was darkening over the far hills of the rough country to the north, where I'd sat on a rocky ridge with Le Moerr and heard the story of my life retold. The sky was that pastel, deepening purple, the colour of mourning, so characteristic of the evening around six in the capital; 'the weeping hour' they call it in the patois, 'when orphans long for mothers'.

She turned to me and took both my hands in hers. 'This won't help either, but I am going to tell you anyway. Remember how I drove all night to get to the capital when the Special Branch raided my flat?'

I was suddenly afraid. 'I remember.'

'Remember my neighbour said they had the ceiling down? Well, I had my notes hidden up there.'

'You always told us to keep nothing, not a single piece of paper.'

'We don't always take our own advice. I kept everything: notes, lists, addresses, phone numbers, notes on our meetings, our code names, the places where you tried to source explosive.'

It was a strange feeling, terrible but somehow full of – what – light? Like slowly coming out of a sleep, or out of some deep place inside myself where I had holed up for a long time.

'You see what I am saying, Charlie? If it hadn't been for me they would never have got to you.'

'But you never knew which of us was hitting the pylons.'

'Constanza reported to Joe, and he would phone me and write.'

I remembered Constanza bent over the table spread with coils, springs, fuses and telling me, 'The less you know about when and where, the better, Charlie.'

'I'm sorry, Charlie. That's why I was so frantic to get you and Constanza away.'

I got up and walked to the window. Le Moerr was not down there and it disturbed me that I should feel abandoned. I had come to depend on seeing his car: I had come to rely on someone watching over me. But I was on my own now.

'Say something, Charlie. Is it terrible?'

'Yes, but things can be terrible and pretty normal. I've found that out. If you hadn't told me, there would always be something more I still hadn't worked out. Will you go back to Geneva?'

She nodded. 'Nothing to keep me here now, is there?'

Bethany gave me a smile so full of loving sympathy that I couldn't bear it. And when she stretched out her hand, I took it. I was glad for her. She had freed herself from something that had harried her for a long time. We had nothing left to say to each other. She knew it, too. She walked me to the door and kissed me goodbye.

It was very late when I got back to the Summerland Hotel and I felt I had been away for years. It was time to leave, I could see that. But leave for where? Miss Tromp and the school and the town waited, but all the substance of the place had been drained away by what I knew about Joe and me, and why it was I'd come to be in McLeod in the first place. I could think of no reason to go back there, ever.

I lay on my bed and below me, somewhere, I could hear one of the girls yelling repeatedly, 'No! I don't want to! No! I don't want to! No! I don't want to!'

Was she screaming because she was afraid, because she was paid to do so, or simply for effect? I was not going to consider any of those alternatives.

There was no taboo that could not be breached when those who swore by it decided it was time to swear by something else.

Maybe Joe was rebel and believer, said Bethany. And maybe it was not possible to do either good or evil; you always did both.

In the room below the girl began to scream again. 'I won't! I won't! I won't!'

But of course she would, if enough pressure were applied; that was how the living world worked. She could even be made to be grateful for the pain inflicted. Moral systems were merely orderly ways of tabulating degrees of terror.

I got off the bed and stamped several times very loudly on the floor and the screaming below stopped abruptly.

'That's better,' I said to myself.

And if she screamed again that night I did not hear.

In the morning I threw my stuff into my bag, yanked out the false back of my cupboard and shoved what was left of the cash into my pocket. I went downstairs to the bar. It was just after nine and Gregoire and his customers were watching the sports channel. On the giant screen, players in blue and red ran between posts, kicked at a ball and fell over.

Gregoire put down his brandy and said, 'Lookee, lookee what the wind's blown in.'

Krystell was there too, but she wasn't drinking tea. She was perched on a stool wearing a black dress, very tight, with a plunging neckline and a rope of what looked like diamonds looped around her pale white throat. Like a noose, I thought, and then I was sorry for thinking that. I wondered if she'd been the woman that screamed in the night.

'Did they ever fix that school those bozos fucked up?' Krystell asked.

As if in a answer, the ball game ended and there was Joe on the screen, the face I had seen on the party T-shirts at his funeral, the wave of dark hair, the gentle and slightly puzzled smile. It was the backdrop to some bloke who was announcing a series of state honours in memory of the late, revered and much lamented Joseph Angel. The Angel Awards, as they would be known, consisted of a gold medal and a large cash sum, and would go to individuals who excelled in the fields of art, commerce and construction – 'arenas of endeavour', the talking head called them, which had been close to the heart of the late Joseph Angel.

There followed a montage of shots of Joe's various interests: the opera company, the ballet dancers, his academy (no sign of the fire now, and the teachers smiling) his vintage-car collection, his yachts, his art collection, and helicopter shots of his mines, his AIDS orphans, his flute, splendid on a cushion of blue damask, graced by a single white rose . . . a parade of glittering achievements which drew from the drinkers around Gregoire's horseshoe bar the ever more intense cries of adulation which people make at a firework display as larger, louder and more richly spangled lights shoot high into the night sky, explode, and rain golden tears.

'Can I get you something, Charlie?' Gregoire gestured at the row of upended bottles, spigots fixed to their glass noses. 'You look like you had a rough night.'

'I'm off, Gregoire. I want to pay you for the room.'

'Off somewhere nice?'

'Don't know. Probably not.'

'You seen the horsemen?'

'Horsemen?'

'Sure thing. Across the road. Since late last night. Sleeping on the pavement, with a little fire and a tent they make of blankets. This morning they come; they ring the doorbell very, very early and when I get out of bed and open the door I find these two. And they're looking for you.'

'How do you know it's me they want?'

'Are you the man who went away?'

It summed me up pretty well. I nodded.

'They've got this with them.'

Gregoire gave me a piece of white A4, folded into fours, opened and closed so many times, at innumerable stops along the way to find me, that the paper had split along the folds. The note was typed and had been written in Miss Tromp's lovely, convoluted English:

> To Whomsoever It May Concern, Greetings!
> The bearers here undersigned, of this missive, seek Mr Charles Croker, late of the village of McLeod in the desert lands of the South. If you may help encourage us or support our quest, you will earn our matchless appreciation.
> God Bless you!

I went outside and on the opposite pavement, across the early morning rush of traffic, I saw them. Old Saul sat in the driving seat and Sinna was fitting a feed bag to the muzzle of one of the donkeys. Her hair was tied up in a flaming red scarf and she was smoking a pipe. Old Saul was still wearing his Princeton sweatshirt and he lifted his whip in greeting when he saw me.

'We have been waiting for you.'

Sinna began to weep, raw, snuffling sobs which she tried to stifle with her scarf and Old Saul did not try to comfort her. She reached out and put her hand on my sleeve. 'You take pictures – of our girl? Who we left with the farmer. Can you remember her?'

I remembered her. 'Chantal. What has happened to her?'

'You went away,' said Old Saul, grimly, 'we come to find you. Do you have the pictures?'

I had left on the table of my darkroom the pictures of Chantal when she played with the old bicycle wheel, the iron rim between her thighs, her dress riding up, her gaze remote and dreamy . . .

'I don't have the pictures. Where is she now?'

They looked at me with astonishment, as if it were not possible I had not heard the news. Old Saul spoke to me like I was some kind of simpleton.

'She is gone, mister.'

'But if she is missing you must go to the police.'

'We have found you again, but we cannot find her,' said Old Saul.

'Yes. We found you again,' said Sinna. 'You took the pictures, and with the pictures we can find her again.'

'But what can I do?'

Sinna took the feed bag off the donkey's muzzle and slung it into the cart and clambered up beside Old Saul. They did not look at me. They sat there utterly silent, as if waiting for something. As if there was no answer to my question.

And then they were off down the road, with Saul's whip

licking the donkeys and the rubber tyres of the cart hissing softly on the tar.

I drove to Bethany's hotel. I wanted to tell her some things I'd worked out in the night. I wanted to say I saw now that it was possible to be utterly faithless and yet brimming with sincerity. Absolutely flexible yet unwavering. To believe in personal liberty and lock up those who oppose you. It is possible to hate murder and yet execute those who you believe will be morally improved by this. You can be yourself a heretic and burn heretics.

It is even quite possible to despise Calvinists while admiring Calvin.

As I stepped inside the hotel, I saw her sitting on one of the settees that faced each other across low coffee tables, dotted around the lobby. Her face was bright. She was talking fast to a man who sat with his back to me. I knew the ears, the hair visible above the back of the sofa. Bethany would talk in bursts, then laugh, put both hands to her mouth as if she'd said something which appalled or amused her. He'd say something back, short and sharp. But his hands were instructive, succinct movements, like a conductor of an orchestra, unfolding the score, bar by bar, so that all should be clear and explicit.

I felt sure Bethany must see me at any moment – but her eyes were locked on the man she had lost herself in. She would nod and nod again, drinking him in, opening to his message, hearing his arrangement of the world.

I took a last look at them, wrapped in their own music, before stepping into the revolving door. It looked like they had a lot to say to each other about how it was when you were disabused of illusions, when you accepted that nothing was easy or simple or just in the living world. When you took things as they were.

At the airport I paid for my rented car, went over to the ticket desk and, using my open return, I booked the next flight out. I knew now what Old Saul and Sinna had come to do: they had given me a message. It wasn't an answer, but a question. I had been shown, incontrovertibly, that things were set and fixed and you changed them only by visiting violence on them, smashing them. That was where Joe scored.

'First hear what the angels say, then shoot them if you must.'

Joe had taken it a lot further. He'd come to visit me, given me time to hear what he had to say, and then shot himself. Suddenly I understood, and I was grateful.

EPILOGUE

The heat was huge, the sun an unblinking eye. The cab dropped me at the door of the town, and I could hear the corrugated-iron roofs ticking like clocks as I walked down First Avenue towards McLeod High. So quiet, so apparently empty – everyone inside, in hiding, taking an afternoon siesta, or playing dead. I dropped my stuff at my cottage, collected the pictures of Chantal from my darkroom, put them into a briefcase, then climbed into my truck and set off for Redwatersridge.

As I approached the farm up the long rutted drive, furry globes of tumbleweed hung on the barbed wire like drying pelts, trophies of some cruel hunt, and the last afternoon sun lay softly on the iron roof of the homestead. Somewhere behind the house I could hear the rusty clank of a windmill pumping water into a reservoir. Three wooden steps led up to a wooden stoop that ran along the front of the house. Beside the door a ceramic plaque showed a Mexican dozing under a sombrero and a brass sign read: *Mac's Hacienda*. I walked up the steps, carrying my leather briefcase, and knocked.

In the far corner of the stoop, propped up against the wall, was the wheel Chantal had been riding. I took a few steps towards it and saw that the rim was encrusted with what looked like dried mud. From somewhere inside the house, a voice called 'I'm coming!' and I went back to stand before the Mexican in the sombrero.

Geena Mackenzie opened the door and she did not look pleased to see me.

'Yes?'

'You won't remember me – my name's Croker.'

'Yes. I don't remember you.'

'I've come looking for someone.'

There was a ruffle of sadness, like wind on water, in her grey eyes.

'Well, you won't find him. Not here.'

It was clear she was not anticipating me, nor misunderstanding me. In her mind there could be only one person I might be looking for and it wasn't the girl. She was also telling me that this was as far as I would get with her. She was ready to close the door and disappear back into the house which stood on the great stage of the desert like some flimsy façade, a prop which could be whisked away along with all the lives it once supported, leaving empty space under a mighty, indifferent sky.

That was the thing about these vistas, the near-absence of the human; people might get small parts in the show, but the show had no director, no shape, no beginning or end, and no interest in the small lives that played out briefly in the empty auditorium. It was a giant cosmic scrapbook and between its stony pages there were pressed the traces of those who had once lived here. And yes, you might accept that disappearance was the norm and yet still believe that the traces left by those lives were important, you might accept futility without allowing it to stop you seeing the signs, preserving them, recognizing them.

It was to stop her closing the door that I stretched out a hand and took hold of it myself.

'I've come looking for her.'

Propping my briefcase awkwardly on my knee, I took from it my pictures of old Saul and Sinna on the day they struck camp and loaded the cart. Saul was leaning back in the driving seat, sending his whip snapping over the backs of the small donkeys. Chantal watching them, her eyes wide, her perfectly oval face with its golden calmness, as she straddled the bicycle wheel.

'Here they are. Setting off after doing some shearing for your husband. Saul and Sinna and their daughter. I took these pictures. I was here.'

'I don't know her.'

'But Mrs Mackenzie, you took the child in. The day her parents left. Chantal is her name. You sent her to wash, I remember.'

She took the prints from me and looked at the picture for a while. 'I don't remember her.'

'But I do. She was with you. And now her parents can't find her.'

She shrugged. 'Maybe she was here once – and she ran away. We have so many of them. They come with their carts, they stay a day or a week and then they go again. Like the wind. Who can say where they are now?'

'Maybe your husband has seen her. Can I talk to him?'

Still she said nothing. She was holding the pictures. Then she began tearing them up methodically into four pieces and throwing the pieces in my face. Then she slammed the door and turned the key and from behind the locked door she said, 'You can't speak to my husband. Never again.'

I drove back into town and went to the school. The figure of the gunman on the school wall was there still. The black bars of stencilling that made his body had faded in the fierce sun, but the important details were clear: the machine gun, the pistol in the belt, the bandanna, the hand grenades strung like shrunken heads from the belt, the giant dagger, the brace of pistols, the combat boots, the wide forehead, the full hair, the muscles, the braggadocio, the bullshit, the aching stupidity, but I had to admit it worked. What a thing to have to compete with. Here was a hero of prodigious glamour and, if you believed all you saw on the screen – and who did not believe it? – a killing machine of superb efficiency. There was much comfort to be had from believing dark, expensive games – better than the sunny horror of the everyday world.

Which was why the kids of McLeod High loved him – had stencilled this hero with his guns and knife and grenades on the school wall. He was the messenger from a culture that understood the necessity of killing and knew it was not barbarism – but a sign of professional standards and enviable wealth, of swagger and panache. Powerful, successful cultures exhibit a considerable capacity for – and take pleasure in – the liquidation of enemies, and even, at times, their friends. Certainly no great power has ever baulked at eliminating its own people. Indeed, as the figure on the wall testified, execution, torture in as many cruel ways possible, has been in leading societies a sport, a pursuit of delight as well as a necessity. You don't get heroes, certainly you do not get saints or some idea of what it means to be holy – without being able to portray and picture and admire and reward murder.

Miss Tromp was in her office and she showed no sign of surprise. Her handshake was warm and firm, and the look she gave me carried, I thought, a hint of relief.

'So the cart people, the nowheres, they did find you. You were somewhere deep in the world and they got to you. When they came here and parked the cart right outside the school gate I thought they were begging for something. But it was you they were looking for. They said they had lost a girl and I had to try to keep from laughing out loud. They lose everything, don't they? It's their way. They couldn't tell me a thing about the girl, not her age or how tall she was or what she looked like. Just that she was missing. All they knew was her name.'

'Chantal.'

'Yes. And that the mister who went away had taken pictures of her. You had given me your address, Charles, and so I wrote them that note and sent them to find you.'

'Beatrice?'

'Yes – Mr Croker?'

'Thank you for sending Old Saul and Sinna to find me.'

She regarded me intently. 'I thought maybe you had got lost, too. So I sent two lost people to find another. I never thought they would do it. It was putting a note into a bottle and throwing it into the sea.'

'Their girl was working over at the Mackenzie farm.'

Miss Tromp was unmoved. 'He's gone, you know.'

'Gone where?'

'They found him one morning, floating in the big dam.'

'What happened?

'Who knows?' said Miss Tromp with the shrug of her burly shoulders, which the townspeople of McLeod reserved for events that left them angry but helpless. 'Things just happen.'

The 'things' she had in mind were the usual: marital stabbings, hunting accidents, road smashes, rapes, beatings and gunfire, and they carried off neighbours or wives or children with as little warning – and as little mercy – as the wind which sent the tumbleweeds headfirst into the fences, or as jackals ripped into the sheep.

'I'll go out to his farm and look for her.'

She nodded, 'I thought so. You won't find much there.'

'I plan to keep looking.'

'Yes, I thought so, too. Is that why have you come back?'

'This is where I live.'

'Will you teach your usual classes?'

'If it doesn't mess up the timetable.'

'The timetable, Mr Croker, is not among my worries. I change it when I like and no one notices.'

I settled back into the school without difficulty. I found my class stonily familiar – my students, sitting more or less as I'd left them. With the same frowns of incomprehension as they studied their cellphones, sat Levant, Birkett and Jessup, pausing in their private reveries only long enough to repeat, 'Long Tall Sally's back!' before losing interest when I asked them to take out their poetry books and look at 'Daffodils' by William Wordsworth on page 26.

I was back and it made them uneasy, but then the world was imperfect and my job was to increase their unhappiness in some useful way.

Anywhere else, perhaps, I might have gone to the police. But I would face disbelief and disinterest. What sort of case could I make that would persuade harassed and underpaid officers at Calvinton, based an hour away, to start an investigation into a missing girl who belonged to a clan of nomadic sheep-shearers and tinkers, whose destiny and desire it was to go missing as often as possible? Chantal's case simply did not rate. It had no shape, no weight. The girl I had once known and photographed had vanished, and if she continued not being there who would know or care? Even her parents, who had reported her disappearance, had themselves disappeared; the farmer who had taken in Chantal was dead, and his wife said she remembered nothing of any girl. End of story.

Accept and forget, said the sensible voices.

I went back again a few days later to the Mackenzie farm and found auction notices wired to the gate. The house was shut, the curtains drawn and the dust in the driveway was thick and smooth. No one had been that way for a while. On the stoop the bicycle wheel lay where I had last seen it.

To anyone else it meant nothing.

Geena Mackenzie had vanished, but that didn't affect in the least what I had to do. I dealt in disappearances. The way to go was to build a case, to look over everything and to make a careful record of all I saw. Traces always lingered if you looked hard enough. I began with the bicycle wheel. I carried it down the steps and set it up in front of the house, propping it so I could shoot through the spokes, framing, in the arc of the wheel, the farmhouse beyond, liking the way the sunlight reflected off the shavings of silver that escaped the rust along the inner rim. I wanted to capture the thick edgings of mud that stuck to the rim edge and wrapped around the spokes, some of which were broken or bent. I photographed the wheel from a number of angles, carefully, scrupulously. Somewhere I knew there was a picture. I knew that – and I had to look hard for it, but also be willing to search for it blindly.

Next, I decided to look inside the house. The door was locked, but that gave me no problem. The sash windows were easily forced and once inside I found it much as I might have expected. An air of dusty order. The rugs on the living-room floor were old kilims; the pictures showed views of the mountains under the blue-grey immensity of sky that diminished all to little specks on the periphery. In the main bedroom on the wall over the bed hung photographs of the newly married couple: Geena and Manus Mackenzie, greys and whites, flowers and foaming bridal veil. The pink candlewick bed cover was thin now. The cupboards and drawers were empty.

In the single spare bedroom I found a small, narrow, wooden bed with a mahogany headboard and green cotton bedspread, and nothing else – or so I thought until I looked beneath the bed and saw a yellow-wood chest, opened it, and found three dolls, two of them bald, the third thin and blonde with bright blue eyes that opened and closed, and a picture book of incongruous English nursery rhymes – *The Cat and the Fiddle, Little Jack Horner, How Many Miles to Babylon?* – brightly printed on heavy cloth pages. And a child's exercise book with the name *Chantal* written in pencil, in large, uncertain capitals, again and again, until either she or her teacher had tired of it. I laid the three dolls side by side on the bed, the thin blonde between her two bald sisters, and photographed them with their heads on the pillow. The notebook I could do nothing with. Try as I might from every angle, it did not make a picture, but I found the single name *Chantal*, traced in clumsy script, unbearable.

I replaced the dolls and the notebook in the wooden chest, climbed out of the window and returned the bicycle wheel to its place in the corner. The next stop was pretty obvious. This was the way you built a case, assembling the evidence – nothing, of course, that would interest the prosecution – too fragmentary, too arbitrary, too slight to convince anyone in a law court. But I had something else in mind. I was interested in proving not that someone had been murdered – though I was fairly certain that was what had happened – but rather in making sure that the scene of the crime was documented, and that the mere idea that there was nothing to be seen here was false. The deserted farm where no one now lived was in truth filled with living presences, and with their possessions, stories, lives and deaths.

The farm graveyard was more or less where I expected to find it. About a ten-minute walk from the house – near enough to be walkable, far enough away not to be a constant reminder. It was fenced off against predators, and the gate carried a notice: *No Souls are Lost in the Lord*.

There were seven graves of departed Mackenzies, adults and children, dating back a century, judging by the dates on the rough headstones. And there was one fresh grave, unmarked. Just a recent mound of sand. Raw, hasty and deserted. This, I was sure, was the grave of Manus Mackenzie, so recently drowned. The grave itself would not make a picture, but the old gate would, hanging long on its failing hinges, and the small, neat notice, the words painted white on a plank from a box that had once held fertilizer, tacked to the crossbars, seen against the huge horizon, and above it the sky like some vast dirigible, swinging its small basket of departed souls. At least that was the way it looked through the viewfinder. But I never knew for sure until I got home and developed my rolls of film.

But that was right. That was the thing: looking hard always, and yet searching blindly for something you could not see, until I found I'd caught it, by accident.

'Ah yes,' I thought, as I lugged my Leica and tripod up on the hill to the dam behind the house, 'there was something magnificent about Joe di Angelo, the bastard!'

At the dam the first thing I saw was the mud. The rains had been heavy over the past month, an unusual thing in a semi-desert where sometimes it did not rain for a decade. The dam was a messy bowl of chocolate-brown water stretching out gently to the few stunted trees around the perimeter. I did not bother to look for tracks; there would be none. But I reasoned that the mud on the rim of the wheel had come from here. And it was here, too, that Manus Mackenzie had been found, floating. My instinct said Chantal had not been buried but hidden near the dam, and in that mass of mud the chances of finding her were remote. It didn't matter. I would picture the scene, little by little, bit by bit. A touch here, a trace there, the story forming in its crucial detail: the mud on the wheel rim, the name in the exercise book. I would make a memorial. It mattered to me that she should not vanish – Chantal was not someone who could be forgotten. It was vital she should be remembered, because without her there was no future.

I set up my tripod to give me a view of water and sky, wanting to see where each began melting into the other, that point where I couldn't say where one ended and the other began.

ACKNOWLEDGEMENTS

Though myths, and movies, long ago outstripped the man, John Kobler's *Capone*, is a vivid portrait of the mobster some called 'Scarface'. Alister E. McGrath's *A Life of John Calvin*, and T.H.L. Parker's *John Calvin*, achieve the same for the man some called the 'Pope' of Geneva. John Witte Jr and Robert M. Kingdon's study, *Sex, Marriage and Family in John Calvin's Geneva*, examines what happens when human desire is regulated by religious martinets. Hugh Lewin's classic prison memoir, *Bandiet*, is remarkable for its account of liberal dreamers enmeshed in the iron idiocies of a police state; a comedy of terrors. My small knowledge of forensics, was much extended by David Klatzow and Sylvia Walker's *Steeped in Blood*; along with a suspicion that high moral scruples have a way of making room for murder. And on the nuances of political betrayal and the pains of solitary confinement, my thanks to Sholto Cross, who faced both, and answered my questions with subtlety and patience.